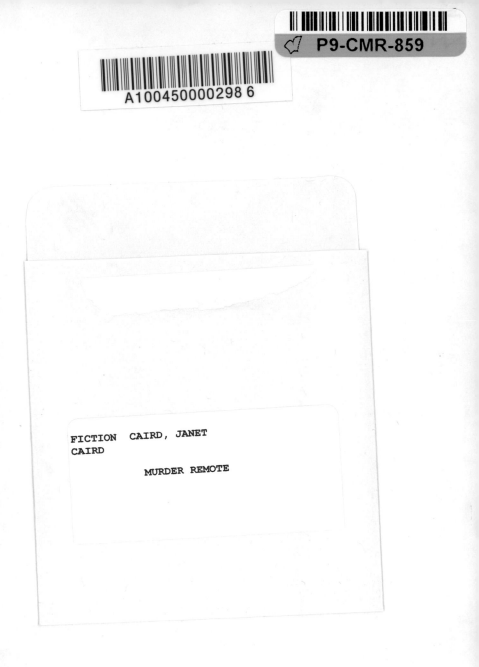

FICTION   CAIRD, JANET
CAIRD

           MURDER REMOTE

MURDER
REMOTE

Other Books by Janet Caird

MURDER REMOTE

JANET CAIRD

PUBLISHED FOR THE CRIME CLUB BY
DOUBLEDAY & COMPANY, INC.
GARDEN CITY, NEW YORK   1973

ISBN: 0-385-00475-3
Library of Congress Catalog Card Number 72–84896
Copyright © 1973 by Janet Caird
All Rights Reserved
Printed in the United States of America

MURDER
REMOTE

CHAPTER 1

The road, climbing, swung dizzily to the right, swooped left, right again and on the leftward curve back, broadened minimally so that in the nook of the bend there was room, just, to pull up, pressed into the low drystone wall bordering the road above the drop to the valley. It was meant, Elizabeth decided, to be a passing-place, though the familiar white diamond sign on the striped pole which should have marked it was missing. And of course she had no right to be parking herself in a passing-place. But the road twisting up the pass ahead of her seemed empty, at least until it was obliterated by drifting cloud towards the summit. And there was no sound of anything following her up behind.

She turned to look back, and wished she hadn't. On the edge of her vision, coming up, she had been aware of fallings from her, vanishings, but had had to keep her eye too steadily on the road to look; but now she saw how the little wall separated her from a precipitous, scree-clad plunge into the valley, a narrow valley, dark and colourless even at this season, with a burn twisting through old heather over black rock; a valley quite empty of anything living, but filled with a total silence. As always on the rare occasions when she encountered it, generally in the high hills, the totality of the silence filled her with astonishment, even incredulity. Normally, when she met it, she would luxuriate in it, hold her breath not to spoil it, feel it seeping into her like a beneficent drug. But not now; now the silence hung about her like a miasma; not an absence of noise, but a withholding of sound; as if the silence had in some way

1

acquired secretiveness from the enormous barriers of rock that rose on the other side of the valley. She had never seen mountains like these before. They rose in great rounded bastions to the cloud-cover, precipitous, sheer as a fortress wall, but huge, with a glint of moisture on them; and even now, even in near midsummer, spaced across the rocks were great hieroglyphs of snow.

If she twisted her neck, she could see between the mountain walls, away down behind her, a green valley that opened to the west, where the gleam of the river told her the sun was shining. She thought wryly with what cheerfulness she had turned off from the main road to take the way through the mountains. "The road is a little steep [*a little steep!*] in some places," Aunt Jenny's letter had said, "but perfectly feasible. At the crest it is most interesting, for it runs across a volcanic crater, or so they say. And when you first see down into Mourie you will be enchanted—such a wonderful view. A real Shangri-la." (For Aunt Jenny, generally fairly crisp in thought and word, was capable of dizzying lapses into the banal.) "That's to say, if it's not raining. Then you only see fog." Judging by the mist ahead, that was what she was going to see, and no Shangri-la. Of course, the mist might very well be purely local; perhaps over the crest there was sunshine.

But she made no move to drive on. Through the open window, the silence pressed in. The mountains loomed, the whole landscape was motionless except where the mist shifted on the crest. A vast reluctance to go on gripped her, an unwillingness to break the silence, to draw attention to herself by movement in this immobile landscape. So she sat for a moment still as the rocks about her.

And then she heard it. A faint droning above the clouds. A plane? The sound grew. No, not a plane. She saw the grotesque shape through the clouds and watched the helicopter grow distinct as it came down above the valley behind her and flew up towards her. She looked at it with distaste, for she hated helicopters; they were like huge horse-flies, graceless, ugly things. Then distaste turned to anger, turned to fear, as the machine suddenly lurched sideways and hovered above her, hidden by the roof of the car. She heard the throbbing directly overhead, and found herself cowering in her seat, trembling while her heart drummed with fear and a sense of outrage. Was this how the field mouse felt beneath the hawk's shadow? But why, why, why should this be done to her? Anger began to outweigh fear. The noise above her changed, slid away. The helicopter came into view again, flying up the valley, climbing into the clouds, disappearing. The droning that had swelled to a roar between the mountain walls diminished, faded, vanished. The silence rolled back and she was able to reason with herself.

There was no cause at all to think that she personally had been an object of interest to the helicopter. It was, after all, only natural that, seeing a solitary car parked on the road, it should investigate. Her too violent reaction had surely been due to the shock of seeing the machine violate the stillness and remoteness, and to the sudden surfacing of that feeling of being watched that haunted her when she was solitary in a lonely place.

She wound up the window savagely, turned the ignition key and drove on. The familiar routine of driving steadied her further; and she scolded herself for the near panic of the past few minutes, and forced herself to think of the helicopter. Had there been any distinctive markings on it? Letters—yes. What, she couldn't say: it was certainly not an RAF 'copter, of that she was sure. Perhaps it was a police helicopter? She'd read somewhere that they were using them in the Highlands for mountain rescue. That would explain why it had hovered over her, wouldn't it? No, it would not. A mountain rescue helicopter surely wouldn't be interested in a car? Oh, stop fussing, she said aloud to herself, and forget it. But she couldn't quite do that, aware of an enduring prickle of uneasiness. Not lessened by the fact that mist was now swirling delicately round the car, and ahead the road vanished into a thick hill fog. But at least she need no longer be conscious of the drop to the valley on her left. As she approached the summit of the pass the valley had risen too and was now only the bed of a narrow burn. Tufted grass the colour of dried bone, and slabs of wet black rock stretched into the mist on either side; she caught a glimpse of the mountain cliffs as the mist momentarily broke up; they seemed to be curving away from her. Perhaps this was the crater-bed of Aunt Jenny's letter.

But geological speculation had to be postponed, for now she was right into the hill fog. Thick and white it hung before her and the road vanished into it some ten feet ahead. She switched on dipped headlamps, but found the play of the light on the mist distracting, switched off, reduced speed to the limit and concentrated everything on steering up the tussocky verge of the road. Fortunately it ran fairly straight except for a sudden right-hand turn where a narrow bridge, parapetless, crossed the burn and where she nearly ran off the road on to what seemed to be a slippery great slab of rock tilted down to the water.

Once over the bridge, she stopped the car and sat for a moment or two to relax, for the tension was stiffening her muscles. She wound down the window and listened. At first the silence was broken by tiny creaks and ticks from the car. Then it became absolute, suffocating, as if the fog were the silence made visible and tangible; for the mist struck cold on her hands and face. It seemed to press closer to her; it was impenetrable. Anything, anyone, might be groping through it, out there; anything, anyone, at any moment might loom out of that white blindness beside her—or before—or behind.

She looked over her shoulder through the rear window at the cloud hanging there so still; and suddenly she was clutching the key with cold fingers, desperate to drive on.

But before the noise of the engine outraged the silence and while she was winding up the window she heard, or thought she heard, for the fog muffled it, a cry that rose and swelled and was cut off in a moment. It froze her into stillness; but nothing came after, nothing at all. Softly she closed the window and drove on, fighting the desire to rush through the fog, concentrating on the road, the rough grassy edge, the relationship of steering-wheel—to car—to road . . . The gradient had altered. She was running uphill again. Pray God she was nearing the crest—once over it, surely the fog would lessen. But here it was thicker, though that had seemed scarcely possible. She was moving at a walking pace; it was hard even to see the edge of the road; her whole body was stiff and cramped; her neck ached; her eyes, prickled with pain, were blurring. A red blotch formed before them. She shook her head and blinked. The redness was still there. It grew, took shape, and she braked with her bumper fractionally away from a small, red road-roller. It was drawn up in what she now saw was a passing-place, and its cheerful, commonplace, prosaic presence suddenly looking out of the baffling hostility of the mist was immensely comforting. She felt the tension go from her, felt herself relax and she switched off and got out of the car. The mist was as thick as ever and little drops of moisture began to form on the tweed of her skirt. She moved over to the road-roller and laid her hand on the clammy red metal, and, keeping it there (for she had an absurd notion that she must keep touching it or the fog would instantly swallow her up), she walked along it to the front, and there was the actual roller, black and heavy, with moisture gleaming on it. She patted it and remembered how as a child she would stand watching the roller on the road, ecstatically sniffing the smell of the hot tar. This, of course, was in a sense a miniature road-roller, not one of the great black monsters that had so impressed her in childhood. It had a high enclosed cabin. The driver would have a wonderful view of the countryside. But perhaps if you were driving a road-roller you weren't very interested in scenery.

She trailed her hand across the roller and began to move back down the other side of the machine towards the car. The mist was so thick that from where she stood it blurred the outline of the car beyond the red shape of the road-roller. There was something wrong with this shape, an excrescence, distorting the smooth outline.

From the open door of the cabin something was sticking out, something small, drooping, dark against the white mist.

A hand.

CHAPTER 2

For the first time in her life Elizabeth felt pure terror; and knew the truth of the old cliché that her knees had turned to water, for she could not move, but stood with her hand on the side of the roller, staring, with a dreadful halting and constriction of the heart. It passed and she stepped slowly forward, her lips dry and her breath coming in little gasps, and looked into the cabin.

Huddled on the floor, crammed in, knees almost at the chin, was the body of a man. He was wearing dark trousers and a short raincoat. Underneath where his left shoulder blade must be, there was a cut in the fabric and round it a red stain. The face was hidden from her; the hair was red—red and wavy. One arm was under the body, the other flung backwards so that the hand was outside. Elizabeth laid a reluctant finger on it as it hung there. It was not yet cold; under the chill given to it by the fog, she could feel the ebbing warmth of life.

So he was not long dead.

She remembered the cry she had heard, so suddenly cut off. As the knife went in?

He was not long dead.

Then somewhere in the fog there was a killer. Who would have heard the car coming up the road. Who would have heard it stop. Who knew she was standing by the road-roller, staring fascinated at the dead man's hand.

Elizabeth jerked her eyes away. The car—she must get to the car and go, go as fast as she dared, go faster than she dared.

6

But she was afraid to stir; afraid lest the movement should catch an eye battling with the mist, somewhere out there.

So she hesitated, leaning against the road-roller, looking at the dead hand while the silence deepened and deepened.

Out on the left, she heard the small rasping sound of a foot slipping on rock. Perhaps far, perhaps near: the fog distorted sound.

And suddenly she was in the car, her trembling fingers fumbling at the ignition key. The engine screeched, she reversed from the roller, pulled round the wheel and set off up the road.

As she passed the road-roller she tried not to think of what lay inside. Beyond it the road vanished almost abruptly into the fog. There was a shadow in the whiteness to her right. A rock perhaps? Unconsciously, she slowed down to look. The shadow moved, solidified, sprang. The door of the car was wrenched open, a man, a scarf wound round his jaw, a lock of dark hair escaping from under the blue beret pulled down to his eyebrows, put out a hand to seize the wheel.

Elizabeth had never thought of herself as particularly brave, certainly not as violent. But a deep instinct in her took over, and with her right hand she thrust at the face looming towards her, pushing with all her strength over the mouth, up against the nose, shoving against it with a vindictive pleasure. The head jerked back, struck the frame of the door; there was a grunt; she gave another vicious shove, and he flung up a hand, toppled over and was again a black shadow in the mist.

Quicker than she could ever have believed, she had the door shut and was driving on, driving faster than would have seemed possible a moment ago. The road levelled, began to go downhill. Soon she could see further ahead. The mist began to break up, became trails of vapour across her way, then it was wisps clinging to the hillsides. The mountains had come closer again and the road ran through a narrow valley, to her left huge bastions, to her right rock and grass rising to black craggy peaks. The road ran round a curve, and down, and before her lay Mourie.

It was like magic. Down there the sun was shining; the burn that gurgled beside her through the bleakness of stone and turf was a pleasant stream down there, and ran through meadows where beech trees were splendidly green, and where there were small white houses. And beyond that was a curving white beach and a blue sea out of which rose the mountains of the islands magnificently dappled with light and shadow, blue also, but with a difference, and with sheets of schist sparkling on the heights. It was so beautiful and so unexpected after the fog, the horror and the fear, that it had an effect of shock on her, and she had to stop the car and sit for some minutes while the full realisation of what had happened took possession of her; for she had pushed it into the back of her mind while driving. Now she was able to face up to it, think about it, decide what to do.

She must report everything to the proper authorities; there would be questions and enquiries of course; she would have done her duty as a citizen, and she could put it out of her mind. Meanwhile, there below her was Mourie, and the sooner she reached it the better.

And just as she had reached this admirably calm and balanced frame of mind, high on the fringe of cloud where the hill fog melted into the blue of the clear sky, she saw it, a sinister bird of prey, the helicopter. She was conscious of it, a black monstrosity in the bright air, all the way down the zigzagging road, till she reached the level strath. Then suddenly it was gone. But the uneasiness and foreboding it aroused were still with her as she approached the white houses of Mourie, and drew up at Aunt Jenny's door.

CHAPTER 3

Mourie, as Elizabeth had seen driving down the road from the pass, was a string of little houses following the curve of a shallow bay. To her right, as she reached level ground, the road had branched off, run over a bridge, and continued under trees towards and past a ruined little church in a churchyard, and then to a modern church, blocklike and uncompromising, flanked by an equally square and uncompromising manse. Elizabeth had kept to the main road and now she was standing at Aunt Jenny's front door, and thinking how blissfully peaceful and normal the scene was—warm sunshine, calm sea, the little white houses so spruce. Most of them were built directly on the street. Aunt Jenny's was distinctive in having a tiny garden-plot in front of it, bright with roses, a huge crimson peony, and—yes—a honeysuckle trellis over the door. Its fragrance hung in the air as Elizabeth lifted her hand to the knocker a second time. But before she had time to touch it, the door opened and Aunt Jenny was there.

They looked at each other with pleasure and affection. Aunt Jenny was tall, had been beautiful, was still comely. She had thick, beautiful white hair, worn in a bun, and clear dark blue eyes. Elizabeth resembled her, in her eyes, and texture of hair, but hers was fair and hung shining round her face. Both had the same graceful line of neck and shoulder and poise of body, though Elizabeth was still slender. Possibly a recognition of her younger self in Elizabeth may have contributed to Aunt Jenny's affection for her niece—probably not; Aunt Jenny was not one who clung to the past. Elizabeth's liking for her aunt went right

9

back to early memories of fun and treats and had grown into a genuine adult-to-adult affection. Now she thought: How well she looks! How glad I am to see her! While Aunt Jenny, kissing her, thought: She's looking tired and peaky. A good thing she's here.

"Elizabeth! So you've arrived! Was it difficult on the road? I saw the cloud on the hills, and thought it might be."

"It was pretty bad. I—oh, Aunt Jenny, something horrible has happened." And to her dismay, she began to sob.

"My dear child! What on earth's wrong? Come in; come in here."

A door just inside the hall was open. Aunt Jenny steered Elizabeth through it, pushed her gently into a chair and said: "Now, tell me."

So Elizabeth did. The telling helped her and when she had finished she was quite calm again. Aunt Jenny was silent for a minute, looking at her, then she said briskly:

"Well, I'd better ring Hamish McIntosh."

"Hamish . . . ?"

"The bobby. If he's in. We've only one policeman here, and lucky to have one, and he's a wide territory to cover. But if he's in, he'll soon be here."

She lifted the phone and waited for the exchange, saying to Elizabeth, "We must have one of the few local non-dialling exchanges left." And after a minute or two, she asked for the police station. There was a pause, and then the metallic distorted sound of a voice at the other end.

"Is Hamish in, Mrs. McIntosh? It's Mrs. Lauder speaking."

A lengthy clattering explanation followed.

"I see. Can you get hold of him? . . . Good. Thank you."

She put down the receiver. "He's down the coast at Ruaidh Point but she'll send a message to the farm and they'll tell him. And now I'll show you your room and you can have a wash."

They went up a narrow wooden stair to a small landing. Four doors opened off it. Aunt Jenny flung one open with a little air of triumph, stood aside to let Elizabeth pass and listened

10

with a smug look of satisfaction to her exclamation of surprise and pleasure.

"Aunt Jenny! What a lovely room! And the view!"

For the window looked out across the bay to the mountains of the islands. It was a small room, with sloping ceiling, white furniture, rose-budded wall-paper, matching bed covers, curtains and chair covers. Aunt Jenny looked at it complacently.

"Do you really like it? I've always wanted a sentimental bedroom. Not for myself of course—I couldn't stand it. But for guests who won't be in it for very long—I don't mean you, Elizabeth; you're to stay as long as you like—I thought it would be all right."

"It's nice. And hot and cold running water too!"

"You sound surprised. We're quite civilised here. We've electricity, as you see, and as far as mod. cons. go, we have everything. For other things . . . well, you must admit the *place* is ravishingly beautiful."

"Every prospect pleasing, and only man being vile?"

"Oh, I shouldn't go as far as that. I'll leave you now. Come down when you're ready."

When Elizabeth had washed and changed she felt better, and was still further cheered to find a tea table set in the window of the sitting-room downstairs and Aunt Jenny waiting to pour out and offer egg and cress sandwiches.

"I didn't know exactly when you'd arrive, so I decided we'd have tea whatever the time. I don't think Hamish will be long in coming. Now that they've given him a car instead of a bicycle, life's a lot easier for him."

"Is that him now?" asked Elizabeth, for a sturdy small black car had drawn up at the gate.

"Yes, it is," said Jenny, and went to open the front door, while Elizabeth watched a large policeman uncoil himself from the little car.

Constable McIntosh was tall, broad, fair-haired, about thirty, with a gentle expression. On Aunt Jenny's invitation he took tea while Elizabeth told her story. When she had finished, he put down his cup and said: "Aye."

11

It was, Elizabeth felt, a less than adequate comment and she looked indignantly at Aunt Jenny. But Hamish McIntosh was rising to his feet.

"Ah well, I'd better be getting up the road and having a look."

"Do you want me to come?" asked Elizabeth.

"Well now, normally I would be wanting it. But you see, on this occasion—well, I will have to be bringing the body down, in the back of the car, most likely, and it wouldn't be very nice . . . I'll get Jock Thomson to come with me. But I'll be having to ask you to come and identify it when we get back. In the road-roller, you said. Yes, I think I know where it is."

And he took his large person and his West Highland voice out to the car, and drove off.

Aunt Jenny watched him go.

"He's a good type," said Jenny, "and I don't envy him his job."

"I shouldn't think there's much for a policeman to do here," said Elizabeth. "It's all too peaceful and idyllic. You told me it was a Shangri-la, remember?"

"Did I?" Jenny looked a little shamefaced. "That was perhaps a little exaggerated. In every community you get malice and back-biting; hatred and prejudice. You should hear the Reverend Murdo MacFarquhar, when he really gets going. I remember one Sunday when he fulminated against whitewashing the cottages and compared them, one and all, predictably, to whitened sepulchres . . . Hamish is the soul of discretion but I'm sure he could a tale unfold of doings in Mourie that would make your hair stand on end."

"Why do you stay here, if it's such a sink of iniquity?"

"Oh, but it isn't. Did I give you that impression? I only meant that you can never judge a place by outward appearances. There's also kindliness, and an immense fund of fellow-feeling here. Besides, I really live here because of that." She gestured to the mountains and sea that filled the square of the window. "All the time I was working in cities and hospitals, I promised myself that some day I'd live where I could see, all the time,

12

sea and hills and clouds and waves. So I came here, and at least the scenery hasn't let me down."

"Meaning the people have?"

"No. I never expect too much from people. And there are some interesting characters about. For instance, Alice Merriweather, who used to be on the stage and who's retired to a cottage here and runs the drama group. And then there's Douglas McBain, the schoolmaster—you'll probably meet him today. He's definitely unusual. The job of schoolmaster here was vacant for ages—more than two terms to be precise. No one apparently was willing to come to such a remote area . . . Alice acted as teacher temporarily—the children loved it—lots of play-acting and art, and not too much spelling and arithmetic—and then about three months ago Douglas McBain turned up, having been appointed teacher."

"Well, what's so unusual about that?"

"Douglas is unusual. He's fantastically highly qualified—a doctorate in classics from Harvard."

"Then why is he here?"

"He's got a thing about the Highlands and depopulation and so on, and feels they're overlooked in every sphere—cultural, educational, economic. And it was his duty to come here and teach, I suppose as a kind of demonstration that a remote area deserves the best as much as a large populous place . . ."

Elizabeth considered this.

"He's not priggish?"

"Not really. A bit solemn perhaps . . . but also capable of an apparently hair-brained enterprise. He's taken it into his head that he'd like to dive for treasure."

"What?"

Jenny laughed. "Oh, it's not unheard of. You know about the Tobermory Spanish ship that they periodically try to find . . . and I believe young men have been finding Spanish gold off the coast of Ireland . . ."

"But where is the treasure? Or is it just a vague idea he's got?"

"Oh there's treasure all right—of a kind. Out there."

And Jenny looked out at the sea lying sparkling beneath the Skye mountains.

"Come on, Aunt Jenny. You're teasing. Just as you used to do with stories when I was tiny."

"Did I? Well, this is a sad story—one of these dark stories I sometimes think Scotland specialises in. You know about the Clearances, when the landlords drove the people from their crofts on the land, to make way for sheep—well, all this peninsula was a fairly prosperous self-contained little community, till the middle of the last century, and then it was "cleared" by a horrible landlord and most of the people went to Canada, some to the States. And the few that were left came down here to the shore and tried to make a living from fishing. It's a common enough story in Scotland."

"What I can't understand is why they didn't protest. Why they so meekly let themselves be dispossessed."

"Ah, that puzzles me too. But in Mourie they did. A ship called into the Sound here to take the dispossessed families away, about 1849–50—I'm not quite sure when, and the night before it was due to sail, the men came ashore again in a small boat, and went to the Big House, and murdered the laird and loaded up the boat with all the money they could find—thousands, according to one legend—and plate and jewellery . . . it was a crazy thing to do; they'd never have got away with it—but their desperation and sense of wrong must have suddenly boiled over and made them blindly reckless."

"What happened to them?"

"The boat sank between the shore and the ship; and the men—and their loot—were lost. All the men from Mourie on the ship, except one; a man called Aeneas Maclean. He had refused to take any part in the killing and he stayed on the ship. Those on the vessel saw them drowning, and they launched a boat and tried to save them, but it was hopeless. Aeneas Maclean risked his life to try and rescue them—I suppose he felt guilty that he alone of the men was left . . . he never wrote back to friends in Mourie, but seemed to cut himself off. The story of what happened that night was brought back by one of the women who returned years after; otherwise, no one might ever have known what happened."

14

"And the money and the valuables are somewhere on the sea-bed out there."

"That's the story. There's a local legend to the effect that the occasional gold coin can be picked up on the beach. I can't say I've ever actually met anyone who's found one—it's generally 'my mother's brother's wife's cousin's youngest boy' who's said to have picked one up."

"But surely it would need a lot of money to be able to organise an expedition to find it?"

"Obviously. But Douglas murmured something about a wealthy and eccentric businessman in Glasgow who might be prepared to back up the search—on condition that if anything was found, it, or its value, was used for the people of Mourie."

"And what do the people of Mourie feel about it?"

"Less than enthusiastic. There's still a kind of guilt about it here in Mourie. People don't talk about it. Mairi Macleod the Shop told me about it once in a moment of confidence. She's never referred to it again. Any time I've tried to get the natives of Mourie to tell me about it, they've always shied off into polite vagueness; they're very skilful at that."

"So there's a split—between the 'natives' and the 'incomers'?"

"What makes you think that?"

"You've a way of speaking about them."

Jenny looked vexed.

"I didn't mean to sound patronising or superior. I'd say we were a very united community. Sometimes one feels almost over-welcomed—but just occasionally one realises one is an 'outsider.' Old causes, old wrongs; their memory lingers; it does in all Scotland, I think, but more persistently here—perhaps because the outside world hasn't the same force here to drive out old memories. People here, walking past a hummock in a meadow, know that was their great-grandfather's house—and will have heard how it was burned before his eyes. They carry a shadow of ancient wrong . . ."

She stopped suddenly and laughed.

"Don't look so serious, Elizabeth. People here can be as gay as anywhere. They don't move around in a sorrowful dream—on

15

the contrary. But they're marked by history—their own history, not national history. But you'll enjoy being here and meeting them—I hope."

She looked out of the window.

"Here's Douglas—he generally looks in on his way from school."

She went into the hall without another word, and could be heard greeting someone at the front door, and soon there followed Aunt Jenny into the room a young, tall, lean and undeniably handsome man, with very dark blue eyes, thick black hair and a clear line to his jaw.

"Douglas, this is my niece, Elizabeth. We were just talking about you."

Not unnaturally, Douglas looked rather less than delighted. Elizabeth decided he was definitely glowering. And he is rather the solemn type, she thought.

"Yes," said Jenny cheerfully. "I was telling Elizabeth the story of the laird's murder, and I was explaining that people here won't talk about it."

"You're not from these parts?" said Elizabeth.

"No. I come from the industrial belt, near Glasgow. But if it hadn't been for the Clearances, I might have come from the Highlands. My forebears were driven from their crofts too. So I know what the people here feel, and I'm not surprised they don't want to talk about it."

"So you feel it's resentment at what was done to them, and not guilt at what they did, that makes them reluctant to talk?" said Elizabeth, aware of a little spurt of hostility towards him.

" 'Guilt?' At the murder? They should be proud of it. For once, the exploited turned against the exploiter. It's just a pity they didn't get away with the spoils."

"But you're hoping to rectify that, aren't you? By finding 'the spoils' and giving them to the people of Mourie."

He looked at Jenny.

"You've been telling her . . ."

"About the treasure seeking? Yes. You don't mind, do you? After all, everyone in the village knows your plans . . ."

16

"No, I don't mind."

"How are things going?"

"I think we've got things moving. Two or three volunteers will be joining me here in Mourie tomorrow. Our backer—if you can call him that—has recruited some people."

"You hadn't thought of getting some of the locals to help?" said Elizabeth.

"At first I did. But they seem very wary of the whole idea; so I expect it'll be outside help. A few students and so on, and some professional frogmen . . ."

"It's all fixed then?" said Jenny. "You've kept very quiet about it."

"It just happened that way. I didn't want to rouse any hostility among the locals . . . It's extraordinary, but it seems to me that since the time they made their rebellion and the boat went down, the place has been sunk in a total apathy. And they're still exploited, by government departments and by people who come and buy up houses and live here like a lot of minimal lairds . . . Not you, Jenny, I don't mean you. You pay your debt to the community. But others who come here for a few days every summer, very lah-di-dah and full of bonhomie."

But Jenny was laughing.

"You're being ridiculous, Douglas, and you know it. If there's any exploitation being done, then the government departments are at the receiving end—they're the exploited—and the same goes for the summer visitors, I should say."

Douglas looked at her and suddenly smiled. He had a totally transforming smile, as Elizabeth noted.

"Perhaps I was exaggerating," he said. "But I do feel the people here have been too meek all along. A touch of violence now and then . . . What have I said?"

For Elizabeth had turned abruptly aside and was looking out of the window. Talking with Jenny, she had not forgotten what had happened up on the hill but at least the memory had slipped back a little in her thoughts. Now Douglas McBain's words brought it all back, and she felt again the sickening

17

revulsion that had gripped her when she touched the dead man's hand.

Jenny was looking grave too; and Douglas stared at them, astonished.

"It's just that there has been violence," said Jenny. "Not a mere 'touch,' though. Elizabeth on her way here found a dead man, and he'd been murdered."

"I don't believe it! Where did you find . . . ?"

"Up on the crest of the pass." And Jenny told him.

When she had finished, he turned to Elizabeth and said: "That was dreadful for you, and I'm sorry," and there was warmth and genuine feeling in his voice. "You didn't see his face? . . . No, don't answer if you'd rather not talk about it."

"I expect I'll have to talk to the police about it," said Elizabeth, "so I may as well talk to you. No, I didn't see his face. But he had red hair."

"A stranger then."

"How on earth do you know that?"

"Because there are no red-headed men in Mourie. You must remember that here everyone does literally know everyone else. And the only man here with red hair is Crane Maclean . . . and it couldn't be him."

"Who," said Elizabeth, "is Crane Maclean?"

"He's just bought Mourie House," and "He's the new laird." Douglas and Jenny spoke together and were silent. There was a glint in Douglas' eye as he went on.

"He would like to be the new laird. But he is not and never will be."

Jenny ignored this and turned to Elizabeth.

"Crane Maclean is the great-grandson of the Aeneas Maclean I told you about—the one who didn't take part in the murder. He ended up in the States and did well for himself. News to that effect drifted back here. But then nothing more was heard of him or his family till this Crane turned up, oh, about ten days ago. Having bought Mourie House."

"How romantic," said Elizabeth. "Descendant of poor evicted

18

crofter returns and takes over wicked landlord's estate. Very satisfactory."

"That's rubbish. It's *not* satisfactory." Douglas' tone was brusque to rudeness, and Elizabeth flushed. She always reacted very sensitively to rudeness. "I call it arrogance," he went on. "Coming back here and flaunting his money—probably made in some dubious fashion—over the descendants of his father's fellow-victims who didn't get away to make fortunes. It's disgusting."

"I don't think you're being fair," said Jenny. "We hardly know him. I've never spoken to him. Have you?"

"Just a passing word. But what's he going to *do* here? Just live at Mourie House? It seems pointless to me. Money means power. If he's got all that he's supposed to have, he could be doing things, influencing events, manipulating people . . . Instead he comes and buries himself here."

He was speaking out of a real emotional pressure. Elizabeth was interested.

"But isn't that just what you've done, buried yourself here?"

He drew a breath, as if restraining himself, and said: "But I'm different. I don't have money."

He spoke lightly, but Elizabeth thought there was a bitterness beneath the words.

Jenny remained unperturbed.

"By opening the Big House again, you might say he was improving the quality of life here."

The peculiar sound that came from Douglas sounded to Elizabeth very like a rude snort, but Jenny ignored it. Perhaps she didn't hear it. She was looking out of the window.

"Here's Hamish's car coming," she said. "Steady, Elizabeth . . ." For Elizabeth had jumped from her chair and was looking out. "You may as well get it over right away."

But Elizabeth didn't hear: the very thought of looking again on the sprawling body, the outspread hand, the red-stabbed stain, was making her heart race and her fingers twist. She had seen death before, and often enough too, in India. Withered, starved death. Why was this so horrible? Because of where it had happened? Because she'd been alone at the finding of it?

19

She felt unreasoning panic rising in her; into it came the gentle pressure of a hand on her elbow, and a voice saying: "It won't be too bad," and Douglas was looking down on her encouragingly and with concern; and she took heart.

The three of them watched the little car come along the road and draw up at the gate. Beside the uniformed Hamish sat Jock Thomson, grizzle-headed and sunburnt. Hamish got out, opened the gate, came up the path, looking correctly and officially imperturbable, but also slightly puzzled. Before he had knocked, Jenny had opened the door, and he was in the room.

It's come, thought Elizabeth. He's going to ask me to go out and look. It would be under some covering, and he'd pull it aside and there would be the face—but of course she couldn't identify the face—only the back . . .

Hamish McIntosh was speaking to her, and she stepped forward, ready to say, "I'll come at once." But stopped as the meaning of his words sank in.

"There was no body there, Miss Cranston. The road-roller was quite empty. There was nothing there at all."

20

CHAPTER 4

Elizabeth left the tiny sheep track, scrambled up the gentle slope of a rocky outcrop and sank into the heather, panting a little. She was on a ridge to the north of Mourie, and was looking across the Sound to the mountains, dark blue and sharp against the clear light in the sky. The sun was hidden behind them and the long midsummer twilight was beginning. On a cloudless night like this, she knew, the glow would never wholly die out of the sky. It would lessen and become gentle and move round the northern horizon and then grow bright and strong and flash into sunrise about half past three in the morning, and it would never be really dark. The sudden early darkness every night with little variation in time throughout the year was one of the things she had not liked about India. Quite often there she would find herself thinking of the long clear summer days of Scotland, pushing out of memory the bleak wet windy chilly summer days—one inevitably idealised what one had left behind. She was beginning to look back at an India without smells, sweltering heat, poverty and sores, and full only of splendid things. Perhaps it was only the place one was in that one could see really as it was—and then possibly only after peeling off layers of preconceived notions. As in the case of Mourie.

She lay back in the heather with her hands behind her head and looked up at the sky and smelt the musty, dusty smell of old heather mixing with the raw smell of the new plants, and thought about Mourie. What had she expected to find there? Basically, a kind of quiet refuge, where for two or three weeks she need do nothing but walk, and look, and talk at leisure; a time to

21

take stock after India, think out things, free for a little, from the pressure of events; to enjoy undemanding affectionate companionship with Jenny; all very soothing, therapeutic and desirable. And the pressure of the reality had been such that she had simply had to get away by herself this evening to relax and be at peace for a little. Aunt Jenny—dear Aunt Jenny—perfectly understanding, had warmly endorsed her wish to go off on a walk by herself. "Of course I don't mind. You're like me, Elizabeth. At times I simply have to be alone, or else I get all fussed-up, as if I hadn't enough air."

Now, as she took a deep, deep breath of the scented air and looked into the empty sky, she thought how aptly Jenny's words described the way she had been feeling. And yet it seemed absurd that in a place like Mourie she should have felt that too much was pressing in on her too closely. Of course, yesterday had been quite a day. The horrible journey up the pass; the discovery on the crest; and the shattering let-down of Constable McIntosh's words: "There was nothing at all." At the very memory she squirmed, for beneath Hamish McIntosh's professional matter-of-factness, there was discernible a note of amusement. He seemed not to be taking the matter so very seriously, and even ventured the suggestion, in a kindly way, that maybe with the fog and the mist and the strain of driving, her imagination . . . ? After her indignant denial he had taken her through her story again, and then left. And Jenny and Douglas McBain had resumed their speculation about the identity of the body, and had agreed that Crane Maclean hadn't been seen about the place for two days. It seemed slender grounds for assuming he was dead, as Elizabeth, weary and upset, caustically pointed out. Jenny, noticing her edginess, had briskly got rid of Douglas, prepared a meal, and packed Elizabeth off to bed. No sooner had she slid between the sheets in the rose-budded spare room than she had fallen in to a dreamless sleep.

She woke in clear shadowless morning light, into a soundless world. There wasn't even a murmur from the sea breaking in slender ripples on the pebbles. She stood by the window, drew deep breaths, and felt completely refreshed. No one was stirring, so she went back to bed and thought, just as she was drifting into sleep: This peacefulness is what I came to Mourie for.

But the promise of the early morning had not been fulfilled. Some hours later she had been wakened by the noise of an ill-maintained motor engine labouring along the road outside her window. It was an old and rickety lorry, painted a faded and flaking blue with "Mourie Agricultural Transport Co" in red letters on the door. At the wheel was a thick-set man with a weather-beaten face and white bushy eyebrows, a cloth cap pulled down over his brow. She was sure he was the "Co." The lorry was towing a battered and overloaded little cart, covered with a black tarpaulin. In the lorry were a young-middle-aged man, three women whose ages ranged from about twenty to about forty, all with rusty red hair, one old woman with chop-fallen jaws, white hair and a malevolent expression, two broad-faced, bleach-haired, mahogany-brown children, one a tiny toddler, three dogs, and an unkempt Highland pony. The tinkers had arrived, and were getting a lift from the pier a couple of miles away, where they had come by boat.

When she told Jenny at breakfast about the tinkers, she found Jenny already knew they had arrived. "We'll have a call from them soon," she said. "They're really Lowland tinkers and they seem to winter in or near Glasgow. I delivered one baby last year, and there's probably another imminent," and in answer to Elizabeth's look of surprise, she nodded. "I do a bit of nursing on a sort of semi-official part-time basis. The nearest nurse and doctor are across the Sound and it's not always easy for them to get here. It keeps up my professional interest." She apparently saw nothing incongruous about the retired matron of one of the most famous teaching hospitals in the country delivering a tinker's baby in a black tent, and this, thought Elizabeth, is typical of Aunt Jenny.

From breakfast on, there had never been a moment, or so it seemed, without someone being shown into or leaving the house.

Mrs. Macleod from the shop had "run across to tell Mrs. Lauder the four-ply heather-mixture wool had come at last." And she was letting her know early in case she wanted some.

23

Introduced to Elizabeth, she had shaken her warmly by the hand and had hoped she was none the worse of her terrible experience the day before, and it was a queer thing that there was scarcely a red-headed man in the whole countryside and yet she was finding one, and wasn't the world becoming a terrible place?

"I didn't know you were a knitter," said Elizabeth to Jenny, when Mrs. Macleod had at last gone.

"I haven't clicked a knitting needle since the war," said Jenny, and chuckled. "Mairi's curiosity must have been at breaking point if she couldn't think up a better excuse for an early visit than heather-mixture wool . . . We'll have a stream of callers today. You may as well be prepared for them."

She was right. Willie McAlister—the Mourie Agricultural Transport Co—had called with two freshly caught gleaming mackerel, "for your niece to let her taste what fresh fish is really like," Mrs. Grant from Ruaidh with a dozen eggs, Kenneth the Post rang the door-bell to enquire if Mrs. Lauder could remember a registered packet having been delivered to her last January . . . Elizabeth couldn't remember all the visitors, but each and every one had hoped she was none the worse and had commented on the scarcity in the area of red-headed men . . . Even the tinkers had heard what had happened. Bella Macphee, arriving at the door with a cheerful and grubby small boy tucked into the shawl on her back, commiserated obliquely with Aunt Jenny on her niece's ill-luck on the way over the hills, before she came to the point of her coming, which was that Peg was near her time and would appreciate a visit. Not one of the callers mentioned the name of Crane Maclean—"They're waiting for you or me to do that," said Jenny—until there arrived in the late afternoon a small woman with a puckered little face, huge dark eyes and a mop of incredible chestnut curls. She was wearing a brilliantly patterned shift dress and Grecian sandals and her beautiful English voice was as remarkable in Mourie as a nightingale's song would have been among the sandpipers on the shore. She burst into Jenny's sitting-room, seized Elizabeth's hands and cried: "You must be Elizabeth! My poor child! What a dreadful beginning to your visit to Mourie! You must have been quite, quite shattered!" She turned to Jenny. "And to think that Crane Maclean should die like this! There is a doom on the Mourie treasure—the long-ago laird murdered for it—and this one when he tries to restore it!" She flung one hand up in a gesture of fatality and there was a tiny pause in which Elizabeth could almost hear shadowy applause. But Jenny remained unmoved.

"Nonsense," she said briskly. "What reason have you to think Crane Maclean is involved? Elizabeth, this is my neighbour Alice Merriweather."

Alice gave Elizabeth a nod and a squeeze of the hand, but spoke to Jenny.

"Mrs. Macleod in the shop said there was no doubt it was him—at least I think she did."

"I'll be very surprised if she said anything as definite as that," said Jenny. "Cast your mind back and you'll see . . . And as you're here, stay and have tea."

Over tea, Elizabeth learned that Alice, as she put it, "belonged to the theatre," had been an actress, had come into a little money, and lived most of the year in Mourie, going down to London in midwinter to "do the theatre" and look up old acquaintances. She was the moving spirit in the Mourie Dramatic Society, which she and Jenny assured Elizabeth flourished splendidly.

The exuberant Alice was followed by a morosely earnest Douglas McBain, who looked in later in the evening to pass on a *Times Literary Supplement* to Jenny ("I've never really time to read it, but I don't like not to take it," she confided), and it was at that point that Elizabeth felt she'd had enough of her fellow men for the time being and had come out.

She sat up. Already she was feeling restored and refreshed, smoothed-out and calm, like well-ironed linen. This was a splendid point from which to view Mourie. On her right there was a tumble of big massive mountains, ben beyond ben, far into the northern horizon. On her left, beyond the trees that fringed the river which ran into the Sound just below where she sat, lay the

25

village. And down there, beneath her and a little to the right, was the tiny ruined church and a little graveyard with stones that tilted and sagged. She would go and visit it.

In five minutes she had scrambled down the slope and was at the double iron gate into the churchyard. Askew and flaking with rust, it was immovable, sunk into a tangle of grass and weeds. But some ten feet along the wall, she found a stone stile over the wall, and was soon walking along a path sketched in the grass from the stile to a tall stone slab. She glanced at the stones on either side—none older than the eighteenth century, most of them nineteenth, and one or two early twentieth. Mostly they were simply upright stones, with a little scroll-work at the top. Two were square columns topped by draped stone urns, lichen growing in the sculptured folds, and sea-bird droppings trickling down them. The names recurred—Macleods, Macdonalds, Macleans, an occasional Mackenzie. Sometimes the words "drowned at sea" brought a faint and faded echo of past tragedy. Near the gable of the church was a little cluster of five small white headstones, and she left the path to look at them. They marked the graves of drowned sailors. Two, unknown from 1917; one, unknown, washed up in 1942; one to Stanley Jones, A.B., aged 19, found in May 1944. And one to an unknown German seaman. These stones were common enough in the west; she had seen them before. But they never failed to move her.

She turned back to the path leading to the tall thin upright stone slab. It was about eight feet high by two wide, she judged, and at first it puzzled her, for she could see no indication of what it was. It was fuzzy with lichen, and as she looked at it, she began to see that it had been carved. Gently she pulled away some of the soft grey lichen, and found the simple incised outline of a cross-head, the short broad arms linked by a circle. It was clearly very old and brought to her an awareness that the little enclosure where she was had been hallowed ground for more than a thousand years and that underneath the uneven turf were many "quiet sleepers" with no stone to mark where they lay. The churchyard was very still, very quiet; the twilight was slowly

26

deepening; not a sheep was to be heard, not a sea-bird; for a moment's space there was total silence.

From the ivy-draped ruined church came a rasping and scraping as of something hard dragged along stone.

And silence again.

It was a simple thing but it filled the quiet place suddenly with uncertainties, menacing possibilities, irrational fear. All this she felt; but even as a child, Elizabeth had always chosen to know what she must fear. So now she stepped firmly through the straggling weeds and across the uneven turf to the door of the ruin and peered inside. The thick branches of ivy sprawling over the roofless walls made a deeper twilight there; there had been burials in it; at one end a massive headstone stood askew; just at her feet, a rusty iron chain was looped round a square of ground where bloated thistles grew out of untidy gravel. But the old church seemed quite empty of anything living, and after a moment she left the doorway and went round the gable end. On the far side there were only two or three headstones, but she felt the turf hard beneath her feet; under the grass there must be a multitude of flat stones; this was clearly the oldest part of the graveyard. Over by the wall were one or two slabs comparatively clear of turf, and she peered at them hoping to find one carved into the intricate patterns of leaf and scroll which she found so beautiful. But they were plain and untouched and she turned away, disappointed and uneasy.

For the charm of the place had gone, banished by the noise she had heard from the church. In the twilight, light and yet not light, the headstones stood distinct and shadowless—they said the returning dead cast no shadow—she felt herself being drawn into a superstitious panic and pulled herself up sharply. Over the wall was the road to Mourie and Aunt Jenny's house; she could hear the distant drone of a car engine—it was an ordinary summer's evening. Ah yes, said an inner voice, beyond the churchyard wall perhaps—but inside it, here . . . ?

She must go; all her pleasure in the evening had gone. So she completed her circuit of the ruin, and came back to the doorway.

And there she saw it. Lying parallel to the wall, and almost

27

clear of encroaching turf, so that she wondered how she hadn't noticed it before, was a beautiful grave-slab, tapering slightly to one end, and carved with an intricate pattern of leaves and tendrils round a great two-handed sword. With a little exclamation of pleasure, she fell on her knees beside it and ran her fingers over the surface for the pleasure of feeling the worked stone. The edge was bevelled, and she felt round it and could distinguish letters carved there. She bent down, her hair brushing the stone, pulling at the turf to disengage the edge, and see if she could read the letters. And suddenly was simultaneously aware of three things. The turf had already been loosened; something was moving inside the church; and she heard the creak of rusty iron, and a half-glimpse of something moving above her right shoulder made her jerk her head back just as a stone from the edge of the doorway fell forward and crashed past her head, so that she felt a gush of air on her cheek. It lay on the slab with tiny flakes splintered from it, and even as she rose in terror she could see how it had bruised the carved tendrils.

But now she was stumbling through the grass over the uneven ground. She could hear no sound of pursuit. Apart from the soft panicky thudding of her hurrying steps, silence had fallen again on church and graves. Nevertheless, she must leave the place, at once and quickly. It was full of hostility, of menace. The weeds caught at her ankles, she stumbled and lurched over mounds and hollows. As she reached the cross-slab she lost her footing and fell sprawling on her face before the tall old stone. With the breath knocked from her she lay for a moment in darkness, her face pressed into the rank grass. Then she fearfully raised her head a little and looked sideways.

And saw a man's foot only inches from her head.

She went rigid with fear, and an American voice, full of concern, said:

"You're not frightened? Let me help you up. Take my hand."

She couldn't do anything else than put her hand in his, and in a moment she was leaning against the cross, looking at him— at a head of dark red wavy hair, very dark eyes, strong eyebrows,

28

tanned skin. A striking, not to say remarkable, face. He looked at her thoughtfully and said:

"Are you all right? You'd better sit down." And he gestured towards a table tombstone standing foursquare on squat legs. But Elizabeth shook her head.

"I must get out of here." Her voice came in a whisper.

"Fine. Then let me help you to the stile."

He put a hand under her elbow and steered her to the wall, and she was glad enough of his help, for her knees were trembling in a ridiculous way. Once over the stile, she sat on the bottom step and put her head down on her knees. When she raised it, he said:

"I'm glad I happened to be passing. My car's down there." He nodded in the direction of Mourie. "I saw movement in the churchyard and stopped to look . . . You're not hurt?"

"No—thank you," said Elizabeth. "It was stupid of me to fall."

"You certainly were going at a fast pace. Had something scared you?"

"Well, yes, I had been frightened." Elizabeth paused. Frightened she had been—horribly. But exactly why? Not simply because a stone had fallen from a crumbling wall. Had she sensed that it had been pushed out deliberately, that it was an attack? That was surely absurd. There had been no one in the church . . . he was looking at her, waiting for her to continue. "A stone fell out of the church wall almost on top of me, and startled me."

"That must have been very upsetting. And now, can I take you home?"

"I think I'll manage to walk, thank you."

Elizabeth stood up, felt her knees sag, and staggered a little.

"Nonsense. I'll take you. If you tell me where to go."

"I'm staying at my aunt's, Mrs. Lauder's."

"I know her. My name is Crane Maclean."

She felt she had known this from the moment he first spoke. But all she said was: "I'm Elizabeth Cranston."

"Let's go then."

Once more he put his hand under her elbow and they went down the track to his car, a large, rakish convertible.

29

Elizabeth sank gratefully into the seat, he got in, started up and they drove off to Aunt Jenny's.

Neither of them looked back through the thickening twilight, so neither saw the figure that stood in the shadow of the doorway, one hand pressed against the insecure masonry. The hand had broken nails and the anchor tattooed in blue and red on the back was like a half-healed wound. Only when the car had disappeared and the sound of it died into silence did someone move quietly from the ruin and round the gable end into the darkness of the tangled ivy.

CHAPTER 5

When Crane Maclean's car drew up at Jenny's door, Elizabeth, through the open window, could see, by the light of the lamp on the mantelpiece, that Aunt Jenny had visitors. She thought she recognised Alice's chestnut mop, and was aware of one or two figures on the edge of the circle of light. As Crane Maclean opened the garden gate for her, he said: "Well, now that you're safe back, I guess I'll be going."

"Won't you come in for a little?" For surely common politeness demanded that she ask him? Even though Aunt Jenny didn't like him? His dark eyes seemed to consider her for a moment and then he said: "Thank you, I'd like to."

So in a matter of seconds, Elizabeth opened the sitting-room door and stood with Crane Maclean facing the startled gaze of three people.

Aunt Jenny's reaction was a not altogether pleased surprise. "Elizabeth—and Mr. Maclean!"

But her words dwindled beside Alice's dramatic cry: "Mr. Maclean! So you're not dead!"

There was a hush. Elizabeth, as she squirmed with embarrassment, could see that Douglas was there with Jenny and Alice. All were gazing at her and Crane Maclean with expressions varying between Jenny's surprise, Alice's wide-eyed (and malicious?) wonder, and Douglas' glowering disapproval. It was an awkward moment. Crane Maclean met it smoothly.

"I'm not—dead, I mean. Why should I be?"

Jenny opened her mouth to reply but Alice forestalled her. "Because of your hair."

31

"My *hair?*"

"Yes. It being red. You see, the body had red hair. So we thought it was you."

"Would someone," said Crane Maclean, "please tell me what all this means?"

"I will," said Jenny, and gave Alice a warning look. "My niece Elizabeth, when she was coming over the hills yesterday in her car, found a dead man. With red hair. And as you were the only one locally to have red hair . . ."

"And hadn't been seen around for some time," Alice interrupted helpfully.

"—the impression got around it might be you . . . You know what small places are like," Jenny concluded.

"I'm beginning to learn," said Crane Maclean. He seemed more amused than angry. He and Elizabeth were still standing in the doorway and he looked down on her. "That was a bad introduction to Mourie. And now this evening's happening . . . it's too bad."

But Jenny was now acting hostess.

"Do sit down, Mr. Maclean. Douglas, come and help me get drinks."

There was a polite little bustle as Jenny and Douglas went to get drinks. Elizabeth sat saying nothing, hearing Alice twittering to Crane Maclean and realising she felt very tired and that what had happened at the church had been a real shock. Soon Jenny and Douglas came back with the drinks, and she took hers gratefully, and when Douglas had served the others, he sat on the stool by her chair. He's handsome too, she thought dreamily, feeling the drink gently bemuse her.

But Crane was speaking to her.

"What exactly did you find up in the hills, Elizabeth? Or would you rather not say?"

As she hesitated, he smiled at her—he had a very persuasive smile—and said: "I'm kind of interested—seeing it was supposed to be me."

So Elizabeth told the story again; and found that with repetition and the passage of time it had become easier to speak of. When she had finished, Alice gave a little shiver and said: "It must have been awful."

"It was." Jenny spoke firmly. "But it's past, and I think we should stop talking about it. I'm more interested in what happened tonight."

"Nothing, really," said Elizabeth. Sitting here in Jenny's pleasant room she had difficulty in recalling the indefinable fear she had felt in the graveyard. "I went to the old graveyard and when I was looking at the carved stone just by the wall of the church entrance, a stone fell from the edge of the door just by my head and scared me and I ran, and fell—and Crane picked me up."

"Is that all?" Jenny sounded disappointed.

"Oh, it doesn't sound much. But I'd worked myself up into a kind of panic before that, and the stone falling was the last straw . . ."

"I couldn't go alone into the churchyard *ever*," said Alice. "I am very sensitive to influences and atmosphere, and I'd *feel* things. Perhaps the stone didn't fall by accident. Perhaps"—she lowered her voice—"perhaps it was *psychic*."

"Don't be ridiculous, Alice," said Jenny. "You know perfectly well the church is crumbling. After every gale there are stones down."

"But there isn't a gale tonight, Jenny. Perhaps someone pushed the stone."

It was said with an air of innocent simplicity, but the words produced a sharp reaction.

"Are you suggesting," said Douglas brusquely, "that someone was deliberately trying to injure Elizabeth?"

"Not injure." Alice was all surprise. "Kill."

There was a horrified pause and then a little babel of voices.

"Alice! That's a dreadful thing to say." "What makes you think that?" "Have you any good reason for such a suggestion?"

Crane Maclean said nothing but looked at Alice with a kind of reluctant respect.

Oddly enough, Elizabeth felt a certain relief at hearing put into words what she had been trying hard not to admit as possible.

33

"I'm not sure myself it was purely accidental," she said. "You see, I thought I'd heard something in the church . . ." And she told them.

"But who would want to . . . ?" Douglas' voice tailed away into incredulous silence.

Alice's clear voice answered him. "The man who tried to get at Elizabeth in her car, up on the pass."

"That's a possibility," Crane agreed. "If he thought Elizabeth would recognise him again—well, he'd want to make sure she didn't. *Would* you recognise him again, Elizabeth?"

Would she? Elizabeth closed her eyes and thought back. She had at times a photographic memory, and now she could see the face, half-covered with a scarf, a glimpse of dark hair under the blue beret, light eyes—no, she would not know him again from his face. But as she sat there with closed eyes, seeing it all again clearly, vividly, ah she saw him topple backwards and throw up one hand, she realised that—yes—she would be able to recognise him again.

She opened her eyes, with her lips parted to say just that. They were all looking at her; Jenny anxiously; Alice's eyes bright, even mocking; Crane—were Crane's eyes wary?; were Douglas' calculating? As she looked at them, deep within her, away at the back of her mind, a little warning mechanism sent out a signal. Three of these four people she had known only for hours, some not for one hour. In her heart she knew the fall of the stone was no accident; she was walking in a web of danger; had been ever since she'd touched the tepid hand up there in the mountain; and she must go warily.

So she said: "His face was covered; I couldn't recognise him again."

The words saved her life, though she didn't know it. She had a sense—but perhaps it was imagination?—of them all relaxing, and they began talking of other things. She leaned back in her chair, breathed deeply, closed her eyes. She would think of nothing for the moment, and simply accept the restorative effect of Aunt Jenny's comfortable room and the drink in her hand.

34

Into this soothing absence of thought came Alice's clear, high voice.

"And will you make Mourie House your home, Mr. Maclean, or will you be another absentee landlord?"

Crane's lips tightened a little with, Elizabeth felt, entirely justified irritation. Really, Alice was positively impertinent!

But as his deep voice replied, only a very keen ear could have detected anything in it other than calm courtesy.

"I hope to spend as much time as I can there, ma'am. But I guess sometimes I'll have to be away on business."

"But you must find it very quiet here, alone in that house with just one man."

Crane was a little puzzled.

"How did you know I'd just one man? No—don't tell me. 'Everyone here knows everything about everybody.'" He smiled at Elizabeth as if sharing his amusement with her. "That's just till we get organised. Jimmy grew up with me—his father was one of my father's staff—he travels around with me and was quite keen to come here. I don't find it too quiet. I'm happy and interested to be in Mourie, where my ancestors came from."

He paused and glanced round at them as if wondering whether to speak further, looked at the floor for a moment and then raised his eyes and said:

"Well, I guess you would be as good people to tell as any, with Mr. McBain here being schoolteacher, and you, ma'am [to Jenny], being so prominent in the community. The fact is, I've a scheme in mind that I figure will be very interesting to carry out, and I hope will benefit the folk here."

"Oh?" said Alice. She and Jenny were politely interested. Douglas, Elizabeth noticed, was silent and wary, looking up at Crane from brows drawn into a forbidding straight line. Crane was speaking again.

"Did you know that when my ancestor, Aeneas Maclean, left Mourie there was a robbery committed that very night at Mourie House? . . . You do know?"

For Jenny and Alice nodded, and Douglas drew his breath

35

sharply and Elizabeth saw his hands gripping the arms of his chair.

"You know then about the ship going down . . . My great-grandfather was very troubled about this, for he was the only man from Mourie to escape. The story has been handed down in my family ever since, and so I got the idea that I'd like to come here and see the place. But I'd like to do more. I'd like to try and get that treasure that's out there in the sea and maybe give it to the people here whose folks didn't get to the States, and get the chance to make their way in the world the way mine did."

If he expected a strong reaction to this statement he got it.

Jenny looked totally taken aback and Douglas, pushing back his chair, sat up looking angry, disturbed and very wary. It was, predictably, Alice who broke the stunned silence and made all clear.

"But you can't do that," she cried. "That's what Douglas is going to do!"

Now Crane looked dumbfounded.

"Oh," he said, and after a moment, "I'm sorry to hear that. I had kind of set my heart on doing it."

They all looked at Douglas. He was clearly reluctant to speak, but at last said stiffly:

"It's unfortunate that our plans should clash. But I have been thinking of doing this for some time. And two or three of the people that I've been hoping will help me have already arrived in the village." He turned to Jenny. "You may have seen one or two strangers about."

"I hadn't noticed anyone," said Jenny.

"I did," said Alice. "A tall man with pale eyes and a rather smaller dark one."

"That's right," said Douglas. "Johnson and Murphy. My friend —our backer—got hold of them."

"So you have a backer." Crane seemed to have got over the first shock and to be taking a calm and rational view of the matter. "I was wondering—forgive me—how you were going to manage for finance. It'll take a lot of money."

"Quite." Douglas' tone was dry and uncordial. "But we have

a backer—a businessman who wishes to remain very strictly anonymous, but who is prepared to give us all we need, on condition that what we find—if anything—is used to benefit Mourie. Just your own idea in fact."

"So it is. But I certainly am sorry that I appear to have come too late. I don't suppose I could join in with you and share in your enterprise?"

Douglas frowned. Elizabeth had the impression that he found Crane's suggestion very upsetting. But he answered calmly enough.

"I'd have to ask our backer."

"I'd help with funds, if they were needed. I've got plenty. In fact, I'm a very rich man."

The statement was simple, wholly lacking in arrogance, and impressive. Douglas seemed to consider it.

"I'll get in touch with our man and ask . . ."

"Because," went on Crane smoothly, "it would be silly to have two groups at work both looking for the same thing—wouldn't it?"

This time there was no doubt about it. Douglas was upset and very angry.

"You wouldn't do that, organise your own search? It's ridiculous. I thought of it first—" And perhaps aware how childish he sounded, he was suddenly silent and sat flushed and grim.

"I just might. When I took over the estate, I established rights over anything there might be there, left from the wreck of the murderers' boat . . . and I don't suppose your backer has done that?"

"I don't know." Douglas was sulky. Then he sat up, his face cleared and he said:

"But of course you're right. It would be silly to have two groups at work. If you work with us, and we find the treasure, you will agree it should be used for the benefit of Mourie?"

"I figured on handing out what I found of the treasure to the descendants of the Clearance victims."

Jenny interrupted:

"You mean actually hand over *objects?*"

37

"Why yes, ma'am. It seems a kind of poetic justice." He turned to Douglas. "What were you figuring on doing?"

"The intention was to sell the stuff and use the money—but that's a detail." Douglas rose to his feet. "I must be going. I'll contact you as soon as I hear from Glasgow, Mr. Maclean. It may take a day or two."

"That's all right. I must go too. Can I give you a lift?"

"No thanks, I'll walk." And in a minute or two Douglas was striding along the road towards the schoolhouse. Crane Maclean and Alice left soon after, and Jenny and Elizabeth both flopped into chairs and sank into the soothing relaxation that follows the departure of visitors.

Jenny broke the silence first.

"What an odd thing—that Crane Maclean should also be interested in the laird's treasure!"

"I rather liked him," said Elizabeth. "He may be disgustingly rich, but he seemed quite modest with it all."

"Mphm." Jenny had always been able to convey an immensity of meaning by this simple utterance. Now it indicated scepticism, muted disapproval and also open-mindedness about Crane.

Elizabeth decided to answer the scepticism.

"Do you feel he's insincere?"

Jenny took her time over answering.

"He *sounds* genuine enough. Perhaps he really is motivated by guilt feelings and a desire to make some reparation to the people of Mourie . . ."

"You didn't suspect Douglas of being insincere when he wanted to do just that."

"No. But Douglas has really strong feelings about the Clearances and so on. I told you why he came here. I find his motives more credible than Crane Maclean's . . . And I'd scarcely call him 'modest.' He really was using threats when he suggested the possibility of a second treasure hunt."

"Yes. Quite suddenly, from being, one would have thought, gentle and rather naïve, he was almost ruthless . . . You must admit he's an *interesting* character—they both are, he and Douglas."

38

"I suppose so. But I'd rather talk about your adventure of tonight." Jenny's voice was suddenly serious. "You would be able to recognise the man who tried to get at you on the road up in the hills, wouldn't you?"

Elizabeth looked at her with respect. "How did you guess?"

"I was sure you were lying, though I don't think anyone else thought so. I just happen to know you well enough to be aware when you're hedging . . . Why did you?"

Elizabeth stirred in her chair, uneasily.

"I just suddenly thought that, apart from you, I didn't really *know* anyone there. And it might be wiser to let it be thought I couldn't recognise him. Otherwise . . ."

"Otherwise someone might have an interest in getting rid of you?"

"Yes—no! That sort of thing doesn't happen . . . does it?"

But Jenny was looking grim.

"I think you were quite right to lie. And as word gets around that you couldn't recognise him—and it certainly will, for Alice is congenitally incapable of holding her tongue about anything—I think the possibility of danger to you will become negligible . . . Are you worried about what happened to you at the church-yard tonight?"

"It wasn't *nice*—but no, I'm not worried. I'd rather forget about the whole thing, and hope other people will too."

This was perhaps too much to hope for. But at least Jenny's estimate of the situation was sound. Not only Alice talked; Douglas, after he left Jenny's, met Kenneth the Post on the way to a night's fishing, and told him, during a polite interchange of weather and local news, that Mrs. Lauder's niece would never be able to recognise the mysterious attacker. "And mebbe that is a good thing for her," said Kenneth sagely. Crane Maclean told the story to Jimmy and said: "And she has no idea who went for her in the car. It would be impossible for her to identify him." When Alice, the following morning, passed the same news on to Mrs. Macleod the Shop, a goodly proportion of the community already knew it. Alice and Mrs. Macleod merely completed the good work. When six people had told it back to Jenny in the course of the morning, she could with some confidence say to Elizabeth: "I think you're safe enough!" And she added thoughtfully: "And if the murderer—if your attacker *was* the murderer—is around, he'll think he's safe. And only you and I know he isn't."

CHAPTER 6

Of course, Elizabeth's adventure up on the crest of the hill, and her inability to recognise her attacker, were not the only items of news to circulate in Mourie after the evening encounter in Jenny's house. Word that Crane Maclean—"himself at the Big House"—was also interested in the laird's treasure was sufficiently exciting to break down the taboo on the subject. There was much low-voiced talk in the shop; among the little groups of men that always seemed to be gathering on the old jetty; and, less low-voiced, in the local bar at nights; though here it tended to die down if Crane or Douglas or either of Douglas' helpers appeared. The whole of Mourie soon knew of the possible rival treasure hunts, and two days after the encounter between Crane and Douglas, a gleaming-eyed Alice came to the cottage to say Mrs. Macleod the Shop had told her it was a sure thing that there would be two fleets of boats out in the Sound looking for the treasure and it would be no wonder if there was not a real sea fight between them . . .

But Mourie wasn't to have this pleasure. Common sense prevailed; and the morning after Alice had brought her report, Elizabeth met Crane Maclean just outside the post office, looking very pleased with himself. He greeted her cheerfully.

"I'm glad to see you. I'd have been to see you at your aunt's if I hadn't been so busy getting things fixed with Douglas McBain."

"You've made a satisfactory arrangement?"

"Sure. Douglas—or Douglas' backer—will get the personnel together—I gather they're already recruited—and pay them. I give them the use of Mourie House for living quarters and share

41

the cost of running the boats, and perhaps pay towards the hiring of them. It's fine."

"And Douglas? What part will he play?"

"Ah—that's one bit I'm not too happy about. It could be he may feel he's been done out of something. I said it'd be a shared command but he said "no"; better just one in charge, and as long as the stuff, if and when found, was used for the people right here, he didn't much mind if he was in command or not. I think it was pretty large-minded of him."

"It was indeed." Elizabeth was aware of her own astonishment as she spoke. Remembering Douglas' very strong reaction to Crane's announcement in Jenny's sitting-room, she found it difficult to believe Douglas could placidly give up his own scheme. But when he looked in at Jenny's later the same day, he was quite unperturbed about it.

"Two of us in charge would have been hopeless. He's got more money and a lot more time than I have—after all, I *am* schoolmaster here. Of course, I'll be involved in it—our backer wants me to keep an eye on things and keep in touch with the men."

"You're being very noble," said Jenny. "Are you sure it isn't that you just cannot bear working with Crane Maclean?"

Douglas seemed to be about to deny this, caught her eye, grinned and said:

"Well, perhaps."

So he is quite human, thought Elizabeth, beginning to feel much more kindly towards him.

All this happened on a Friday. On Saturday there was much activity. Three cabin cruisers towing three small boats equipped with outboard motors appeared in the Sound; the treasure fleet, as Alice dramatically called it. Six strangers came over the pass in a dormobile, and joined Johnson and Murphy, already established in Mourie House. On Sunday of course everything stopped and the strangers watched in amazement as the whole village sedately went to church to attend the monthly service taken by a minister from Skye, the charge at Mourie being vacant. On Monday more men arrived; excitement grew. On Wednesday Crane called in at Jenny's yet again (he had taken

42

to dropping in for coffee at eleven—a time, Jenny remarked, when he was sure not to meet Douglas) to tell Jenny and Elizabeth that all was ready; the natives of Mourie alone remained calm, though they did display a certain interest; their phlegm, in the presence of so much activity aimed, after all, at their benefit, was remarkable. Elizabeth mentioned it to both Crane and Douglas. Crane shrugged his shoulders and said maybe they resented strangers coming in and upsetting things. He hoped they'd get friendlier the longer he stayed. Douglas said it was to be expected. Exploited as they'd been for centuries by avaricious landlords, how could they be anything but sceptical?

But at last the diving started. Out on the Sound, two small boats, one a cabin-cruiser, the other with an outboard motor, tilted slowly up and down in a gentle swell, figures moved, and then, to a little murmur of wonder and interest from the small crowd on the shore, the helmeted, clumsy shape of a diver went over the side and slowly disappeared.

Crane, who had been watching through field-glasses, turned to Elizabeth and said:

"Well, now all we can do is wait and see."

Elizabeth heard the current of excitement in his voice, and his eyes were gleaming, as if from some hidden knowledge. Only for a moment. Then he grinned at her and said:

"I'm kind of looking forward to the moment when I can go to these people and say—'This is for you.'"

And he took her arm and turned to go up the beach.

But the small crowd which now faced them didn't part to let them through. It consisted, for the most part, of oldish men, with one or two middle-aged women, and in the forefront an old, a very old, woman. Or perhaps, thought Elizabeth, she isn't so very old; for wind and sea had tanned and wrinkled her face; she wore a black skirt midway down her calves, black stockings and shapeless black buttoned shoes, and over her head was a grey shawl that she clutched to her chest with brown hands; an anachronistic, a timeless, figure. The men wore thick jerseys and caps, and shapeless trousers tucked into Wellingtons, and one of them now spoke to Crane Maclean.

43

"It's a fine day, Mr. Maclean, a fine calm day."

Crane stood still and answered genially:

"Indeed yes. A very fine day."

"It is lucky for you that it is such a fine day, seeing you brought the divers here from the Clyde, and you will not be wanting them to waste their time."

Crane paused a little before replying:

"I am very pleased they can get on with it. But they didn't come from the Clyde. They come from Liverpool."

"Is that so? Well, well, they have come a very long way. Will they be long, do you think, in locating whatever it is that they are looking for?"

Crane's hand still held Elizabeth's elbow and she felt its grip tighten. She thought she heard him draw a little sharp breath. Then he dropped his hand, and she heard him say pleasantly, and patiently, perhaps a little too patiently:

"But you know what we're looking for: the laird's treasure."

Elizabeth saw the watching faces suddenly smooth themselves into blank immobility. It was like a barrier clicking down—or a sea-creature closing its tentacles—a withdrawal of contact. But Crane seemed not to notice and went on:

"And you know—some of you at any rate—that when we find it, I mean to give it back to the people I feel ought to have it."

There should have been at least a flicker of interest in the still faces turned towards them. But no; they remained smooth, shut. No one stirred, until an old man, white-haired, his jersey wrinkled over his thighs from the stooping of his back, said mildly:

"And are you sure the things from the Big House *are* out there?"

"Would I have these men there if I wasn't sure? But though I'm certain the stuff is there, that doesn't mean I'll find it. It may take some time. And we don't want a lot of outsiders coming and prying into what we're doing. So I'd be grateful if you keep quiet about it, don't tell any visitors or outsiders what we're after."

"But if they ask us, Mr. Maclean, what these divers are doing out there, what would we be saying? I would not like to be telling a lie."

And he looked round for approbation. A few heads nodded desultory approval, but it was at Crane, a somewhat non-plussed Crane, that they were all looking. Before he could speak, the first man's voice was heard: "Well now, Donald, you would not need to be telling a lie. You could just say that Mr. Maclean here was engaged in underwater research, and that would be quite true, and would not be giving anything away."

There was a murmur of agreement and Crane relaxed. "That would be the perfect answer," he said, "and I hope that's just what you'll say. It was a good suggestion, Mr.—?"

"McKay. Angus McKay. And I hope you will be very successful in your search."

And now the little crowd did part to let them through. But as they moved forward, a voice, cracked and scornful, said: "You'll find nothing."

It was the old woman who spoke.

Crane answered her, gently and courteously:

"Why not, ma'am?"

"Because the laird's treasure is not out there. It is—" But she dropped the hand she had raised to point, and, muttering something in Gaelic, swung round and pushed her way out of the crowd and down the street past the shop. Elizabeth noticed that the men gave her a wide path through and didn't look at her.

Angus turned to Crane and said: "Don't be heeding her. Morag is not quite right in the head, and you don't want to be paying any attention to her. Some people say she can cast the evil eye on you, but that's all nonsense."

"It is not all nonsense." Old Donald's voice was firm. "And I noticed you weren't meeting her eye yourself. And you know quite well what happened to Jamesina Macpherson when she annoyed Morag at the ceilidh just before Andrew went away."

"Well, well, we'll not be bothering Mr. Maclean with these stories. But don't you be paying any heed to her, Mr. Maclean."

"I won't," said Crane, and at last he and Elizabeth were able to make their way back up to the road.

45

Crane left Elizabeth at Jenny's door, regretfully declining to come in on the grounds that repair work up at Mourie House required his attention. Elizabeth found Jenny standing at the sitting-room window, absent-mindedly creaming butter and sugar in a mixing bowl while she looked out at the divers' boats.

"I see they've started," she said.

"Yes. There was quite a little crowd down on the shore watching."

"There would be. What were their reactions?"

"Politely interested would best describe it, I think. Wary, too. I think Crane was a little disconcerted by their lack of excitement. There was an old woman—Morag, I think was her name—who said the treasure wasn't out there anyway . . . and who's supposed to have the evil eye. Do they *really* believe that, Aunt Jenny?"

"Some people do. I think poor old Morag may believe it herself. She lives away out at Ruaidh Point on a tiny croft with a few sheep and hens, and she makes up herbal concoctions and people slink out shamefacedly to buy them. They're quite harmless. I suppose she must be one of the last of the 'Wise Women.' But I'm sure she's wrong about the laird's treasure."

"I'm sure she is too. I'm certain Crane Maclean would check on the story pretty thoroughly before beginning operations . . . it must be costing him an awful lot."

"A fool and his money," said Jenny sententiously, "are soon parted. Though I don't think Crane Maclean is a fool. More a rogue."

Jenny had always been prone to sudden prejudices against people, and Elizabeth didn't take her remark too seriously. But she too was certain that Crane was no fool. She could sense in him a drive and purposefulness much greater than the present project would have seemed likely to generate. After all, it could really make no difference to him whether or not he found the laird's treasure; there must be a deeper pressure. Some kind of guilt he was working out? Some ancestral, unconscious impulse? He was, at any rate, an interesting character, and she fully intended to learn more about him; and was quite ready to admit

46

to herself it would not be a purely intellectual exercise; even now she could feel the gentle pressure of his hand on her arm. As for his eyes—she'd always been susceptible to eyes . . .

Giving herself a little mental shake, she decided to go out for a walk, for it was a beautiful day. She strolled on down the village street. Quite close to Jenny's house was the school, a low, old-fashioned building of grey stone, the small-paned windows set high in the walls. It stood back from and above the road, and a playground surrounded by a stone wall sloped down almost to the street. As Elizabeth passed, she looked up at it. Douglas McBain's head was just visible at one of the windows, looking moodily out to sea.

He's probably glumly watching the divers, thought Elizabeth. He always seems to be disapproving of something. If he sees me, I'll wave to him.

Just then he did see her, and a delighted smile lit up his face. He raised his hand in greeting. She waved back, and walked on, thinking what an attractive smile he had: if only he smiled more often. But being schoolmaster in a place like this must be a lonely sort of job. Especially if you were as brilliant as Jenny said he was. So what motives drove him to stay? Really, whoever would have thought that Mourie would have provided such fascinating characters? She strolled on, answering greetings from everyone she met, past Mrs. Macleod's shop, past the post office, until she was beyond the last of the little houses of Mourie.

The road now turned inland to avoid the rocks and cliffs of a headland, and after a few hundred yards Elizabeth was walking through one of these bleak patches of landscape that, she was beginning to learn, could suddenly happen up here. She was looking across a stretch of bog and moor rolling away to the high hills on her left, without a tree or a house, and a few sheep the only living creatures. It was bleak but beautiful, with wide drifts of bog-cotton, white and soft as swansdown, and patches of brilliant red campion and blue cranesbill, and here and there the dark scar of a peat-trench. The sun shone, the air was clear and unsullied, there were puffs of the fragrance of bog-myrtle

47

and Elizabeth's spirits soared to a state of mindless happiness and she walked on unheeding time or distance.

The landscape changed where a ridge of rock struck down from the hills to the sea. The road ran into a cutting through rock, out of the sunlight into coolness and dampness, moss and ferns and trickling water. Not only the coolness made her shiver. She suddenly felt lonely and vulnerable and remembered the churchyard; and the fog-shrouded pass upon the hills. All sense of happiness fled, and she wondered if she should turn back, decided this would be cowardice, and went on. The cutting narrowed, the rocks pressed in, the sky was distant and the air gloomy, and looking ahead she saw a dark figure sitting on a boulder by the side of the road.

Now she was really afraid and her steps slowed down. But she continued to walk forward; and in a minute or two drew a breath in mildly hysterical reaction. For the dark figure turned its head to peer at her and she was sure it was old Morag. She was now close enough to see the old woman's expression, which was sufficiently malevolent to make Elizabeth remember the tale of the evil eye. But when Elizabeth was actually beside her, the lines of Morag's face relaxed, and Elizabeth realised that her vicious appearance was largely due to her short-sighted peering. She wondered if she should speak a greeting, and decided to compromise by smiling at her. But as she passed, Morag rose up, slowly, stiffly, and said: "It is a fine day."

Elizabeth stopped.

"Yes indeed. A beautiful day."

Morag was now standing beside her, and Elizabeth could now see that she was indeed very old, and that more than wind and sea had laid the wrinkles on her cheeks. Nevertheless, her eyes, though the irises were fading, were full of life, and she stood straight and upright. She carried in one hand a black plastic bag bulging with potatoes and topped by a wrapped loaf. The other hand held her shawl round her head and shoulders.

"Can I carry your bag for you?" said Elizabeth, on a sudden impulse.

Morag looked at her.

"I am not needing to be helped with the carrying." A pause. "But you can take it for part of the way."

She handed the bag over to Elizabeth with the air of one conferring a privilege and added, "But I will be walking more slowly than you would be doing by yourself."

"That doesn't matter," said Elizabeth, and they set off together up the road. It swerved gently round to the right, and soon they were out of the cutting and looking down past bog-cotton and dried heather and weather-worn grass to the sea again, and a green point covered with the close-cropped turf of the machair, and on it a small, low white house with a thatched roof on which blades of grass sprouted green. At one end was a tarred black lean-to shed with a crooked door; at the other, a neatly built peat-stack. Hens scratched round the house, there was a stretch of cobbling before the door, and a path had been trodden over the machair from the road to the door. Beyond the house, the machair ran down to a bay of yellow sand between two rocky points, where a dazzling sea broke on the shore.

"That is my house down there," said Morag.

"It's a beautiful spot," said Elizabeth.

"Yes." Morag accepted her remark as no more than due. They walked on. Elizabeth, glancing at Morag, got the impression from her closed and distant look that she didn't want to talk, and said nothing. When they reached the place where the path led from the road to the house, she stopped and made to hand the shopping bag to the old woman. But Morag ignored it. Instead, she gave Elizabeth a long look from her very old clear eyes and said:

"Would you like a cup of tea? I will be making one when I go in."

"Thank you," said Elizabeth, and followed her over the buoyant turf of the machair to the door of the little house.

Morag shooed away the hens that ran to cluster round her feet in their usual silly friendly way, opened the door, beckoned Elizabeth in, chased out a persistent and hopeful-eyed speckled biddy, and closed the door. They were in a tiny flagged lobby with a door to right, left and in front; plank doors with the kind

49

of iron handles and latches that Elizabeth remembered from her uncle's farmhouse. The door on the right was open and Morag went through it, Elizabeth following. The room rather surprised her, for she had expected something rather primitive—not exactly a hearth in the middle of the room, but stone floor, and a kettle swinging from a chain above a peat fire. But the room was comfortably organised, with two rag rugs on well-polished linoleum, a wooden table worn hollow with scrubbing, a sturdy wooden armchair on one side of the hearth, a rocking chair on the other and a comfortable settee under the front window. In the recess which must once have held a box-bed was a sideboard on which stood a radio. Morag filled the kettle from the tap at the sink under a small window at the back of the house which looked out on to the sea, and put it to boil on a neat Calor gas cooker. But the fire in the grate was peat and the cottage was warm with the fragrance of it which had hung on the air outside too.

"Sit you down," said Morag, busy setting out old-fashioned white and gold cups on the table. "It will not be long till the kettle is boiling."

So Elizabeth sat in the wooden chair and looked round the room. On the high mantelpiece there were two heavy brass candlesticks, a clock in a black marble casing, a little black wooden elephant with ivory tusks and a model of the Eiffel Tower with a thermometer in it, registering an impossibly low temperature. Above the mantelpiece hung an enlarged and fading photograph of a smiling young man wearing a seaman's cap; below it, on the left, one of a young man in a graduation gown and hood. Propped up behind the Eiffel Tower was yet a third photograph, of another young man, wavy-haired, smiling, with strongly marked features, wearing an anorak. Three generations? Husband, son, grandson?

Morag handed her a cup of tea and a biscuit from a tin gaudy with rosebuds. She sat in the rocker and drank her tea. She had laid aside her shawl. Her thin hair was completely white. She saw Elizabeth looking at the photographs and said:

"That is my husband, the big one. And my son when he was

50

capped. And my grandson is on the mantelpiece." She drank her tea and went on:

"My husband was drowned at sea when my son was still young. He was a good son to me. But he is dead now too." Elizabeth saw the old wrinkled hand shake a little and the cup trembled on the saucer. But the quiet voice was steady enough. "Yes. He died last year."

"I'm sorry . . . And your grandson?"

But either she had not heard, or did not wish to hear, for she rose and said:

"Will you be taking more tea?"

But Elizabeth had seen the time.

"No, thank you. I must go, or I'll be late for dinner. Thank you very much for the tea."

But Morag totally disregarded her, took up her cup, refilled it and said:

"I have something to say to you, so you will please sit down again."

And Elizabeth did so.

But Morag was not to be hurried. She took her own cup over to the stove and refilled it and then she put another peat on the fire and then she sat down and rocked gently for a moment or two, without saying a word. It was only when Elizabeth made a movement as if to stand up again that she put out an authoritative hand, saying:

"Wait now, and I will tell you what I have to say," at the same time looking fixedly at Elizabeth. Perhaps it was the effort of focussing her eyes, but they suddenly were dark and luminous and seemed to be seeing more than the immediate surroundings. Elizabeth, looking into them, jumped as she felt Morag's hand—oddly cold—touch her own fingers.

"There is no need to be jumping at my hand on yours." There was a smile in the old tired voice. "If I had the evil eye"—a tiny chuckle—"I would not be using it on you."

She drew back her hand, and beckoned to Elizabeth. "Pull your chair closer. That is better. Now—I was seeing you down

51

at the shore with that man who has been sending the divers down?"

"Yes, I was there."

"Well now, they are telling me he is after what the people here call the Laird's Treasure."

"Yes, that's so."

"Well now, I am telling you he is wasting his time. The treasure is not there." She stopped and looked at Elizabeth as if expecting a comment. There was a note of urgency, almost hysteria in her voice, and as Elizabeth remained silent, looking at her and wondering what to say, she turned her head away with a little jerk of disgust and muttered something in Gaelic. Then she turned back and caught Elizabeth's arm.

"I tell you, it is not there!"

"Mr. Maclean is sure it is. He's been told by everyone it's there . . ."

(But how was he so sure? She must ask him.)

"But it is not, I tell you. And you must tell him."

This is absurd, thought Elizabeth, divided between irritation and concern for the old woman, now apparently veering towards the impotent anger of the very old.

"But why are you so worried about it?" she said at last, gently. "If there's nothing there, in a few days they'll stop looking, and there'll be no harm done."

But this also was disregarded. "They will never believe what I say. But I have been here longer than any of them." She began to mutter in Gaelic again and then returned to English. "But if you told him, he would be believing you."

But Elizabeth rose to her feet, gently detaching the hand clutching her arm.

"I promise I'll tell Mr. Maclean that you are sure the laird's treasure isn't there. And now I must go. My aunt will be waiting for me."

But Morag followed her to the door and caught her arm again.

"I see you are not believing me. But I tell you I *know*. Have they not told you I have the sight?"

52

And she thrust her face up to Elizabeth's; and indeed her eyes were very dark and full of some kind of knowing.

It was too much. Elizabeth felt as if she were in a dream where she was caught in a situation from which she could not break out. But she was still gentle.

"No one told me that. But I must go." And she managed to reach the outside door and open it. The speckled hen immediately walked in, cocking a beady eye, and unheeded by Morag. She was now clinging to Elizabeth with both hands so that, short of a near brutality, it was impossible to escape. Again she thrust her head up and peered into Elizabeth's face, lowered her voice and said:

"If I was to be showing you the treasure, where it is, would you be believing me?"

"Yes," said Elizabeth, seizing a chance to end the situation.

"Well then, you come back here tomorrow—you would be better to come in your motor car—and I'll take you to the place. Will you promise me you will come?"

"I promise," said Elizabeth. Morag released her, and soon she had crossed the machair and reached the road. She looked back and waved to the dark figure in the doorway, but Morag made no answering gesture. Next time she looked back, Morag had disappeared but a speckled hen was running out of the cottage door with raised wings.

She was late for dinner and would have been later, if she had not been given a lift in a rickety van owned by the shop and driven cheerfully and erratically by Mrs. Macleod's nephew Roddy, an amiable young man who in the short distance—for it was only three miles or less to Aunt Jenny's house, managed in the nicest way to find out where Elizabeth came from, what she meant to do next, her opinion of Mourie and her marital standing— "But you'll surely be going to get married before long?" What he did not touch on were the two topics uppermost in the mind of Mourie—her discovery on the pass and Crane Maclean's enterprise. She remarked on this to Jenny as they ate, but Jenny found nothing odd about it.

"He wouldn't waste time discussing something everyone knows

about already. It was new information he wanted—and got—about you. Everyone coming into a community like this is terribly interesting to the inhabitants. They know all about each other so a new person is a godsend. You have to learn to live in a glass bowl here. It's 99.9 per cent impossible to keep anything secret."

"So if the whereabouts of the laird's treasure was known to one person, it would be known to everyone?"

Aunt Jenny stared at her.

"But it is known. It's in the Sound."

"I know. But old Morag . . ." And she told Jenny about the morning's encounter.

Aunt Jenny was interested but dismissed Morag's claim to knowledge of the treasure's true whereabouts.

"She's very old, and lonely. And yes—some people would say she has the sight—and the evil eye, as you have heard. And she does lay claim to mysterious sources of knowledge . . . It's all a compensating mechanism, I'm certain, to make up for her loneliness. It's increased since the death of her son. He was a good son, in that he sent her money and came to see her from time to time. He took a degree in Glasgow and went to work in London. His wife never came. She was ashamed of the old woman and his humble origins, I think. Once he brought his son, just a boy. I believe the boy—he must be a man now—does occasionally write to her."

"I saw his photograph. She has three photographs—husband, son and grandson. Is she very poor?"

"She has National Assistance and she manages. People are kind here. She gets presents of fish and home baking and so on. If she's as lonely as she is, it's largely by choice."

"I told you I've promised I'll go again tomorrow . . ."

"You must go. But she'll probably have forgotten all about the treasure. She's like that—for a day or so she'll be obsessed with a notion. Then she'll forget it . . . What's wrong?"

For Elizabeth had put down her knife and fork and was looking down at her plate.

"Nothing really. It's just . . . well, she's so old, and no one really caring for her, and her mind slipping . . ."

"But I don't think she's miserable. She has her own place and her independence and is still part of a community. And if she's lucky, it'll be like that to the end . . . Come on, cheer up. You can't take all the woes of the world on to yourself."

Melancholy did linger with Elizabeth for some time. But by evening it lifted, and when Douglas suggested she should go to the dance being held in the village hall in aid of Dramatic Club funds, she accepted cheerfully. The hall was a large wooden hut on a high and exposed site above the sea. When they got there, the dance was in full swing, with fiddle and accordion pouring out a reel tune. Elizabeth was surprised to see so many people, and such a wide range of ages. The air was thickish with smoke and occasional whiffs of whisky drifted past. Tea and sandwiches were being served at one end of the hall, but there was a fairly steady coming and going by the men through the two doors open to the evening sunlight and it was clear that stronger fare was available somewhere outside. It was good fun and Elizabeth danced reels and waltzes and Dashing White Sergeants with a variety of partners, including Roddy the Shop, who hailed her like an old friend, but most often with Douglas, who turned out to be an excellent dancer. She was enjoying herself thoroughly; this lighthearted unthinking kind of pleasure had been missing from her scheme of things for too long.

And then Crane Maclean came through one of the open doors, dark against the clear light. And with his arrival, the whole feeling of the place altered. A kind of wariness settled over the company, manifested, it seemed to Elizabeth, in a forced bonhomie. Angus McKay, who was acting off and on as Fear an Tigh, keeping things going, seeing people had partners, and generally acting as a master of ceremonies, bustled up to Crane and said—a little too loudly?—"Well, now, Mr. Maclean, we are glad to see you here."

The dance went on. Crane professed ignorance of the dances but the hall was full of people ready to teach him. It was some

55

time before he danced with Elizabeth. It was an old-fashioned waltz and as they took the floor he said: "I've been waiting for a dance that I know, where I'll have you to myself. In these reels, you never have the same girl for more than a minute."

They circled the floor once or twice and then he said: "Let's go outside for a bit and breathe the good air."

So they went out and sat on an outcrop of rock and looked over the Sound to the sunset behind the mountains of Skye. Black on the shining water was a little boat. They could see the man in it silhouetted against the light as he pulled in his lines. And the sight prompted Elizabeth to ask:

"Did the diving go successfully today?"

"It depends what you mean by 'successfully.' We didn't find anything. But I didn't expect to do that at the first attempt."

"You're quite sure, of course, that the treasure is there?"

"Of course it is." Douglas had come out too and was standing behind them. He sat down beside Elizabeth and went on, "Why do you ask?"

She told them about Morag.

"I'm still satisfied it's out there," said Crane, nodding towards the Sound. "I went into the matter pretty thoroughly before I came here—old records and traditions and so on. *Will* you go and see the old woman again tomorrow?"

"I promised. But Aunt Jenny thinks it's all just a delusion of old age, and that she'll probably have forgotten about the treasure by tomorrow."

"At her age she might very well get fanciful notions about things," said Douglas. "Shall we go back in? I'd like to dance this reel with you, Elizabeth."

By midnight the hall was a thick haze of hot smoky air, and very crowded. Crane, Elizabeth and Douglas decided to leave. Crane drove off in his car, and Douglas and Elizabeth walked to Jenny's. It was a dark night, for clouds had gathered behind the hills and blotted out the afterglow. The sound of the sea was more insistent, and white crests were tumbling on the shore.

"It's going to be a wet and windy night," said Douglas, and

by the time they reached Jenny's door the first drops were falling.

Jenny welcomed them cheerfully. She had been prevented from going to the dance by a call from a shepherd's cottage beyond Ruaidh. "But it was a false alarm. It's her first and she's a bit nervous. I saw Morag at the door of her cottage and she returned my wave of the hand. Come in, Douglas."

But Douglas refused, regretfully.

"I've some work that must be done before tomorrow," he said. "I'll see you in the afternoon, probably. Good night."

As he turned from the door, the rain was falling heavily and the wind rising. When Elizabeth went to bed the wind was roaring across the house, the waves crashing, the rain rapping on the window. Out at Ruaidh Point the booming of the waves and the screaming of the wind penetrated the thick walls of Morag's cottage and filled her bedroom with a shadowy thunder that disturbed her not at all. The tumult swamped lesser sounds. It muffled the click of the latch as the front door was opened and shut again quickly, and deadened the stealthy footfalls on the flagstones leading to the room where Morag slept. Here there was total darkness, for the window was curtained by thick stuff that moved as the wind thrust through the frame. A narrow beam from a torch cut through the blackness like a razor, and played for an instant on the old, wrinkled, chop-fallen face. For a moment the eyes opened but doubtless the light blinded them and Morag never saw the man with the cold pale eyes who held the torch, and never knew what it was that suddenly blotted the light from her eyes and took the breath from her body. She was old and had little strength. Once or twice the blankets and the patchwork coverlet twitched. And then were still.

In the darkness, the man lifted up the cushion, and for a minute or two the light probed at the face and the open, un-seeing, unchanging eyes. A hand felt for her heart. Then the muffled steps withdrew, and the light went through to the other room, swept round it, lingered for a moment on the mantelpiece,

57

and was then switched off. The front door opened and shut again. A dark shape, bent and distorted by the gale, loped with long strides up the path to the road and into the cutting. The wind, rising to a gust, drowned the noise of the car starting up, and swept moaning round the silent little house.

CHAPTER 7

The next day, a day sparkling after the storm, with a northern, cold clarity of tumbling waves and sharp-edged mountains, with every stalk and feathery blossom of the grass standing out in the light, Elizabeth kept her promise and went to Ruaidh and found Morag in the dark quiet little room. She closed the wide-open eyes, and drew up the sheet, and then she went out into the sunlit day, saddened. The speckled hen led the others up to her in a puzzled hungry rush, and she went into the shed, found grain in a galvanised bin, and threw them a handful. Then she drove back to Jenny's and told her of Morag's death.

She heard the news regretfully but calmly. "It's not unknown for an old person to die alone like that. So often they live by themselves in remote cottages. I'll phone Dr. Marshall and he'll get the ferry over from Skye. And I suppose we must try to contact her grandson."

"The photograph of her grandson that stood on her mantelpiece isn't there any more," said Elizabeth, in a small voice. "When she didn't answer my knock, I went into her kitchen—and I saw the photograph had gone."

"I expect Morag took it down to look at and forgot to put it back." Jenny looked searchingly at her niece. "What's bothering you, Elizabeth?"

"I couldn't see it lying around. You don't think there might have been an intruder in the cottage . . . ?"

"No I don't. Don't let your imagination run riot, Elizabeth." Momentarily she was a grown-up aunt addressing a small niece.

59

"The photograph will probably turn up somewhere in the cottage. And now I must phone Dr. Marshall."

Which she did. And the due processes took place. And in two days the men of Mourie carried Morag to the churchyard, a simple and solemn procession, and she was buried. Efforts to find her grandson were unsuccessful; a telegram to the address found among her letters elicited from his landlady the information that he had gone on holiday and left no address. His photograph didn't turn up either, but no one worried about that. The cottage was shut up until such time as he could be found; the hens went to a neighbour's croft; and the little house was left to the sound of the wind and the sea, and its sturdy walls absorbed and held the secret of Morag's death as they had absorbed and held so much.

And might have kept the secret for ever until only an unevenness in the machair showed where the walls had stood, if John Maclean the Ferry hadn't gone peat-cutting.

This did not, however, happen immediately after Morag's death, which indeed caused very little upheaval in Mourie. The community, having seen her decently laid to rest, paid the due tributes of kindly comment on the old woman and continued with the daily round. Her death simply fitted into the pattern and was neither ignored nor emphasised. Elizabeth remarked on this to Jenny. "Life is beautifully simple and well organised here."

Jenny laughed. "I'm not so sure about that. People always make the mistake of thinking remoteness means simple-mindedness and it's not so."

"In some ways," said Elizabeth, "they seem very obvious in their approach to things, like the way they're keeping a constant watch on the divers to catch the first glimpse of the treasure they hope is coming to them."

For she and Jenny were sitting in the sunlight among the rocks of the headland on the north side of the bay and above them they could see Angus McKay and Kenneth the Post lying on the turf, watching the diving boats.

"There's always someone on the watch," went on Elizabeth. "They change over regularly."

"You'd think they didn't trust Crane to hand over the spoils," said Jenny.

"I'm sure they needn't worry about that."

"I'm sure too. But it's all a bit puzzling. The more I see of Crane Maclean the more puzzling I find it, that he should devote all this energy to looking for this legendary stuff to give to the people of Mourie."

Elizabeth didn't answer this, for she knew Jenny's attitude to Crane was still rather cool. Instead, her own thoughts having strayed to Morag and Morag's words about the treasure, she abruptly asked:

"Didn't you say coins have been picked up from time to time on the shore?"

"That's the story. But as I said I don't know of anyone who's actually *seen* such a thing."

But they both saw one themselves that night.

Jenny and Elizabeth shared a weakness for sitting up late reading and drinking tea. Jenny was absorbed in a weighty and improbable romance about ongoings at the Court of Charles II (*To Bed to Bed, Fair Madam*) and Elizabeth was totally lost in the gentle moral agonies of the *Heir of Redclyffe,* when a hammering at the back door made them jump. Jenny looked up from her book momentarily bewildered. Then she put it down resignedly and went through to the back. Elizabeth heard a man's voice loud and worried and Jenny's soothing and calm. Then she put her head round the sitting-room door and said: "Peg's in labour and they want me to go. I don't know how long I'll be."

"I'll come too," said Elizabeth, "if I won't be in the way."

"You might even be useful. You could at least keep the rest of the tribe at bay, and leave me in peace to get on with things."

In ten minutes, she and Sandy Macphee were standing in the road while Jenny got the car out. It was about a quarter past twelve. There was a stiffish breeze blowing—not stormy, but

61

enough to mettle the Sound with white wave-crests and spume and to draw sound from the stiff grass and low bushes and to make Elizabeth shiver in her thick pullover and Sandy hunch his shoulders under his worn and ragged jacket. In the car, he leant over from the back seat and kept up an anxious patter of conversation. From him there came a smell of smoke-saturated clothing and sweat. Jenny listened to him, asked one or two questions and finally said:

"You're in the usual place?"

"Aye. At the mooth o' the Mourie Burn. Yon level stretch past the trees."

Elizabeth realised they were following the road towards the old church, but before they reached it, Jenny swung off to the left on a track that soon disappeared in the turf of the machair. The headlights swung and dipped as the car took to the grass. Presently the beam caught a group of three low black tents, like clumsy up-turned coracles, centred on a fire where flames flickered beneath a big black kettle. Through the opening of one tent the faint glow of a hurricane lamp spilled on to the grass outside. Shadows moved across the light, and as the car stopped they heard from the tent a choked cry and a murmur of voices. When Sandy heard it, he froze into stillness, listening, then clutched Jenny's arm, gabbling:

"That's her. For God's sake, dae something, missis."

Jenny released her arm gently.

"Don't take on, Sandy. You were just like this last time and it was all right. Peg's a healthy lassie."

"Aye. But this time it'll mebby no be a' richt."

Then, as another cry rose past the sound of the wind in the trees . . .

"Oh Goad," he said, dropped his hand and stood shivering.

"Away in, and have a drink, if you've got any," said Jenny, and, picking up her bag, she made her way into the tent, followed by Elizabeth.

There was more room inside the tent than Elizabeth would have thought possible. A hurricane lamp hanging from one of the supports and swinging in the wind filled it with moving shadow.

The covering was black tarpaulin stretched over long withies, curved in and bound together to make an arched framework. It was just possible to stand upright in the middle of the tent. Round the side were bundles of rugs, two or three stools and some pots and pans. Tin mugs hung from nails in the framework and in an up-ended box were a loaf of bread and a tin milk can. On a mattress on the ground a red-headed girl was tossing and turning, her face flushed and her eyes glittering. On one side stood an older woman and on the other a young woman was kneeling, and as Jenny and Elizabeth entered, Peg clutched at the other's hands and clung till her knuckles whitened while her body heaved, and sweat glistened on her forehead.

The older woman turned to Jenny and said: "Ah'm gled to see ye, mem. She's no' havin' an easy time: no' like the last baby. Ah've got the kettle boiling and the basin ready here."

She had a broad face with high cheekbones, and dark eyes, and her hair was caught back tidily. She had an air of competence which her motley huddle of tinker clothes could not conceal. It was clear Jenny respected her.

"We'd better have the basin filled then, Nancy, and I'll get my hands washed." And while Nancy busied herself, Jenny knelt down by the mattress.

"Hullo, Peg," she said, and Peg turned on her, her eyes brimming with tears of relief and weakness.

"Oh, Mistress Lauder, Ah'm gled tae see ye." She was breathing quickly and now she released her hold of Bella's hands and clutched at Jenny's. "Ah'm feart. It's different from last time."

Jenny patted her hand gently.

"You're not to be upset, Peg. Let me see how you're doing."

And she pulled down the tattered rugs and blankets and felt the heavy, heaving body with kind, skilled hands, while the lantern swung and the wind tugged at the tarpaulin. When she finally drew up the bed-clothes she said cheerfully: "You're doing fine, Peg, but the baby won't be here for some time yet. Meanwhile I'm going to send my niece for some medicine."

She drew Elizabeth out of the tent and said in a low voice: "I'd like you to go back to the house and telephone Dr. Marshall

63

over in Skye. Tell him what's happening, say I'm not happy about the way it's going, and ask him to come. You'll have to keep ringing for some time before Mrs. Robertson at the exchange answers. But she will—eventually. Don't let anyone here know why you're going back—I'll say I've sent you for some medicine."

So Elizabeth drove back through the windy night to the cottage and did at last succeed in rousing Mrs. Robertson at the exchange and persuading her to put a call through to Dr. Marshall — "But don't be upset if he is a bit cross when he answers. He does not like having his sleep broken." And when Dr. Marshall did at last answer, he was very gruff indeed; but calmed down when Elizabeth explained the situation.

"Mrs. Lauder wouldn't waken me up at this godless hour without good reason. I'll try to come, but with this wind, there may be difficulty with the ferry. But I'll do my best."

When Elizabeth arrived back at the tents, she found the fire had been banked up and was blazing high. There were lights in the other tents now and a general feeling of anxiety and uneasiness. Jenny, watching by beside Peg, heard Dr. Marshall's message with a sigh. "I was just afraid the wind might interfere with the ferry. We'll just have to do the best we can. See what's happening outside. Bella lost her nerve and went out sobbing, and she's probably told the rest that Peg's dying. Which she's not—yet."

Nancy, who had been bending over Peg, turned and called quietly to Jenny, and Elizabeth left them both busy about the mattress on which Peg lay. Outside, the fire was dancing in the wind and sitting beside it was the old woman Elizabeth had seen in the lorry on her first morning in Mourie. She sat looking into the flames; one long lean hand hanging loosely from the wrist caught the light and her face was pitted with moving shadows. As Elizabeth stood uncertainly in the entrance to Peg's tent, the hand beckoned her forward to the fire and a voice croaked: "Is she bad?"

"I don't know," said Elizabeth.

"Her in there"—jerking her head at the tent behind her—

64

"Bella, said she was bad and like tae dee. But she's a silly wumman. Peg's no'! Peg's a guid lassie."

She cocked her head to listen to the sounds from Peg's tent—a quiet moaning, almost swept away by the wind.

"Aye, she's bad." There was a kind of satisfaction in her tone that Elizabeth found shocking, but before she could say anything, the flap of the tent opposite her was lifted and a child, a little girl of about seven, came out, barefoot and crying, "Ah want ma mammy."

The old woman spoke into the flames without turning her head.

"Ye canna see your mammy noo."

The child stood and cried, quietly and hopelessly. Elizabeth went up to her and took her hand.

"Don't cry. What's your name?"

"Lizzie."

"That's my name too. Come and sit by the fire."

She sat on a wooden box by the fire and took the child on her knee and sensed again the smell of smoke and sweat. The child's hair was tousled but quite clean. At first she sat stiffly in Elizabeth's arms, then the thin little body relaxed and Lizzie sat looking into the fire with big worried eyes.

And so the night wore on, and before long the brightness of the fire grew less as daylight came. The wind shifted slightly, the twilight of dawn lay on the little camp. And still Peg tossed and moaned and sometimes cried out, and there was no baby. Sandy came out of a tent, sat by the fire, heard Peg, covered his ears with his hands and slouched off into the shadow of the trees. Old Mysie's eyes swivelled round at him as he went, and she spat derisively into the fire. "Aye, aye. That's the men. Canna face thir ain wark." She suddenly addressed Elizabeth. "Her in there—Nancy—she'll no' let me in. She fair fancies hersel' as a howdie-wife. An' me that has helpit mair weemen than she ever set eyes on, aye, an' in ways she doesna ken. But they'll need me at the end o' the day—ye'll see. Even if it's juist fur the layin'-oot."

She leaned forward and thrust her face at Elizabeth. "Ye

think Ah'm a cauld-herted auld bitch. Ah'm no'. But a body doesna like tae be thrust oot . . . Noo, Ah'll mak some tea."

It was when they were drinking the hot sweet smoky tea that the climax came. There was a scream from Peg's tent and through the entrance Elizabeth could see hurried movement from Jenny and Nancy. The child on her knee stopped gulping at her mug of tea and began to tremble. And Mysie put her mug on the ground and stood up.

"It's time fur *me* noo. An' fur something else in yon tent than hot water." She looked at Elizabeth. "Ah'm going in there with *this!*"

And she thrust a hand down her jumper and pulled out something small and gleaming threaded on a dark cord. It was like a little round pendant and she held it up and swung it to and fro. Lizzie, in Elizabeth's arms, went rigid and hid her face. For a moment the old woman looked like some kind of priestess, standing there with the thing swinging before her, and the light climbing in the sky behind her and the trees tossing. She seemed to be entering into some part and acting it out. She swung the little round object to and fro, casting sly sidelong glances at Elizabeth, and when the sun, rising above the hills beyond the trees, struck a glow from the pendant, she held it up, stalked over to Peg's tent, and entered, a ragged old tinker woman with wrinkled stockings round her ankles and bauchled shoes—and yet momentarily in the dawn light, clothed with a weird dignity. The child uncovered her face and said: "Is she awa'?" And Elizabeth was aware that Bella had come out from her tent and was standing beside her at the fire.

"Things are bad, if she's taken *yon* in." Bella spoke in an awed whisper, but Lizzie heard, and began to whisper.

"But what *is* it?" Elizabeth realised she was whispering too. The wind had momentarily died into stillness, and from Peg's tent there was silence—a chilling silence.

Bella knelt by the fire and held her hands to it.

"It's a—it's a kind o' charm. Mysie's man—ma grandfaither—got it frae a drooned man. He found him on the shore doon there. It was in his hand and ma grandfaither took it. It was in

66

the war—the auld war—the man was a sailor and he's buried back there in the kirkyaird. An' ma grandfaither had a hole made in the thing, and wore it till he died; and Mysie got it. An' it's a luck-bringer—and worth money. But ma grandfaither said it was never tae be sold. It's no' often we see it. Only if things is bad."

"Are you telling me," said Elizabeth, "that Mysie thinks that—that object can help Peg to have her baby safely?" She hoped the scorn in her voice was not too obvious.

But Bella whispered back seriously: "It micht—it *will!* Ah tell you, it's a powerfu' charm."

She flung a branch on the fire and it burned up brightly. The daylight was fully there, the pale dawn sunlight flooded the encampment. Bella looked sideways at Elizabeth.

"Why no' gang after her, and see whit happens?—naw"—as Elizabeth made to speak—"Ah'll no' go. But Ah'll tak the bairn frae ye."

She took Lizzie gently on to her knees, and Elizabeth rose from the fire and went over to Peg's tent and through the low entrance. The tent, with the swinging lantern, was darker than the clearing outside. The air was hot, the little shelter heavy with the smell of sweat and raw humanity and disinfectant. Nancy knelt by Peg's head on one side, Mysie on the other. Jenny was standing, looking serious. She turned as Elizabeth stole in and whispered: "No sign of the doctor?"

Elizabeth shook her head and raised a questioning eyebrow. "I'm a bit worried. She's getting very tired . . ."

Peg's face was white, drawn and shining, and her red hair was ragged against the mattress. She had the look which Elizabeth had seen among the village women in India in childbirth, of being abandoned to forces that she neither controlled nor understood. Pain, struggle, fear were grinding her strength away.

Peg's half-naked body heaved, the muscles stiffened, thrust, there was a shriek—and nothing happened.

And then Mysie took over. She took Peg's hands and placed them round the ridiculous little object swinging from the string. "Hold that, ma lassie. It's powerfu'. It'll gie ye the strength

67

ye need." There was no malice in her voice now. It was all confidence and reassurance. Elizabeth looked at Jenny, wondering, waiting for a brusque and sensible rebuttal of the old woman. But Jenny was kneeling by Peg, she was adding encouraging murmurs to Mysie's words. And as Peg cupped her hands round the pendant Mysie caught her wrists and Peg's body heaved and pushed and heaved and pushed, and her mouth opened and she shrieked—and Jenny said:

"Good girl, good girl. The head is here."

And between Peg's thighs Elizabeth could see the tiny, wet, red-haired skull appearing.

She turned her head to hide the tears in her eyes.

In a matter of minutes the baby, sticky and yellow, alive and perfect, lay in Jenny's hands. For a moment there wasn't a sound in the tent. A deep silence, broken by the baby's first cry.

The five women had eyes for nothing else than the squawking little scrap of humanity, and between them flowed a primeval surge of triumph. Jenny was looking at the baby with a kind of wonder. She caught Elizabeth's eye and said:

"I've delivered hundreds and I still don't get used to it."

Nancy was—yes, she was glowing, triumphant in sharing the process of birth. Peg lay back, exhausted and satisfied, and opened her eyes to ask the inevitable question: "Is it a laddie?"

"A fine wee boy." Jenny was the unemotional and competent nurse again. Mysie rose up, and strode out, putting the string round her neck, tucking the pendant into her jumper, saying not a word, but casting at Nancy and Jenny a withering look of scornful triumph. Jenny saw it and laughed: "Mysie has certainly shown us up . . . Nancy, get some warm water, will you, and we'll bathe the baby in a minute." And to Peg, "I'm just going to cut the cord, Peg, and he'll really be on his own, and in a minute you'll get him to hold."

The moment of high feeling had gone, ebbed away, lost in practicalities. Elizabeth slipped out of the tent to find Mysie. She was standing by the fire, looking down at Bella and saying to Lizzie: "You've got a wee brither: an' yer mammy's a' richt—thenks tae me." She turned to Elizabeth. "Is that no' richt?"

"Oh yes," said Elizabeth, "it is indeed . . . May I see the—what you gave Peg to hold?"

Mysie was reluctant. She looked at Bella.

"Tak the bairn intae the tent. She's tired." And when they had gone, she said: "It's no' tae be laughed at."

"But I wouldn't dream . . ."

"Aye. Weel, ye see, it's no in itsel' sae wonnerfu'. But it cam tae us in a deid man's han'—and that's whit maks it a powerfu' charm . . . ye'll no touch it?"

"No."

So Mysie dived into her grubby jumper again and hauled out the powerful charm. It swung at the end of the string, and Elizabeth saw it was a coin—a gold coin—a sovereign. It spun round before her eyes and she saw the St. George and dragon.

"It was in a drowned man's hand?"

"Aye. A sailor. Ma man found him doon there, in the war, the First War. Lying on the sand. And he had a haud o' this."

Surely this was one of the coins reputed to be picked up on the shore. She must tell Crane about it . . . but Mysie was putting it away again.

"There's no mony fowk Ah show it tae. Ye'll be carefu' whae ye tell aboot it?"

"Yes, I will. Very careful."

Mysie said nothing more, and at that moment the sound of a car made them look towards the road. John Maclean the Ferry's dented old Morris 1000 came bumping gently over the machair. Out of it came a man in a duffle coat, grizzle-haired, weather-beaten, carrying a small case. He strode purposefully over to Elizabeth.

"Which tent? I'm the doctor."

Elizabeth pointed. "In there. But the baby's come."

He grunted, glanced at her from under bushy eyebrows, and went in.

Elizabeth was left alone by the fire in the clear bright morning air. She was aware of a feeling of anti-climax after the emotions of the night, and smiled wryly to herself, thinking how she had looked forward to peace and quiet refreshment in Mourie, and

69

what she had actually found. Bella came out, built up the fire, put on the big black kettle. It was clear that the sense of fellowship built up during the night was going. She was withdrawing into her tinker wariness again. Presently Nancy called from Peg's tent, "Would you like to see the baby?" and Bella and Elizabeth went in.

Peg was propped up on rolled-up rugs and pillows. There were, Elizabeth noticed, clean sheets on the bed. Had Jenny brought them? Peg was looking blissful, holding the baby. Bella looked and admired and so did Elizabeth and again there was a sense of age-old happiness, of something very basic, in the little tent, all centred on the pucker-faced, ugly little creature in Peg's arms.

The doctor broke the little silence.

"Well, well, Peg Macphee, I'm glad it's all over. And Mrs. Lauder did very well by you. I'll call to see you tomorrow. And now we'd better all get on our way. Where's that rascal, Sandy?"

"Ah'm here, Doctor, Ah'm here," said a deprecatory voice from just outside. "Can Ah come in? Is it a' ower? Is—is she a' richt?"

"She's fine, Sandy," said Jenny. "Come and see your son."

Sandy shambled in, looking shamefaced and sly. He stood by the mattress, and Peg held up the baby. For a moment his face was expressionless. Then he grinned broadly, and poking delightedly at the bundle in the shawl with a grubby forefinger, Sandy greeted his son: "Aw, the wee bugger," said Sandy. "Aw, the wee bugger."

CHAPTER 8

Back at Jenny's cottage, Dr. Marshall was invited to have break-fast, and was glad to accept. They talked, of course, of Mysie's intervention in the delivery of Peg's baby, and Elizabeth was interested and amused to find that Dr. Marshall did not treat it with complete scepticism; not that he gave the slightest credence to any mysterious property of the charm; but the tinkers' belief in such a property might very well, he felt, have had an effect on Peg and given her that little bit of extra strength . . . eh? What did Mrs. Lauder think? Aunt Jenny was non-committal, but said she'd long since given up explaining everything in nursing or healing as being purely physical . . . and if Peg and Mysie felt that the trinket Mysie guarded so jealously had magic powers, perhaps for them it *did* have magic powers—and would the doctor like more toast and marmalade?

It was a pleasant meal, and when it was over and the doctor had gone to find John Maclean the Ferry and to attempt the crossing back to Skye, Aunt Jenny bolted the front door, warned Mrs. Robertson at the exchange not to put through any calls unless of an urgent medical nature, and she and Elizabeth prepared to go to bed.

On the way upstairs, Elizabeth said:

"Do you know what Mysie's charm really is?"

"No. I just got a glimpse of it. And I've never seen it before, or even heard of it."

"It's a very special thing for them at the camp . . ." She told Jenny what it was and added, "It seems to back up the local story of coins being picked up on the shore . . . and to be

71

evidence that Crane isn't wasting his time and that the laird's treasure is there . . ."

"Very probably. But let's talk about it later. I'm tired now." And in a matter of minutes they were both in bed and asleep.

Elizabeth wakened to bright sunshine—bright afternoon sunshine streaming into the rose-bud-spattered bedroom and making it glow. From the tiny front garden voices rose up to her open window. She recognised Crane's—deep and strong—and a wave of pleasure ran through her. She thought: "I'm beginning to like him too much." For in the meetings she'd had with him—casually, meeting him in Mourie's one long straggling street, down watching the diving, at the dance in the hall, over coffee at Jenny's—she had found him enormously attractive, so much so that she had deliberately assumed a cool, calm collectedness which she was far from feeling. Now she lay and listened to his voice, and thought of his red hair and dark eyes, and his mouth, firm and full—and at this point she drew herself up, mentally and actually; sat up and heard Jenny calling upstairs:

"Elizabeth! Someone to see you. Are you awake?"

"Coming!" and she slid out of bed, put on a new shift dress that she knew set off her hair and eyes particularly well, pushed her feet into sandals and went down, knowing she was looking good. An opinion pleasantly confirmed by the look in Crane's eyes when she appeared in the doorway of the sitting-room. Jenny noted it too—with no great satisfaction.

"I've come to ask if you'd like to come for a run in the car," said Crane. "I've got a picnic—it's a fine day. What about it?"

"I'd love to," said Elizabeth, avoiding Jenny's eye.

"Fine," said Crane. "Then let's go. Good day, ma'am." And he gave Aunt Jenny a courteous little half-bow—he had extremely good manners towards older women, Elizabeth had noticed—but it had little effect on Aunt Jenny, whose attitude towards him remained detached and cool.

They drove through Mourie, Elizabeth's hair blowing in the wind, for the convertible was open to the sunshine. Mrs. Macleod the Shop, looking over the screen at the back of the window, saw them passing and said: "Well, well; so Mrs. Lauder's niece is

72

riding about with that man Maclean . . ."; and John Maclean the Ferry gave them a wave and a friendly grin; and then stood looking after them with a calculating pursing of the lips. There were other hands lifted in greeting, and Elizabeth said:

"I like the way people greet each other here."

"It's sure good to see," said Crane. "They're honest, simple folk, and I'm glad I'll maybe be able to help them."

" 'Honest'—yes, probably," said Elizabeth, "but 'simple'?"

"Well, I guess so. Look at the way they sit up on the headland watching us all day, as if they thought we might make off with their treasure . . . Besides, only the simple ones would stay on here."

"Don't you like it here after all?" Elizabeth asked. "Are you sorry you came?"

"Not at all. Please don't think that. I think this is a marvellous place, and I'm happy to think I can spend at least part of my life here, and come whenever I like for as long as I like to relax and enjoy myself away from work."

"What is your work?"

He gave her a rapid sidelong look, and then, with his eyes on the road, which had narrowed and was now running along the cliff top, he said: "That's not altogether a simple question to answer. I majored in physics, but I didn't carry on with a science career. My father wanted me to help him out in the business—and it interested me, so I did. He had a stake in a lot of things—electronics, tele-communications, and so on. Sometimes we'd get involved in jobs for the government, and I took on more of that—and in fact, it was when I knew I was to come to Europe on a government assignment that I decided I'd visit Mourie; and then I got the chance of buying the estate."

"Is your father still alive?"

"No. He died a couple of years ago. My mother died when I was just a little boy. But the business goes on prospering . . . that's how I felt I could come and do what we are doing at Mourie . . ."

Elizabeth was silent, thinking over what he had said. Not that it told her so very much more than she knew already; she

73

had guessed that he was intelligent and used to power. She looked at him; with his red hair flaming in the sun, his mouth half-smiling, he was formidably attractive. How long had it been since she had driven in a car beside an appealing male? Careful, she thought, or you'll be in love with him; and thought further, and why not? It's about time you had some emotional excitement again.

And suddenly she was back, a first-year student again at Edinburgh, and in love for the first time. Robert was in his second year, doing political economy. He was a new kind of person for Elizabeth—public school in the English sense, well-mannered, with an allowance of his own; perhaps she had been dazzled a little with all this: but it was not only that. In her third term they met and fell in love. The summer vacation meant separation—and long letters. Robert travelled with his wealthy manufacturing father; Elizabeth went home to the Border manse. And when they met again at the beginning of the new term, everything had changed—on Robert's side. She sensed it from the first moment of their meeting, and pride made her stop seeing him. For a whole term she was sure her heart was irrevocably broken; a dreary prospect of dedicated spinsterhood (dedicated to what?) stretched before her . . . and then she met Tom. The relationship with Tom had been happy and undemanding and manageable till after Finals—and then it had all become fierce and tense—on Tom's side. And now it had been her turn to reject someone—she still felt guilty thinking of it . . .

"Come back," said Crane's voice beside her. "You're miles away. Where were you?"

"In the past—my student days."

"What did you do at college?"

"I did history."

"And then?"

"I worked in the National Library."

"Did you like that?"

"Very much. Until I met someone who made me feel it was running away from things, and so I gave it up."

"And then?"

74

"And then a friend of mine who worked in a mission in South India came home: and I went back with her as a voluntary worker—well, I was paid my expenses."

"To teach history?" He sounded almost amused.

"No, English. But in actual fact, I was a dogsbody and helped at everything—including the hospital."

It must have been something in her voice that made him say: "That was bad?"

"Sometimes. I'd like to forget it."

"O.K. We won't talk about your past any more . . . Would you look at that!"

For the road, now high above the sea, swinging round a bend, laid before them mountains, islands, sea and curving shore. Nearest to them were the peaks of Skye, blue and shimmering. And beyond, other islands, other mountains, a dimmer, delicate blue-grey; the peaks of Rum, and Eigg beyond and further still, blending into the sky, the hills of Mull. And just below the road, an untrodden sandy shore and a peacock sea rippling against it.

He had drawn up the car in a passing-place and they looked in silence. Then he said: "If we could find somewhere hereabouts to eat our picnic, then we could look at this all the time. You keep your eyes open, while I drive."

Soon they had found it. A burn trickling down from the high hills had cut out a little glen through the rocks and birches and ferns. Fox-gloves and lavender-blue cranesbill grew in it. The burn went under the road beneath a narrow bridge with stone parapets and then fell in a cataract of rippling peat-brown water to the shore. By the bridge was a grassy patch where they parked the car before climbing up to a knoll out of sight of the road, looking over the little glen to the sea and islands. Yellow tormentil grew in the grass and a little white flower whose name Elizabeth did not know. There was a humming of bees, a trickle and tinkle of water from the burn, and for a second or two a blue dragon-fly hung in the air above the birches. It was a moment of perfection, and Elizabeth was almost angry when Crane, after a glance round, dumped the picnic basket, sat down and said cheerfully: "Well, I'm hungry. What about eating?"

75

If something went from the day along with the dragon-fly, what remained was good. Crane's hamper held some wonderful food: salmon, crisp salad, fresh rolls and butter; and a bowlful of strawberries. There were a bottle of wine and a flask of hot dark coffee. Lying back when they had finished eating, Elizabeth said: "That was no picnic; that was a feast. How do you manage to get strawberries?"

He laughed. "We buy them—order them in Inverness and they come down by van. You must have seen the vans in Mourie."

"Yes of course, but I've never seen strawberries in Mourie."

"They cost a lot. That's one of the things about being rich." He spoke jokingly. Even so, it jarred a little, a very little; it was the second time he had mentioned being rich. But after all, why not? Why should there be a taboo on talking about your own wealth? It was one of the things she had been brought up not to do—was it of the slightest importance? But Crane was still speaking—"You can have anything you want, any time you want." He turned and laid his hand on hers. "Right now, I don't want anything else than to be here—with you."

She began to talk a little too quickly. "But you must have been almost everywhere—Japan—the West Indies—" For these were two places she had not seen and wanted to. He gave her a quizzical look, sat up and said:

"I haven't been to Japan—yet. The West Indies—yes. They're very beautiful—especially if you go to smaller islands. But not any more beautiful than this—only warmer."

Elizabeth was leaning back on her elbows, and she said: "It's a good thing the climate in Scotland is what it is—or we might be over-run with summer visitors."

Crane put back his head and laughed.

"That's a very Scottish remark. You just don't want people breaking in on you. You'd rather keep yourselves shut in among yourselves even if it means you're poor."

"I didn't mean that," said Elizabeth. But her voice tailed off. For what she had meant was not of the slightest importance. She was simply talking for the sake of talking—a protective device—against what? Herself, Crane, the rising tide of feeling in her? She was aware of his eyes on her, and she suddenly jumped to her feet and said: "Let's follow the burn uphill."

A sheep track led down into the glen to the edge of the burn, which was nowhere more than a yard wide and ran swiftly in and out of pools, tumbling over shallow ledges of rocks. The sunlight, filtering through the birches, splashed over grass and flowers and sparkled back from the water. As always in a wooded space, she had a sense of a stage being set, of something waiting to begin. She wished she had stayed on the open hillside. Scrambling up the track, less than a foot wide and dimpled with the imprints of little cloven trotters, made conversation impossible. Nevertheless she found herself prattling on— I'm babbling, she thought, like the burn.

The path became steeper, climbing up past a miniature waterfall. At the top, out of breath, she leant panting against a birch tree. Crane, following, saw her with the light on her hair, the long line of her neck, the shadows dappling her dress, the outline of her young body—and all at once he was standing in front of her, his hands grasping the gnarled branches on either side of the trunk, looking down at her. She kept her eyes away from his, looking aside into the water and began to murmur some comment on the effect of the light. But she felt his hand under her chin turn her face towards his and heard him say: "Look at me, Elizabeth."

She could do nothing else; saw his eyes laughing down at her; and then felt his mouth on hers. What had she expected? Why had she been putting up all the defensive chatter? It was a tender, gentle kiss. And then he was looking down at her again and laughing.

"You're not scared, surely?"

She shook her head, speechlessly. No, she was not scared. Only unbelievably happy. For surely she was in love with him. Had she perhaps been so from the very first? Whether he was in love with her didn't matter—yet. Something of this he saw in her face, for the laughter died out of his eyes. He took her in his arms and kissed her again, not gently and not tenderly. The sunshine, the

77

trees, the running water—all were blotted out in a singing darkness . . .

Into which came the cheerful sound of whistling and a voice saying heartily: "Well now, isn't it the lovely day today?"

And twisting her head round towards the voice, she saw Roddy from the shop standing on the track above them.

Her instinct was to jump back from Crane's arms. But he felt the movement and whispered in her ear: "If you do that, you'll look guilty." He released her slowly and they both turned and watched Roddy come down the sheep track. He was smiling blandly and saying:

"I wasn't expecting to meet anyone I knew here. I have just been up on the hill to see if there was anything there in the way of fishing in the lochan. I do that when I find the shop is beginning to be a bore to me. But of course it is too bright a day for the fishing. So I guddled one or two in the burn and here they are."

And he swung forward for their inspection a string of three or four speckled brown trout, still wet and gleaming.

Crane, quite unembarrassed, looked at them and said: "Not bad."

Roddy made to pass them and said: "Well now, I'll not be keeping you . . . I'll likely be having to wait for some time on the road before I get a lift back." And he looked beyond Crane and Elizabeth in a detached way.

"Oh, but we . . ." said Elizabeth, and stopped. It wasn't for her to offer a lift. Nevertheless, she didn't want to go further up the glen. It would be an anti-climax. Roddy's arrival had effectively dissipated the magic of the afternoon. Crane seemed to understand, for he pressed her hand gently and said:

"I guess it's time we were going back too. We'll give you a lift, if you like."

He began to talk to Roddy about fishing, and the two of them went down the path ahead of Elizabeth. She followed, still bewildered by the tangle of emotions—sheer happiness; furious exasperation at Roddy's appearance now modulating into a wry amusement and a feeling that this had been one of the most extraordinary days of her life, from the beginning in Peg's tent to the ecstatic moment under the birch tree. She said almost nothing in the car, and heard little of Roddy's flow of conversation as he leant over from the back seat. They dropped him at the shop and he slid two cold and slippery trout on to her lap as he left. At Jenny's front door, Crane answered the question in her eyes with a smile and a shake of the head.

"I don't think I could face your aunt just now. I'll see you to-morrow."

Elizabeth went in, presented the trout to Jenny and managed to answer her questions with effective vagueness. But she was aware that Jenny's eyes were bright with conjecture as she said in an off-hand way:

"Douglas called in not long after you'd left."

"Oh?"

"*He* was wondering if you'd like to go a picnic with him—I suppose it's the fine weather has inspired all the young men to go picnics. Of course, he hadn't a fine hamper; just a rucksack with sandwiches and a thermos . . ."

"Oh. Was he very disappointed?"

"I think he was. He went away looking rather glum. By the way, did you tell Crane Maclean about the coin?"

"The coin?"

"Mysie's charm."

"No." Elizabeth looked self-conscious. "I forgot all about it."

"Mphm," said Jenny, and this time Elizabeth didn't try to inter-pret.

When she stood by her window that night watching the after-glow behind Skye, she thought, nothing can take away, ever, a day as wonderful as this one. And she stood in a deep contentment watching the light shift along the horizon.

The following day, John Maclean the Ferry went peat-cutting.

CHAPTER 9

Elizabeth woke up still in a glow of happiness. She was to see Crane that day. It was very disappointing when he rang up to say he had to go away from Mourie to Inverness on business connected with the diving—some kind of crisis—but he hoped to be back by night. And Jenny, of course, asked who was on the phone and why; Elizabeth hoped her disappointment wasn't too obvious but thought it must be by the pointed way Jenny said nothing.

Midway through the morning she went for messages to the shop. Mrs. Macleod greeted her cheerfully, served her and as she counted the change said:

"And did you have a nice picnic yesterday?"

"Why yes," said Elizabeth. "How did you know?"

"Roddy was telling me he had met you. It was a lovely day for it, though myself, I would rather eat sitting decently at a table."

What else had Roddy been telling her? Elizabeth took her change and left hastily. Outside the shop she met John Maclean the Ferry. He hailed her cordially and said:

"You are none the worse of the excitement of yesterday?"

For a moment she could only think of Crane, and she stared non-plussed. Then she remembered:

"You mean Peg and the tinkers? No, I'm none the worse. Did the doctor get back all right?"

"Yes he did. I'm thinking my car is the one that has come off worst. She's in at Angus' just now for him to look her over—and had to be towed there too. I wouldn't be minding but today I had made up my mind to go peat-cutting up at the top of the road and now I will not be able to go."

"I could take you," said Elizabeth. "I've nothing special to do. It's a lovely day, and I'll take something to eat and a book to read."

"Well that is very good of you. Very good of you indeed. If you are sure it is not too much trouble. I will just go and get my things and I will be ready."

So in half an hour, Elizabeth was driving back up the road to the pass, for the first time since she had arrived in Mourie. A day or two ago she would have hated the idea, but now she was totally lighthearted as she drove up towards the heights. The view was behind them as they climbed except for momentary glimpses as they zigzagged up. Above them the mountains lowered, loomed nearer, until at last the road swung into the desolate sweep of wet rock, peat and coarse stunted grass surrounded by sullen hills at the summit. Elizabeth was appalled by the desolation and when she saw the red road-roller incongruously outstanding in the gloomy landscape, she began to wish she had not come. Perhaps John Maclean sensed this, for he said: "I can easily walk the rest of the way if you let me down here—you wouldn't be needing to go any further. . . ."

"Where do you want to go?"

"Up there by the machine . . . but there is no need for you to go right up . . ."

"I'll go."

For it would be sheer weakness to avoid the road-roller. What she had found there was in the past; over and done with. And to prove it she would go right up and look into the driving-cabin— and exorcise once and for all the horrid after-image so firmly imprinted in her mind's eye of a hand hanging limply out of it . . .

So she drove up to the parking-place and drew in in front of the cheerful little roller. She sat for a moment with her eyes fixed on her hands on the wheel before looking straight at it. And of course, it was just a red road-roller and there was nothing nightmarish about it. In fact, under the sunlight it was rather—yes, jolly.

John Maclean had got out of the car and was taking from the

boot the toirsgian, the long-handled spadelike implement with which he would dig out the peat in neat oblong blocks.

"I'll be going over there"—he pointed southwards over the soggy moorland. "Do you see where there is that big hummock of grass? Well, I will be starting the cutting just from there. And thank you very much for giving me the lift up here."

A thought struck Elizabeth. "How long are you going to be here?"

"I was thinking I would do about three hours—it is hard work, the peat-cutting."

"Can I help?"

"Ah, there is no need for that . . . and don't you be wasting all that time here either. I daresay I could get a lift down . . ."

"Not at all. I'll climb up the hillside there as far as I can and find somewhere to sit and read in the sun."

So she took her book and food from the car, followed John to the hummock where he proposed to do his peat-cutting and then went up a sheep track which he pointed out skirting the peat-bog up to the crest of the hill above. It was a tough scramble, sometimes through tricky patches of scree; and the sun was hot. Halfway up the slope she reached a little hollow, with dry bleached grass, soft to sit on, and sloping rock to lean against.

She decided this was an excellent place to stop, and she sat down, lay back, and looked up at the sky, happily aware of the light breeze stirring the tough grass that gently prickled her bare legs, a smell of earth and stone, the blue depth above and the kind warmth of the sun. Presently she sat up and looked across the peat-bog to a wall of hills rising in precipices and scree-slopes to the sky. On the left, her own hill-slope curved round to meet these and close the horizon. To the right, she could see the road running across the valley floor, and the car and the road-roller. Beyond the road was utter bleakness—not even peat—naked wet slabs of rock cut into shallow crevasses, that stretched to more hills, which rose dramatically to a black, conical crest. A little uneasy shiver ran through her, and she thought: If I were John Maclean I'd hate to come here alone; I'd feel an intruder; and then, looking down at him working with a slow regular

82

rhythm—in with the toirsgian, lean on the handle, up with the peat . . . an ancient activity that fitted the ancient landscape— she decided he certainly would have a matter-of-fact attitude to the hills and moor which were his natural environment. Presently he stopped cutting, straightened his back, answered her wave of greeting and sat down to eat his sandwiches. Elizabeth ate too. The sun grew hotter, and a haze began to fill up the valley. She lay back against the warm rock and drifted into a soothing fog of sleep . . .

It was only for a few minutes. When she sat up and looked down at John Maclean he had started working again. She clasped her hands round her knees, left her book lying unopened beside her, and allowed her thoughts to wander happily—India, Mourie, Crane . . .

She became aware that John Maclean had stopped working. He had dropped the toirsgian and was staring down into the cutting. Then he stepped back, looked round as if bewildered, back at the cutting and then began to run stumblingly uphill towards her, his face raised and one arm waving in a desperate summons.

She snatched up her book and slid and slithered down the slope to meet him. When he saw her coming, he stood still and waited for her; white-faced, panting, all he could say was:

"Down there—in the cutting."

They went down together. Elizabeth had a foreboding that made her skin tingle. For her, it was a horrible recognition, not a shock. The revealing sunlight showed it with brutal clarity: in the wall of the cutting, a hand, grubby with dark stains of peat, making a hopeless, helpless gesture; a hand she knew she had seen before, touched before . . .

She and John Maclean looked at each other, questioning each other. John gestured to the toirsgian and said: "Will I?"

"Yes—yes. Uncover it."

He began cutting the soil carefully away. Elizabeth took each neatly cut block, and laid it aside. They worked in silence, and at last there it lay, uncovered from head to foot: face-down in the chocolate-brown peat, the body of a red-headed man wearing a raincoat with a hole under the left shoulder blade, as Elizabeth had already seen it.

Suddenly she wanted to see the face. John Maclean stooped over the poor bedraggled thing. Slowly he turned it over. The face was a muddy mask and he took a handful of sphagnum moss and wiped the dirt from the dead face.

A young face; a good-looking face, with the red of the hair glinting through the dirt. Elizabeth, staring down into the peat, thought: I should know him. I've seen that face somewhere . . .

She heard John's voice:

"Are you all right?"

"Oh yes. I'm all right . . . we'll have to get word down to Mourie."

Into the silence of the hills came the noise of a car driven hard up from Mourie. They swung round to look. It was Crane's car, with Crane at the wheel, and Elizabeth began to run over to the road, calling and waving. In a matter of seconds he had stopped the car and was striding over the heather towards them, tall and reassuring. Elizabeth, as they met, cling to him, her self-control momentarily gone, distress and shock overwhelming her.

"Crane, I'm so glad you're here. John, cutting peats, uncovered"—her voice shook for a moment—"uncovered the man I found up here and whose body vanished. You remember?"

He listened in silence, his face quite expressionless. Then, putting his arm round her, he said:

"You poor child! This must have been an awful shock. Where . . . ?"

"Over there. Oh, Crane, I'm so glad you came."

He looked down at the body silently, showing neither pity nor revulsion, weighing what was to be done.

"You're sure this is the man you saw before?"

"Quite sure. There's the same wound in the back, and the red hair."

"Ah yes, the red hair." Crane sounded almost amused, but was immediately grave again. "We must let the police know." He looked at her with concern. "Are you all right now, Elizabeth?"

"Yes, yes. I am."

84

"I hate to say this, but I'm on my way to a pretty important business appointment—I told you about it already. I've been held up at Mourie all morning, and now it's getting late, and I must be there today . . . But if you don't feel up to it, I'll drive you down to Mourie."

"No, Crane, I'm all right. I'll drive down at once. But what about you, John? It would mean you being left alone with . . .

"I'll not be worrying about that. I was a wee thing upset at first but not now. It is not the first body I have seen—I was in the Navy during the war. No, no, you just go down and tell Hamish and I'll just wait here till he comes."

Elizabeth and Crane made their way to the road in silence. Elizabeth was still niggled by the thought that she had seen the dead man before. But where? Recently, she was sure of that. But he'd been dead before she ever reached Mourie . . . then it came to her. A photograph!

"Morag's grandson!"

She spoke out loud, stopping suddenly in her tracks. Crane looked at her in amazement.

"What did you say?"

"Morag's grandson!" She clutched his arm. "The dead man. It's Morag's grandson. I saw his photograph in her house."

"Are you sure? Quite sure?"

He spoke very gravely.

"Yes—no—yes, I am quite sure."

He turned and put his hands on her shoulders, looking down at her very solemnly.

"Then you're not to tell anyone you know him—promise."

"But why . . . ?"

"Don't ask questions; just promise me. No, I can't explain. But for your own sake, promise. Tell no one."

She looked back equally seriously. His eyes were very dark, very anxious.

"You won't tell me why?"

"No. But promise, *please!*"

"All right, I promise. But you must tell me why, sometime."

To this he gave no answer, and they didn't speak again until she was in her car and he leant in and said:

"Take care of yourself."

He watched her set off to Mourie and then he drove away in the opposite direction.

Silence settled back over the hills and the moor and the rocks, and the lonely figure of John Maclean and the dead man lying in the peat.

CHAPTER 10

Once behind the wheel, Elizabeth began to feel her equanimity returning and she was able to think of what had happened comparatively calmly. The rediscovery of the body, the shock of recognising it as Morag's grandson, had been upsetting enough. But on top of that had come Crane's insistence that she say nothing about this recognition; and that she found very disturbing; for it seemed to imply that Crane knew a great deal more about the affair than anyone had hitherto suspected.

But driving down the road to Mourie demanded too much concentration for her to think about what had happened more than in snatches. So when the worst of the bends and curves were past, she drew into a passing-place to try and sort things out. For once, she looked at the Skye mountains and the sea with unseeing eyes, too absorbed in her thoughts.

For if she was honest with herself—and she had to be—she had to admit that Crane's behavior could have sinister implications. Firstly, it was clear that he had some knowledge of what lay behind the killing. Furthermore, she couldn't help remembering that according to Jenny and Douglas he hadn't been seen in Mourie for two days round about the time of the murder—could he be involved in it? This was a horrible thought, but she had to face it. And even if he were not involved in the actual killing, the fact that he knew something about it must introduce an uncertainty, a doubtfulness into their growing relationship . . .

As for herself—she was now carrying round a double secret: the identity of the body, and the fact that she could recognise the man who had attacked her in the car—and at least she knew for certain that that was not Crane.

Away down in the valley beneath her she could see a little red blob that was the phone box just outside Mourie, and it reminded her that Hamish McIntosh must be told of the discovery. This time there would be no avoiding identifying the body as the one she had found in the road-roller—and she only hoped it would not be difficult to conceal her additional knowledge. Just when she had hoped all that was behind her, here it had boiled up again —it was too bad. And now in a thoroughly bad mood, she drove on down to the phone box.

Once she had told Hamish, she thought, as she pushed the coins into the box, she would go to the cottage, make tea, and do nothing more about it. Let the proper authorities get on with it . . .

Mrs. Robertson at the exchange eventually answered and put her through to the police station. But Hamish McIntosh wasn't there; he had had to go down the coast to the very end of the road. But his mother promised to try and contact him as soon as possible, and yes, she would pass on the message, and wasn't it a terrible thing indeed, and what a shock it must have been and dear, dear, Elizabeth had been unfortunate in what had been happening since she came to Mourie; and if Elizabeth would excuse her, she would try and get hold of Hamish . . .

Elizabeth got back into the car, seething with frustration. So much for her hopes of Hamish taking over. For if he couldn't be got at for hours, she couldn't leave John Maclean alone up there; she'd have to go back—but before she did that, she would go to the cottage and relax for a bit.

But as she drew up at the cottage gate, she met Douglas. When he saw her, his face lit up and she smiled back. Then he looked more closely at her and said:

"Is anything wrong?"

So she told him about the finding of the body and Hamish's elusiveness, and ended:

"I'm feeling very fed-up and I'm going in to be soothed by Jenny."

88

"She's not there," said Douglas. "I met her a few minutes ago and she said she was going to see Peg and the baby. Why not come to the schoolhouse, and Mrs. Farquharson will give us tea. And then, if Hamish is still not around, I'll come up with you."

"Will you? Oh, Douglas, that really is good of you."

Mrs. Farquharson, Douglas' daily housekeeper, welcomed Elizabeth with cordial dignity. Not a native of Mourie, she was very conscious of her position as schoolmaster's housekeeper and this did to a certain extent inhibit her social life. Douglas told her what had happened, she expressed concern, and went off to make tea, while Douglas showed Elizabeth into a comfortable sitting-room. She sank into a chair with a sense of relief, and Douglas said:

"Just relax there for a minute or two. I've one or two phone calls to make—the Education Office at Rosstown and so on—but I shan't be long."

He was soon back, and so was Mrs. Farquharson with an immaculate tea-tray and fresh scones and butter. Deliberately, they avoided talking of the events of the afternoon; and Douglas turned aside Elizabeth's references to the diving operations. They talked instead of Alice's determination to produce a play during the summer visitors' season, and of the social life of Mourie in general. Then Douglas saw her glance at the clock and said:

"I'm remembering; I'll go and phone the police station again."

But they still hadn't been able to contact Hamish. So, reluctantly, Elizabeth rose and said: "Then I'll have to go back up the road."

"But I'm coming too," said Douglas. "If you like, I'll drive."

"Would you? I'm sick of going up and down that road."

They drove through Mourie and into the sunlit height of the hills which was so beautiful and unfolded horror. It wasn't *fair*. Why should it all be spoilt for her?

Her gloomy train of thought was interrupted by her hearing a sound—a throbbing, like, and not like, a plane—a sound she'd heard not so very long before—a helicopter! And there it was, slipping out of sight over the crest of the mountain ahead of them. Elizabeth gave a little shiver.

"Did you see it, Douglas? A helicopter. I hate them. There was one came up the pass and hovered over me the day I arrived. I've always thought they were nasty, sneaky things."

Douglas smiled. "A purely subjective judgment. It's probably a naval one. We've got used to things like that since they built the base up north."

But Elizabeth was in a grumpy, gloomy mood. " 'Base!' They've even got to spoil this wonderful coast with their beastly bases! It's too bad"—she made a leap from the general to the personal, a mental habit of hers which, in her more serene moments, she tried to control—"I came here after India—which at times was pretty beastly—to relax and be cossetted—and all this happens. It's too bad."

"It is bad luck," said Douglas, "tho' I've never understood why people should think that the remoteness and smallness of a community should equal peace and sweetness all round. The contrary could be the case . . . anyway, I'm glad you came."

To this Elizabeth made no reply, but she began to cheer up a little; and felt kindly towards Douglas, for his coming with her made much easier the business of driving up to join John Maclean.

They were now approaching the crest and the little road-roller was in view ahead of them; and in the gap of the hills, the helicopter was sliding away behind the hills beyond. As its droning died away, the landscape became still and quiet again except for their car.

At the roller they stopped and parked.

"It's over there," said Elizabeth, but made no move to go.

"Come on, then," said Douglas. "I'm sure John won't be sorry to see us."

But still Elizabeth did not stir. With one hand on the bonnet, she stood looking over the moor to the peat-cutting. And knew in that moment that something was wrong.

There was the meticulously stacked line of peats that John had cut; there the jumble of turfs where she had flung them down as they uncovered the body. She could even see the long handle of

90

the toirsgian sticking up from the peat. But otherwise the moor was empty—bleak and bare and menacing and empty.

She began to run, awkwardly stumbling and splashing. Douglas, catching her anxiety, followed.

A little way beyond the peat-trench they found John Maclean; lying with his face buried in a clump of heather, one arm beneath him, the other flung above his head, his body limp.

Of the other body, there was no sign. Only the empty sodden grave where it had lain. For the second time it had gone, irretrievably and for always. Weighted at head and foot, tossed into a deep and lonely lochan on the lower slopes of Ben Eighe, it vanished for ever.

CHAPTER 11

The attack on John Maclean the Ferry had a profound effect on Mourie—an effect of which Elizabeth only became aware a day or two after the event, when all the to-and-fro-ing was past, and poor John, desperately ill and in a coma, had been transferred, dramatically and with notice in the national press, to hospital in Aberdeen for specialist treatment. The shock of the discovery of his unconscious body, the desperate journey down that hateful hill road yet again under a weight of anxiety and distress, the summoning of Dr. Marshall, the revelation of how deprived Mourie was of emergency facilities taken for granted elsewhere —all combined to produce in her a state of near illness, which Aunt Jenny firmly coped with by putting her to bed for a day and not allowing her to see anyone except a detective sergeant from Inverness, who was apparently so intimidated by Aunt Jenny's monitory presence (she was the hospital matron again from head to foot so that you could almost see the dark blue uniform and stiffly starched white cap) that he asked the minimum number of questions: merely sufficient to confirm that Elizabeth was convinced that the man in the peat-bog and the body she had found in the roller were one and the same.

She was quite happy to spend a day in bed, reading and dozing. In the evening, she heard voices downstairs and soon Jenny appeared with a box of chocolates in one hand and three tattered paper-backs in the other.

"The chocolates are from Crane, the books from Douglas. And they both hope you'll be feeling all right tomorrow, and they'll see you then."

"That was nice of them."

"Mphm. I didn't think when I asked you here you'd have such a disrupting effect on the community."

"Disrupting?"

"Douglas McBain's in love with you. No, don't protest. *I* know the signs. Even the children in school have noticed the change in him. Ishbel McAlister told her mother he was 'all dreamy and just looked out the window all day.'"

"What nonsense!"

"Maybe so. But he's a nice steady young man, though of course he can't afford to have rich chocolates brought specially from Inverness for you."

And Aunt Jenny, dumping chocolates and books on the bed, swept out of the room.

Elizabeth, greedily munching her way through the chocolates, lay back on her pillows and looked over the Sound to the hills. Perhaps Douglas was in love with her; but she thought not. True, she was aware of his interest in her: she knew he watched her—she had more than once been aware of his listening in to her talk with other people—but love? Still, better not argue with Aunt Jenny, who rather prided herself on her skill in reading character. She herself liked Douglas; he was formidably good-looking, but she knew she could never have been in love with him, even if Crane had not been there; Crane, who was, not more handsome, but different, so that being beside him—or away from him—just thinking of him, made her whole body tingle. And if he wasn't in love with her—or on the way to being—too bad for her. But she rather thought he was. She carefully chose and bit into a truffle chocolate, opened the least intimidating volume (on Highland folklore) from among Douglas' books (did he really think *The Aftermath of Jacobitism* or *Whither the Highland Economy?* was relaxing reading?) and settled down for a lazy afternoon.

But the next day, stern reality returned. Aunt Jenny came back from her shopping at Mrs. Macleod's looking concerned. She piled the messages on the kitchen table and said: "I knew they'd be upset, but not so much as this."

"Meaning . . . ?"

"The attack on John Maclean. Their interest in your adventure coming over the hill on your arrival was keen, but uninvolved. They were sorry you should have had such a horrid experience, but still, it was very interesting—a kind of entertainment almost, which didn't impinge closely. But this—an actual physical attack on someone they know—that's different. They're feeling bitter and angry—I'd almost say they were in a dangerous mood."

"I notice you say 'they,' not 'we' . . . so you feel outside their concern?"

"I told you before. Something happens, and you realise that you are different from the people who've lived here always—whose fathers and grandfathers lived here. Stands to reason one must always be a little outside."

"You said 'dangerous mood'—who could be in danger?"

"Well, that's the question. It's an unfocussed anger. One or two are apparently muttering that they don't know much about Crane Maclean's friends and companions—the divers and so on. They do rather 'keep themselves to themselves' along at Mourie House. They were even hinting that Crane himself could have come back and attacked John—though of course the police have interviewed him and the people in a car he passed on the way down, and it just wasn't physically possible."

"You mean to say they thought Crane . . . that's preposterous."

"Of course it is. It's all quite irrational; I'm convinced that the attack on John Maclean was accidental, in that he just happened to be there when the body turned up again and was removed—and until he's conscious again no one can say how it vanished. They even thought of a helicopter—there was a mountain rescue one out that day, but it's in the clear. I think John was left for dead, and he's lucky to be alive; but the killing doesn't seem to have any connection with Mourie."

But it does, thought Elizabeth, it does. And again she wished she had not given her promise to Crane not to reveal the identity of the body. For it would have been a comfort to be able to discuss the matter with Jenny. Why had he been so insistent? She still felt uneasy when she thought about it, and hoped that when she saw him again—for she hadn't spoken with him since they had parted

94

up on the hill—that he might explain why he had made her promise. Jenny was looking at her questioningly, and said—"Yes?"

"What?"

"I thought you were going to say something."

"No. Just that it's all preposterous."

All day she went round in a pleasant excitement of expectation waiting for Crane to arrive. But he didn't. Just before lunch the phone rang, and she heard his voice, very distant and faint.

"Elizabeth? I just wanted to let you know that I've had to go off on business again."

"So soon?"

"Yes. It's a nuisance, but there's no help. It's about legal points in connection with—with the divers' work. You understand?"

"Yes, oh yes, I understand."

"I won't be able to see you today. I hope tomorrow. Good-bye, my love."

And she was left listening to the hoarse humming of the phone. Jenny, looking at her as she came from the hall, said: "That was Crane."

"How did you know?"

"By your face. Are you getting serious about him?"

Elizabeth felt her face muscles stiffen into a frown, and Jenny went on:

"I know. It's your business, not mine. I just wanted to say that if it is serious, I'd try to like him."

As if to cover up this unwonted lapse into emotionalism, she said briskly: "I hope the feeling in the village dies down quickly."

Elizabeth had not taken Jenny's account of the atmosphere in Mourie too seriously. But when she went to the shop herself later on in the day, she came back every bit as worried as Jenny had been.

"The atmosphere's quite changed in the village," she said. "Mrs. Macleod was terribly gloomy, and the other customers greeted me in an almost melancholy way."

"I told you," said Jenny. "They're upset about John the Ferry. It's at a time like this that one realises one isn't *really* a part of

95

the place. The real inhabitants draw into a knot of grief or protest and one is outside."

"Mrs. Macleod mentioned the diving in a very grudging kind of way and said she didn't believe anything was there anyway. Really, I wish the locals would stop being so miserable about the whole thing." She spoke more vehemently than she had intended and Jenny glanced at her sharply. "There's Crane— and Douglas' backer—spending heaven knows how much on this project, for the benefit of Mourie, and what do they do? Mutter in corners, say there's nothing there, and sit upon the headland watching Crane and the men as if they thought they were up to some kind of jookery-pookery. It's disgusting."

"Talking of Douglas," said Jenny, "here he is coming up the path."

"Then I'm off," said Elizabeth. "At this moment I just could not stand his particular brand of solemn earnestness. I'll slip out of the back door and go for a walk."

This she did, tip-toeing through to the kitchen and out of the back door before Jenny could protest, and creeping down the back path and out of the little gate in the wall.

Some minutes later Douglas, standing by Jenny's window, saw Elizabeth in the distance with the wind blowing her hair.

"Your niece is very beautiful," he said to Jenny, and heaved a sigh, continuing to watch her till she vanished behind a sand dune. The sigh puzzled Jenny. It was less a lover's sigh of longing, and more one of regret; and she found herself thinking of it more than once in the course of the evening.

Elizabeth had slanted her way to the beach and then turned to walk along the firm sand in the direction of the river mouth. The movement, the touch of the wind on her cheek, the sea, soon made her feel less bad-tempered. But it was horrid the way people seemed to be hanging back, ready to denigrate, ready with discouragement, and showing a silent wary watchfulness instead of the enthusiasm one might have expected. And if a sense of outrage at the attack on John the Ferry were to break out in some kind of violence—that would be disgusting. And Crane would be entirely justified in throwing the whole thing over.

She wondered if he knew of the feeling in Mourie. Ought she to tell him? And yet she was strongly aware of a calm sense of competence—almost, but not quite, arrogance—in him. It was part of his attraction for her. And she was almost sure he would be alive to all that went on.

Although she had spoken to him, she had not seen him since the attack on John Maclean. She wished she could—and in circumstances free from complications. She was beginning to realise the difficulties of achieving any kind of privacy in a small community. Everything that happened loomed enormously. Apart from their picnic—into which Mourie in the person of Roddy had abruptly erupted—she had scarcely spoken alone to Crane; and there was so much she wanted to know.

She tossed back her hair and walked swiftly along the shore, her disgruntledness giving way to lightheartedness. For surely all this gloom and disagreeableness couldn't last for ever, and when—if—Crane's scheme came off, all would be well; she did not define to herself quite what that would mean.

Presently she came to the river mouth, where the river had cut a dozen shifting channels through the sand. She turned and walked up the edge of the nearest one and soon came to the rough bents and low alder bushes at the top of the beach, where the river ran in a well-defined bed. A tiny track led up the side and she followed it, and began peering into the water, for she had been told that in the fresh-water mussels found at the mouth, pearls were occasionally discovered. She was in a mood to be distracted by some such ploy and she went on looking into the water, and occasionally poking into the pools with a dry stick she picked up, until she was right under the arch of the bridge that carried the road to the church. And here at last, where the water was dark and shadowed by the arch, she did see a little cluster of mussels and knelt down on the bank to try to reach them.

And just then she heard voices. And one of them was Crane's.

But Crane had been going away on business?

He had got back early . . . for it was unmistakably his voice.

"So we'll take the boats out about midnight. That'll give us two clear hours of darkness—more or less. There's no moon just now."

"And we come back to the bay or the jetty?" A Cockney voice; one of Crane's men, surely.

"Maybe to both—you see . . . why, Elizabeth!"

For Elizabeth, uneasy at eavesdropping, had clambered up the low bank and now stood in the roadway. Crane's car was drawn up in a passing-place just at the bridge. He was on the bridge, talking to a lean-faced man with pale eyes whom Elizabeth had seen once or twice in Mourie, whose real name was Johnson but whom everyone called Johnny. Both men looked surprised to see her—Johnson even discomfited.

"I came up from the shore along the burn," said Elizabeth, "and heard your voices."

"Well, it's good to see you," said Crane, and it sounded as if he really meant it. "I guess that's all, Johnny."

Johnson, with a muttered, "Good night, Miss Elizabeth," walked off up the road, and Crane turned to Elizabeth.

"I thought I'd take some of the boys out fishing tonight. Some of them are keen to try their luck."

She hadn't meant to say it, but the words would be spoken. "I thought you were to be away on business today."

"Business?" For a tiny moment he seemed at a loss. "Oh, that. I got a phone call that made it unnecessary."

Then why hadn't he come to Jenny's? But all she said was: "Have the divers had any success yet?"

"Not so far. That's why I thought a little fishing expedition—a kind of busman's holiday, I guess—might cheer them up. There's not much for them to do, and I don't want them getting drunk and doing anything foolish in the village . . . But how are you? Have you quite recovered?"

"Yes, thank you, quite."

"Say, would you like to get in the car and come for a run around? It seems a long time since I saw you—and then it was at a bad moment . . ."

"Oh, Crane, I'd like to—really I would—but I think I must

get back to Aunt Jenny's. I walked out rather rudely, and it's just on supper time."

"What a dutiful niece!" He was smiling at her, teasing. "What was the trouble?"

She hesitated. "I was in a bad mood, about you, really. Well, not exactly. About the grudging attitude to what you were doing. It got me mad."

"What do you mean?"

"The way they watch you; suspiciously."

"That doesn't worry me. You get that in most remote communities. Why, there's places in the States that make Mourie seem the most co-operative genial spot in the world. Besides, they're not basically unfriendly. I guess it's a hangover from the bad old times. You know what Douglas says. They suffered in the past—or their forebears did. They're simple folk, and I guess they find it hard that anyone'd want to help them that way."

"But my aunt says that since the John Maclean affair, they're not just apathetic, or suspicious; they're hostile."

"I can't believe that. Once we find something, they'll be all right. Don't worry, Elizabeth. Come, I'll run you home."

She got into the car, and he took his place beside her. But he didn't drive off. Instead, he turned to look at her, and said:

"You're upset about something. Is it this talk of hostility in the village?"

She nodded.

"Don't worry. They can't hurt me. Elizabeth, I do believe you really care about what happens to me!"

He put a hand under her chin and turned her face towards him. Then he took her in his arms, and kissed her—a hard, swift kiss—released her abruptly, put the car in gear and set off.

They drove to Jenny's in total silence. Elizabeth couldn't have spoken even if she'd wanted to. At Jenny's she got out, shut the door and leaned on it for a moment looking at him. He put out a hand, laid it over hers for a moment and then drove off.

99

Elizabeth went slowly up the path to the house, and only when she was inside realised that she knew no more than before why he had made her promise not to say anything about Morag's grandson.

CHAPTER 12

Inside, supper was ready and Jenny was placidly waiting for her.

"Have a nice walk?" she asked.

"Yes. I went along the shore and up by the river, and felt a lot better. Sorry I walked out like that, but all this—this *girning* about Crane gets me down a bit."

"So I see. But I think you're taking too much on yourself, Elizabeth. I'm sure Crane Maclean can handle things very well by himself."

To this Elizabeth said nothing, for it was of course perfectly true, and she could not tell Aunt Jenny that everything about Crane Maclean had suddenly become of immense importance to her. She ate her supper, saying little beyond a few cursory remarks, and maintaining, she felt, a convincing appearance of restored calm good humour, though inwardly in a turmoil of happiness, uneasiness and uncertainty. Jenny, looking at her eyes shining and sensing the undercurrent to her desultory talk, thought: She met that man when she was out. Damn! For Jenny, though she had said she would try to like Crane, was not finding it easy; she did not think he was one to make Elizabeth happy; and knew Elizabeth to be in a state where nothing an elderly aunt said would have the slightest effect. Looking back down the corridor of years, Jenny thought, "I'm glad I'm not young any more," remembering Maurice Chevalier's song.

After the meal, Jenny had to make a call a little way out of Mourie. Elizabeth, feeling restless, went round to Alice's.

She appeared pleased to see her, and they sat and chatted

idly but pleasantly over drinks and coffee. Alice twittered and flitted from topic to topic in her usual apparently scatter-brained way, though Elizabeth was beginning to think she was not as scatty as she liked to appear. So she was not as surprised as she might have been a few days earlier when Alice suddenly said—in the middle of a discussion on theatre in the round—"By the way, Elizabeth, what exactly is the arrangement between Douglas and Crane Maclean as to control of the diving in the Sound?"

"A kind of dual control, I think. Crane is more actively involved, Douglas has a kind of watching brief. Why?"

"Oh, nothing really—but—well, you know that man, the tall one with the light eyes, what do they call him—Johnny. He and Douglas have been meeting each other quite often down in that hollow in the dunes there. You can see a corner of it from here, but from the window upstairs you can see almost right into it."

"You've been watching?"

"Oh yes. I'm a very inquisitive person, and it struck me as unusual: they have quite long conversations—earnest ones—and they never leave together, and always by different paths; and I can't think they'd be discussing anything but the diving, and if so, why so secretly? Behind Crane's back."

"I don't know . . ."

"Anyway, yesterday I saw them meeting. So I decided I'd go for a walk on the dunes too. And I took a track that leads down to the hollow and . . ."

"You eavesdropped?"

"Well—let's say I overheard them."

"And they were saying?"

"Well, that's the disappointing thing. Nothing at all important. Douglas said, 'What about a fishing expedition at night?' and Johnny said, 'That's a good idea,' and then I got a panic in case they'd find me listening, so I just walked on . . ."

Elizabeth laughed.

"What did you expect to hear? Probably they agreed to meet like that simply to avoid questions and speculation in Mourie— you know how everybody's every action is noted—and they *are* going fishing tonight. Crane told me."

"Oh." But Alice was not entirely convinced. "Anyway, I intend to keep an eye on them. I'm not awfully *fond* of Douglas. Jenny likes him, but I think he's *stodgy*."

Elizabeth left soon after and found Jenny back home. When she told her of Alice's interest in Douglas' meeting with Johnny, Jenny exploded.

"Alice is sometimes impossible. She dramatises and exaggerates everything. I suppose it's having been an actress makes her like that. It's quite absurd."

Elizabeth really agreed with her, but felt disinclined to start a discussion. Instead, she pleaded tiredness and went to bed comparatively early. Once in her room, she flung up the sash of the window as far as she could and sat on the window seat, leaning her head on her arms and looking out over the sea.

Now she would seriously, yes, really seriously think about Crane and herself; for since her meeting with him that evening, under all the excitement ran a cold little trickle of uneasiness. It was trivial, it was unimportant—and yet—and yet . . . Twice Crane had cited urgent business as a reason for not being able to see her; twice she had subsequently met him when he might have been expected to be far away. Well, so what? People did alter appointments, arrangements were upset. Why was she bothered? Pique because Crane hadn't come to Jenny's to see her? Or a change in his tone, an over-casualness as he explained? Whatever it was, it had left a feeling of uneasiness, of doubt; and there was still the unresolved question of the promise he'd insisted on. But then again, Crane's words—"So you really do care about what happens to me"—had carried, it seemed to her—she had always been sensitive to tones of voice—a kind of incredulous surprise—as if he'd long since given up the idea of anyone really caring what became of him . . . It came home to her, forcibly, that she knew practically nothing about him. It was time she began to use her mind about Crane and herself, instead of sailing along on a tide of delicious emotion. Douglas McBain, she thought, she had no difficulty at all in assessing and judging—and knew him to be honest, priggish (but that was unjust), earnest, kind, probably *dull*. Crane was anything but dull—but what else did she *know* about him? Only surface things—that he was rich, efficient, good company—and apparently with a quixotic streak if his plan for Mourie was any guide. It was time she thought about herself and Crane.

But she didn't. Looking out at the Sound, now a muted, evening blue, the sky colourless but luminous with wisps of shining cloud lying behind the darker blue of the hills, she was hypnotised into a sensuous lassitude, where half-thoughts and lazy images drifted through her mind: Crane and treasure and the sea; ships, shells, a strange marine creature she has once seen called a sea-hare—very vulnerable, very touching in its slow defencelessness—Keats's line about the sea-creatures' "undulating home"—no, she couldn't start thinking coldly and logically about anything, least of all Crane and herself and what future, if any, there could be to a relationship between them . . . So she sat watching the light change and withdraw, and the clouds begin to thicken, and finally she undressed in the twilight, slipped into bed and was almost instantly asleep, her window still wide open to the murmuring air.

When she woke, suddenly, she was certain that some sound had brought her out of sleep. The room was dark, for the sky was heavily overcast and the afterglow blotted out. Her window was a lighter square in the darkness of her room. The sound of the sea was muted to a regular breathing. Yet there still seemed to echo in her ears some kind of disruptive noise. She got out of bed, stole silently over to the open window, and stood listening. Only the sound of the sea. Then, beneath her window, to the left, a stone rolled under a foot and a voice whispered hoarsely:

"Take care! We're not wanting the whole place awake!"

Another, half-laughing, answered:

"Don't be fashing yourself, Rory, there's no one awake in Mourie but ourselves and those down yonder."

Noiselessly and cautiously, Elizabeth leaned out of the window and looked, but there was nothing to be seen. Past the gable of the house on her left, there ran a rough track that came down from the moor behind; sometimes cows and sheep were driven down it. Along the fence of Jenny's garden grew thick fuchsia bushes. People standing close into the fuchsias would be invisible to her at the window; and this must be where they were. She heard a foot shift again and the second voice say:

"Och, I'm getting weary. No one has come along the road at all, and I don't think there was any need for us to be posted here. Angus McKay has great ideas about strategy—thinking himself a Montgomery, no doubt. We could all be sitting in the shed on the jetty and keeping each other company."

"Yes, and talking and blethering like yourself now, and the sound carrying over the water. Besides, we're here to see the signal from the headland, not just to keep an eye on the houses. I'm telling you, it was a good thing we were keeping watch or it's no saying what trickery they might be up to. Taking the stuff up at night and making away with it maybe."

"If we could just be having a wee smoke now . . ."

"You are the fool, you, Kenneth McKenzie! The light of a match would be carrying like a lighthouse and warning them off altogether, and if we are to catch them, we must surprise them."

A moment's silence and then the unseen Kenneth spoke again.

"I am hoping there will not be anything unpleasant happening. I would be sorry if any harm came to Mr. Maclean. He has always been a very pleasant gentleman."

"But Mr. Maclean might not be knowing at all that they had gone out tonight. It might be a plot on the divers' part, or that Johnny fellow—I do not like him. "Man"—and Rory's voice took on an unctuous solemnity—"it is awful what the love of money will be driving people to. As the apostle says, it is the root . . ."

"Quiet! See yonder."

From the headland came three tiny flashes of light.

"They're coming! Watch your big feet and try not to make a noise like a cart-horse. Have you got your stick ready?"

She saw two figures come out from the shelter of the fuchsias, cross the road and begin to run heavily along the grass verge of the shore towards the old jetty; and then she was fumbling in the dark, pulling on slacks and blouse and anorak, fastening her

105

sandals. She crept downstairs, groped along the passage and gently opened the unlocked door. Then she too was running along the verge towards the jetty.

For there had clearly been some ghastly mistake. Someone had got the idea that Crane's people were going out secretly to bring back the treasure—or some of it—convey it away secretly, and deprive Mourie of its promised wealth. This would link up with the smouldering resentment over the attack on John Maclean; and heaven knew what might happen if an unprovoked attack were made on Crane and his men as they came ashore. It was all too stupid, really, and showed how much suspicion and resentment were simmering in Mourie when no one, apparently, had for one moment thought there might be a totally innocent explanation for Crane's people going off in the boats that night. Anyway, she'd tell them that it was merely a fishing expedition and no harm would be done.

She ran swiftly and lightly, hoping to catch up with the two men. But they had vanished in the darkness and she arrived at the jetty without seeing them. There she stopped for a moment, to draw breath and listen. It was an old jetty not much used; the stones were worn and uneven, with here and there rusty iron rings embedded in them. Near the top, there was an old stone building, with a steeply pitched roof, which might once have been a small warehouse. Beyond it was a rickety black wooden shed. Peering into it one day, Elizabeth had seen that it held a few old nets, tyres, empty oil drums and a small anchor. As she stood listening, she heard a low murmur of voices and it seemed to come from the shed. She could just distinguish its squatting bulk beyond the towering mass of the stone building. She picked her way down the jetty, quickly, but carefully too, mindful of the iron rings and the low stone bollards. Not carefully enough. Just as she judged she must be at the door of the shed, her foot caught in cold iron, and she would have fallen headlong had a figure not moved out from the darkness by the shed and caught her in strong arms, that not only saved her from falling but held her prisoner, while a hand fiercely laid across her mouth kept her from crying out. She heard the door of the shed being kicked

106

open and the next moment she was inside in a hot stifling air and total darkness, aware of a pressure of bodies all around her.

There was a murmur of surprised voices.

"Who's that?" asked someone.

"I wouldn't be knowing—it's a lassie."

Into the silence came a little yelp as Elizabeth bit hard against the fingers over her mouth. The hand dropped and she said clearly:

"It's Elizabeth, Mrs. Lauder's niece."

"Miss Elizabeth! And what might you be doing here?"

She thought it might be Angus McKay speaking, but couldn't be sure.

"I heard voices under my window—"

("I told you you were just a big blether," Rory's voice whispered in the dark.)

"—and I gathered there was to be—that you thought someone was trying to sneak away some of the treasure—but they've just gone out fishing: that's all."

"Just fishing?" It was a different voice. If only there was some kind of light! It was horrible speaking in the darkness like this, and her arms were still held right to her ribs. She turned and spoke into the face she could feel breathing down her ear.

"Would you please let me go?"

"Will I?"

"Aye. Let her go." Angus' voice again? "So they're just going fishing? How do you know?"

"Crane—Mr. Maclean told me."

"Aye. She'll know the rights of it if anyone does." A new voice with a snigger in it that made Elizabeth flush with anger. There was a thud, a gasp, and then Roddy the Shop, unmistakably, said softly: "You'll hold your tongue, Duncan McKay, or I'll throttle you."

Angus, if it was Angus, said:

"Well, if it's just fishing they've been, it'll be easy to prove. And if it's the other business, then we'll get that sorted out too. And there need be no harm done to anyone, but just a little explaining."

107

"Maybe we might learn something about John Maclean too. Maybe Miss Elizabeth could tell us something."

It was the sniggering voice again; cold and vicious this time, and producing a thick silence.

"I don't know what you mean."

"Neither does he." —Roddy again.

"Yes I do. She says she found a murdered man on the way here, when she first came; but Hamish McIntosh finds nothing. And she says she has found it again, but when they go to get it, it isn't there; only John Maclean lying at death's door. I should think she could be telling us quite a bit about things if she wanted."

It was a second or two before Elizabeth grasped the full implication of what he was saying. She opened her mouth to protest against the monstrous suggestion that she was somehow involved in murder, but at that moment there was a rush of cool air and another dark figure slipped in through the opened door. Before it could be closed a voice said:

"Could we not leave the door open? It is very hot here at the back."

"All right. But we'll need to stay quiet and not talk. And keep a hold of that girl."

"I cannot! She's away!"

For Elizabeth, sharply twisting her body and digging her elbows savagely back, had broken loose and was through the door. She took a great gulp of cool night air and then ran up the jetty, meaning, once she had reached the road, to slip in between the houses to dodge pursuit. But two figures loomed out of the darkness coming down the jetty. That way was cut off; she darted into the gap between the end of the hut and the gable end of the stone building, burying her face in her shoulder and hiding her hands behind her, lest their paleness would show against the black of the hut; she could feel the weathered wood beneath her fingertips. Dark shapes rushed past going up the jetty. She heard voices.

"Did you see anyone pass you?"

"No."

"We'll look all the same. Rory, go down that way."

Between the back of the shed and the wall, about four feet high, which ran down one side of the jetty was a narrow gap. She edged her way along the end of the shed and into the gap. Under her feet she could feel wisps and tangles of seaweed. From the other side of the shed she could hear hoarse voices, desperately trying not to speak too loudly. Perhaps she would be undiscovered in this gap? It was no use trying to go over the wall—there was a fairly high drop, either on to slippery wrack-covered rocks or into the water, depending on the tide. She edged her way further in. The gap between shed and wall ahead of her was blotted out by solid darkness, and she heard a footstep scuffling in the dry seaweed. There was only one thing possible to do, and she did it. Quite silently, with the agility of desperation, she swung herself on to the wall and lay flat along the top. Another step sounded in the gap ahead of her; there was a mutter of Gaelic; the figure retreated and she heard the words:

"She's not behind the shed."

She would wait till the noise died away, for it was not likely they would spend much time looking for her. Then she would steal up the jetty and go down to the water's edge on the shore; and, always providing Crane's boats hadn't in the meantime come to the jetty, she would shout some kind of warning from the beach.

A footstep rustled in the gap . . . she lay still as stone . . . was aware of movement beside her . . . and a hand groped up the wall and grasped her shoulder. Then she was down in the gap again and Roddy the Shop was holding her in a firm but gentle grip.

"Oh, Miss Elizabeth, what for were you getting mixed up in all this? If I let you go will you promise not to try to warn Mr. Maclean and the boats?"

"No, I will not. Let me go."

But it was no use. She was too firmly held. And now someone else was whispering through the darkness. It sounded like Angus McKay.

"What's going on?"

"It's me, Roddy; with Miss Elizabeth."

109

"Well now, we'll just be getting back into the shed and wait quietly."

And there she was, no better for her break-away, except that it was Roddy who held her. No one spoke. They crowded in, some panting a little; the door was closed, and the air began to grow hot and stuffy again. Her head began to ache, her mouth was dry and she suddenly felt dreadfully miserable. Then the door opened again and a hoarse voice said:

"They're not far off, by the sound of the oars."

"Right." Angus was clearly in command. "Quietly, all of you, and get out on to the jetty. But keep close to the buildings!"

"Have I to be staying here?" Roddy sounded plaintive. "I don't want to miss anything."

"Well, you can bring her out, but keep hold of her, and don't let her make a noise.

The fresh air was wonderful, but a kind of panic laid hold of Elizabeth as she stood by the door, Roddy's hands pinning her arms to her ribs. The men gathered in the shelter of the buildings were practically invisible. No one approaching from the sea would realise they were there; the cloud-ceiling had lowered and a sea-mist was thickening. She could vaguely distinguish movement; she sensed gestures; beside her a hand swung a cudgel; she shivered, aware of raw violence waiting to be released. Then she heard oars, and a blurred sound of voices, and one, and then a second boat loomed out of the dark.

A frozen stillness held the men on shore. The first boat bumped gently where the jetty sloped beneath the surface. She could just distinguish four figures; one bent over the jetty— securing a mooring?—one had stepped ashore; tall, she thought she recognised him.

"Crane!" shouted Elizabeth. "Crane!"

Roddy clapped a hand over her mouth, but she knew what to do. She bit hard, and kicked savagely backwards and upwards. Roddy gave a groaning gasp, and she was away, and running down the jetty shouting, "Crane! Crane!"

There was an angry hubbub of voices behind her, and thudding feet, but she was well ahead. Now there was a beam of light making a path for her; and then she was beside Crane and his arm was round her, and he was speaking calm and caressing words to her, while his torch played over the puzzled, angry faces, and for the second time, he and she faced the men of Mourie.

"Elizabeth! What's going on? Why are you here at this hour of the morning? If it comes to that, why are you here, gentlemen?"

His tone was at once mocking and wary, and the expressions on the faces of the little crowd confronting them changed and grew grimmer in response to it. Elizabeth spoke.

"They think you were trying to sneak away some of the treasure: they wouldn't believe you had just gone fishing. I came to tell them."

"You're a good girl, Elizabeth." He raised his voice a little. "She's right, you know. We have been fishing. You can see the fish if you like."

Now they were beginning to look sheepish. But they still didn't move, and they still held their sticks and cudgels knuckle-tight.

Crane spoke again; this time there was no trace of mockery.

"Did you really think I'd try to sneak off with it? After what I told you I meant to do?"

They looked at each other and then at the ground. From the front of the little crowd, Angus spoke.

"It was just—when we heard the boats were going out with yourself and your men . . . but if you say it was fishing you were, then of course we believe you."

"Come and see for yourself." But as yet he didn't stand aside. "But I still can't understand it—I thought there was trust between us."

They shifted uneasily, and Roddy blurted:

"It was the John Maclean business. It has upset us all."

"I realise that. It upset us, and we're strangers. But why should you think I'd deceive you?"

No answer. A hung head or two; some sidelong glances. They know something, thought Elizabeth; and waited. So did Crane; the men in the boats behind her stopped moving too. For

111

an instant, some revelation hung in the air; was rejected; Rory's voice said:

"Three boats went out. Only two have come back here."

"One of us got a blow on the head from an oar; he's not feeling too good, and that boat went straight into the bay beyond the river, beside the house. Johnny thought he could manage it all right. The rest of us came to the jetty; we meant to leave most of the fish in the shed for you to take your pick." A pause. "If you want to have a look in the boats, you're welcome."

Up to that moment he had held her protectively against him. Now he dropped his arm gently and took her elbow and moved aside, shining his torch into the boat. The light gleamed and glanced on and off the fish lying in it; picked out oars, lines, bailing-tin, rope, glinted on bilge-water beneath the bottom planks; a boat come back from the fishing, and nothing else. Crane jerked his head towards Angus and the rest, inviting them to come and look.

And come they did, reluctantly: Angus, a man she didn't know; Rory, whose voice she knew, whom she now saw clearly for the first time, a black-haired man, big hands tautly clutching his shinty-stick weapon. They looked into the boat, sheepish and hang-dog, and turned back saying nothing, merely nodding when Crane said: "Satisfied?"

Then he spoke to Elizabeth. "I'll take you home." He flung a word to the men behind him, and then the two of them walked up the jetty and past the group of men, now apparently drained of animosity. Crane spoke to them in a friendly way:

"Take all the fish you want." And then gave them never a backward glance.

As they walked to Jenny's house, he said:

"Why did you come to the jetty, Elizabeth? Did they hurt you at all? Were they dangerous?"

"I think they could have been. No, they didn't harm me . . . It was just a chance I heard two of them talking under my window . . . and I didn't like to think you might come to some harm."

112

"Ah, Elizabeth, it's a long time since I heard anyone say they didn't want harm to come to me . . ."

In his voice, there was the tone she thought she had heard that afternoon on the bridge. Regret? Nostalgia? Tenderness? As if another Crane had suddenly emerged. It was only there for a moment. Casually he went on: "You mustn't risk anything on my account. Here we are at the house. Will you be all right?"

"Of course. Good night, Crane."

She waited by the gate for a brief moment or two looking after him till he disappeared in the darkness. When she turned to open the gate, the dark figure of a man was standing just beside her. She gave a loud gasp of alarm, and then saw it was Douglas; but for a moment she had not recognised him, so cold and menacing was his expression in the almost dark. At her exclamation he seized her arm and said:

"What was Crane Maclean telling you?"

"Nothing. Let go of my arm, Douglas. He'd been out fishing with the men, and there was a misunderstanding with some of the Mourie men."

"How did you come to be on the jetty?"

She was angry.

"That's none of your business, Douglas. Good night."

And without a backward glance she went up the path and into the house. Once up in her room, she looked out. Douglas was still by the gate, a darker blotch in the darkness. He turned and looked up at her window, and then moved away into the night; but in the direction of Mourie House, not the schoolhouse.

She lay long awake, as the light grew stronger, thinking, thinking hard. For her mind had been jolted into brisk activity. First there was the shock of revelation of hearing the malice and suspicion voiced by Duncan McKay in the crowded shed. So much for her illusion about the general and wholesale friendliness of Mourie! How many people were thinking and feeling as he did? Even Roddy's swift attack on Duncan McKay couldn't erase the anger and shock produced by his words. But still, that was a matter purely personal to herself. What puzzled her more, and kept her thoughts going round and round, was a conviction that they

113

hadn't gathered on the jetty simply to prevent Crane sneaking away the treasure. There was more to it. There had been looks exchanged, suggestions of a hidden purpose—she remembered Morag's insistence that the laird's treasure was *not* in the sea; and Douglas' remark that Mrs. Macleod had said she was sure it wasn't there . . . and yet there was old Mysie's charm, a sovereign found on the sand . . . Supposing the treasure was not where Crane thought . . . but why should the people of Mourie let him go on looking, if they knew it was a waste of time? She thought it over and over; and finally decided that come the next day she was going to ask someone—she wasn't sure whom—some straight questions—and find out once for all if the treasure was indeed lying in the Sound. There was, surely, no harm in asking—as to getting answers, that was, she was well aware, a totally different matter!

And Douglas—how and why had Douglas come to be at the cottage gate at such an hour? He had not asked what was going on. He had been interested in what Crane and she had been discussing. Had he known all the time what was happening? And she thought again of the bleak animosity of his expression when she first turned and saw him. Or was that merely the effect of the darkness?

There was something else to think about too; and she found herself coming back to it again and again. As Crane had held her close and protectingly, something hard, so hard as almost to hurt, had pressed against her side. Crane had been carrying a gun. Why?

CHAPTER 13

She told Jenny next day of the night's doings, for she would certainly have heard about it in the village. Jenny made little comment, except that she disliked the idea of so much suspicion and latent violence in Mourie. From Crane came an affectionate phone call to ask if she was all right; he hoped he'd see her later on but there was trouble over diving-gear and he might be kept busy all that day. She came back from the phone a little listlessly. Jenny said:

"I'm going to see Peg's baby. Like to come?"

"Yes indeed."

"You haven't seen him since he was born."

"No, I haven't."

"Don't forget to cross his tiny palm with silver."

From a distance, the little camp under the trees had a pleasing rustic air, like an early nineteenth-century engraving of the "Scotch Highlands." But Aunt Jenny greeted Elizabeth's remark to this effect with one of her sceptical snorts.

"Picturesque it may be. It's also unhygienic and in my opinion, no fit condition for human beings to live in; and I'm not made any happier by thinking it's quite possibly a lot better than their winter quarters—probably some shocking slum in the heart of Glasgow or a leaking caravan on an insanitary site on the outskirts. They're very *cagey* about saying where they live in winter."

The car bumped over the turf, watched by everyone in the camp. As soon as Elizabeth stepped from the car, Lizzie ran up and thrust a grubby hand into hers. Peg was sitting by the fire on a log. She looked a little pale, but was otherwise cheerful and dis-

115

played "wee Hector," lying in a battered pram, with much maternal pride. Elizabeth put some silver in the tiny hand. Already Hector had lost the crumpled unfinished look of the newly born. Having admired him, she left Jenny to talk to Peg and went over to speak to the others by the fire.

Old Mysie gave her a morose glance and a grunt. Nancy greeted her with courtesy and then went over to join Peg and Jenny. Bella rose and asked her to sit down and Lizzie came and squatted beside her. The smoke rose from the fire, the sun shone through the trees, and a haze lifted from the sea.

"It's a lovely morning," said Elizabeth.

"Aye," said Bella. "It wis a dark nicht."

Lizzie looked up at Elizabeth.

"There was that much fog, you could hardly see thae trees. You could get lost if ye went ower far intae them."

"Yes, I suppose you could. Unless you knew the country *very* well."

"Like ma faither. He went oot last nicht, but he didnae get lost."

"Mair's the peety." As if to emphasise the words, Mysie spat expertly into the fire.

Astonished, Elizabeth looked at Bella, who stirred uneasily and said in a whisper:

"Ma granny's no' vera weel the day."

"Naethin' wrang wi' me." She glared at Bella and relapsed into a grumpy silence.

Peg and Nancy and Jenny came over from the pram, and Nancy asked if they would like a cup of tea. It was hot, sweet and smoky, reminding Elizabeth of "proper picnics," which means a wood fire, and a kettle balanced on the top, and tea brewed in the kettle, and never a thermos flask in sight . . . She was drawn back from her nostalgic daydream by the appearance of Sandy slouching over to the fire from his tent in a shame-faced way as if uncertain of his welcome. He nodded to her and to Jenny and said:

"Ony tea fur a man?"

"Oh aye." Nancy filled him a mug and he stood drinking it.

116

"Are you pleased with your son?" asked Elizabeth.

"Oh aye. He's a fine wee fella," and evidently encouraged by Elizabeth's gesture of sociability he sat down in the circle round the fire and took a hearty gulp of his tea.

Through the smoke, Mysie glowered malevolently at him, rose up and stalked into her tent. They all looked into their tea and were silent and no one paid any attention except Sandy, who half-rose and then sat down again muttering something about a crabbit auld bitch.

But Aunt Jenny dealt with the situation briskly and firmly. "What is wrong here this morning? You're not yourselves at all."

"Oh, it's naethin', naethin' at a'." And Sandy took another swig of tea.

But Nancy spoke up.

"Ye ken fine ye can tell Mistress Lauder here. She's a guid frien' tae us an' Ah'm shair the lass here is no gaun tae tell tales either."

"Aye. Ah weel, it's like this. Auld Mysie's upset because—ye ken thon thing she keeps hingin' roon her neck? Thon gold kin' o' medal that she says has some kin' o' magic aboot it?—silly auld . . ."

" 'Silly' naethin'," said Peg sharply. "Ah'm tellin' you it saved ma life."

"Ah weel—mebby. Onywey, she's fair mad, because Ah've fun' anither."

"What?" Jenny and Elizabeth spoke together and—"Where?" said Jenny, and "When?" said Elizabeth.

"Last nicht, in . . . alang the shore there. And Mysie's fair mad, because she's no the only yin wi' a bit charm like that— and she's as crabbit as a bear wi' a sair heid."

"But where and when, Sandy?" said Jenny firmly.

"Ah've telt ye. Last nicht. On the shore—that way." And he jerked his head in a vaguely northern direction.

"I'm surprised you weren't afraid to go out along the shore in a fog like last night," said Jenny, not looking at him. "It was on the sand bar out there that Jimmy McKell was drowned in the fog two years ago."

117

"It wisna' exactly on the shore . . ."

"Tell them as it happened, Sandy," said Nancy. "It's ower chancy a business, and we could dae wi' some advice."

"Aye. Ah well, it wis like this. Ah went oot last nicht tae see if Ah could mebby lay hauns on a bit salmon"—he stopped and looked wary—"Ye'll no' tell?"

"No, we won't tell."

"Weel, Ah wis lucky; tho' mind you it's no just luck. Ye need some skill at it . . . onywey, I got a fish; and then Ah went tae pit it in the cave."

Elizabeth looked a question at Jenny, who said: "Sandy uses the cave a little way along from here—where the point comes out to the sea—as a larder. Isn't that so, Sandy?"

"Aye. Ye see, miss, it wouldna just be very canny tae hae a fish aboot the camp here. Someone micht see it and be telling tales . . . But hoo did ye ken, mistress?"

Jenny laughed. "I just guessed. But go on with your story."

"Aye. Weel, Ah cam doon ontae the shore, fur it wis a thick nicht—leastways, doon this side it wis—but Ah kept alang the shingle, sae's tae ken ma wey, an' Ah cam tae the cave wi'oot much bother. An' at the wey in, Ah stopt fur a minute . . . D'ye ken the cave?" He addressed Jenny.

"Oh yes. You go through some big scattered boulders and come to it. I know it goes back a long way but I've never been right to the end of it."

"Aye. They say there's a wey up at the back tae the gairdens at the Big Hoose." He gave them a cunning look out of the edge of his eyes. "Mebby it's true. Aye. Weel, Ah wis standin' there at the rocks, just rememberin' which rock wis which, tae mark ma wey in, fur it wis gey thick, when Ah heard first oars dippin', and then a boat being drawn ower pebbles, an' then voices. An' Ah went further in among the rocks and cam tae the cave, an' Ah felt ma wey tae . . . Ah pit awa' the fish. But then Ah couldna get oot, fur Ah heard them again—voices, and feet on the stanes."

He stopped speaking and looked into his mug. Nancy silently rose, filled it, and handed it back to him. No one said a word;

118

they were all, Elizabeth realised, relishing the telling of the adventure; and Sandy was enjoying himself too. She remembered Douglas saying that the tinkers were great tellers of stories: "the last flicker of a tradition," Douglas had said. But Sandy had begun to speak again.

"Ah went back and climbed ontae the ledge"—his eyes blinked as he realised he'd given away the hiding-place of the salmon—"an' waited. An' the voices an' the feet cam nearer, and then licht makin' a circle in the fog. An' then fower men. Ah couldna see their faces, but one talked wi' an awfu' English twang—and they wis cairryin' twa boxes. The first twa had a box between them and the second twa the same. They werena big boxes, but they seemed heavy. An' when they were weel intae the cave, they pit them doon, and stood and stretched as if their backs an' airms wis sair."

He paused again, and looked over at Nancy as if seeking guidance.

"Tell them, Sandy, tell them."

"Ah. Weel, it wis when they lifted up the boxes again that things went wrang, as ye micht say. Ah couldna see a' that weel, but the first twa, they ige a heave an' up wi' their box an' awa' further in tae the cave. An' then the next twa mak fur tae lift up theirs, an' there's a kin' o' a crack an' a sort o' rattle an' they pit the box doon and wan says: 'The bottom's givin' way!' An' the ither says: 'An' some's fallen oot,' wi' a kin' o' screech in his voice, as if he wis awfu' worrit. An' the ither says: 'Here's a bit rope tae pit roon it.' An' then they're doon on their knees an' fumblin' awa' at the box. An' then wan says: 'Have ye got them that fell oot?' An' the ither casts aroon wi' the licht and scoops aboot wi' his haun amang the sand on the flair, an' he's pickin' up things an' shovin' them in his pocket, an' then he says: 'Aye, Ah've got them all.' An' then wan o' the first twa comes back and says: 'Are you not coming? Is anything wrong?' So they say: 'The bottom of the box broke but we've tied it up with rope.' An' he says: 'Was anything lost?'—awfu' worrit-like. An' they say: 'We've picked it all up.' And with that they lift their box and awa' intae the cave, efter the ithers."

He broke off again—this time, Elizabeth was sure, purely for effect. As if supplying a cue, Bella said, "And whit did ye dae then?"

"Ah cam doon, an' Ah tried tae feel ma wey tae whaur they'd been busy wi' the box. Ah could feel the sand churned-up like, but that wis a'. Sae Ah decided Ah wud wait till the daylicht and see whit wis tae be seen. Ah sat doon in the shelter o' a rock, weel oot o' sicht, in case they cam back. But they didna. An' that maks me think they had found the wey through the cave tae the Big Hoose. Ah hadna a' that lang tae wait till it wis licht—though it took a whiley fur it tae come richt intae the cave. An' then Ah listened and heard naethin', and cam oot and looked fur the place whaur a' the fuss had been. It wisna hard tae find; ye could see in the sand whaur they'd set doon the box and whaur they'd been grubbin' aboot wi' their fingers pickin' up whit fell oot."

This time his silence was not for effect. He doesn't want to go on, thought Elizabeth, and noticed a kind of urgency in the others as if they were willing him to go on. He looked from one to the other and then said unwillingly:

"Aye. Weel, Ah felt amang the sand masel', an' Ah felt something sma' an' roon' an' hard, an' it wis this."

From his trouser pocket he pulled out a small gold coin; a sovereign that shone in the sunlight on his grimy palm; oddly primitive, holding all eyes; a gold coin.

To Elizabeth it was more—it was proof—was it not?—that Crane had been lying last night—lying to Angus and his friends—lying to her . . . But no, she wouldn't jump to conclusions; perhaps some of the men had slipped back in the fog, and got at the gold, and brought it away, cheating Crane as well as everyone else . . . no, it didn't seem feasible . . . Her mind began to whirl: why should Crane want to cheat the people of Mourie? How had they guessed what he was at? Why had he worn a gun?

But Jenny was asking Sandy to show her the coin. Now she had it in her hand and was looking at it. She turned it over, and her face changed. She lifted the coin closer to her eyes and looked at it keenly; glanced at Elizabeth and then handed it

120

back to Sandy. "It's a gold sovereign. Take care of it, Sandy. And I wouldn't tell anyone else about it."

"Ah'll no tell onybody. Ah'm no happy aboot it. An' her"— jerking his head towards Mysie's tent—"she's that crabbit, it's spiling a' things. Can ye no speak tae her, mistress? Ah'm no trying tae—tae dae awa' wi' her thing. Mine's just something Ah picked up oot the sand. Hers . . ."

"Mine wis foond in a droond man's haun'." Mysie had come out of her tent and was standing behind Jenny. "That maks it different." She too appealed to Jenny. "Is that no' richt?"

"Yes. Yours is quite different, Mysie. Can I look at yours?"

Mysie hesitated; then pulled out her coin on the end of its string and, sheltering it in her hands, let Jenny look at it. She turned it over, examined it and then closed the old woman's fingers over it.

"Keep it safe, Mysie; and don't be angry with Sandy. He's quite right. His will never be special like yours."

She turned to Peg. "I think my niece and I must go now. But I'll be back soon to see the baby. Take care of yourself. And Sandy—keep very quiet about what you saw in the cave."

They didn't drive straight home. Jenny had a professional call to make at a cottage up the glen through which the river flowed. The road ran past the Mourie House grounds. The entrance to a gloomy drive that curved sharply to the left was barred by a rusting, massive iron gate between square stone pillars topped by stone eagles that years of Atlantic gales had weathered into misshapen pterodactyls. The house was invisible from the road, and the grounds were bordered by a high stone wall in remarkably good repair. The river came down through the grounds, and where it left them, the road crossed it on a solid stone arched bridge. As they drove along by the wall, Elizabeth thought: Crane has never suggested I go to the house. I've never heard of anyone going.

"Has anyone from Mourie ever been to the Big House?" she asked Jenny. "I mean, since Crane took it over."

"Not that I know of. The van from the shop delivers there, but that's all." She glanced at Elizabeth. "It's not so very strange.

He hasn't a woman in the place to stimulate the social side of things. The housekeeping—cooking and so on—are all done by men . . . He's let it be known that after the business of the diving is over, the house is to take up a more normal role in local life. Perhaps he's waiting to get married . . ." There was possibly a little malice in her words.

Elizabeth didn't answer. Jenny came to the cottage high on the moor, went in, gave an injection, and when she came out found Elizabeth still lost in thought and silent. But she spoke when Jenny drove on instead of turning back.

"Have you another call?"

"No, but if it's good weather I always drive up to the road-end when I come here."

Three miles further on, the road became a rough track running down into a hidden valley in the hills. Once there had been a croft there; the stump of the house, the remains of byre and sheep-fank were there; and two rowan trees and the outline of what had once been a garden. At the far side, the river came through the hills in a deep cleft and fell in a waterfall, and then ran through level ground which had once been good grazing. Now bare, empty, sad.

Jenny turned the car, rolled down the window, and she and Elizabeth looked out at the hills and the sea; from the strange, bleak beautiful shapes to the north, past the peaks of Skye, to the tumble of hills and rocks to the south. Elizabeth's clenched fingers slackened. Jenny noticed and said:

"I like to come here when I'm tensed up. It relaxes me." She inhaled great gulps of air noisily. "Isn't the air wonderful?" And then said quietly: "I thought you were a bit upset by Sandy's story."

There was no point in putting up a pretence.

"Yes, I was. It looks as if the men of Mourie were right, and Crane *was* trying to take away the laird's treasure secretly . . . though I can't think why he should want to . . . and there might be some other explanation."

"Possibly. There *must* be another explanation."

"What do you mean?"

"The emigrant ship sailed in 1849 or 1850. The sovereign Sandy found is an Edward VII one; Mysie's is 1888. So . . ."

"You needn't say more." Elizabeth's tone was bitter. "Whatever is out there in the Sound, whatever they've been looking for, it is not the laird's treasure."

CHAPTER 14

It was late in the morning when they got back to the cottage, for they sat for some time in the car talking and puzzling over Jenny's discovery. Elizabeth was grateful that Jenny kept the discussion impersonal; she made no reference to her niece's relationship with Crane, and concentrated on trying to disentangle the business of the treasure. She conceded it was just possible that Crane might have thought it was indeed the laird's stuff he had found; but flatly refused any credit to Elizabeth's tentative suggestion that perhaps he was the victim of a plot on the part of some of his men . . . and even as she put forward the idea, Elizabeth knew it was almost incredible. But she found herself trying to defend Crane; clutching at any suggestion that might explain what had happened in as favourable a light as possible. But under Jenny's quizzical gaze, she had to give up the attempt. Crane had hoodwinked the people of Mourie; had apparently been using the story of the laird's treasure as a cover for something else; had played a mean part in raising the hopes of Mourie's inhabitants; had in fact exploited poor and humble people . . . Douglas no doubt would have said it was just the continuation of a long exploitation.

But wasn't Douglas just as much involved as Crane? Or didn't he know what the divers had found? Had he too been using the people of Mourie?

When she put this to Jenny, she protested, anxious to defend Douglas as Elizabeth was to defend Crane. Douglas could very well be completely ignorant of what was going on. Yet even she had to admit that there might be a possibility that Douglas too had become an exploiter.

And yet, and yet . . . even as she and Jenny discussed the matter, Elizabeth remembered the men always on the watch on the headland; their faces in the light of the torch on the jetty the night before—they hadn't the appearance, or the feel, of people easily open to exploitation. They rather gave the impression of following some quite clearly conceived purpose. She remembered the moment last night down there by the boats when the two groups of men had faced each other and it seemed as if something was about to be revealed . . .

"It's not as simple as that," she said. "I mean, it's not just Crane or Douglas or both using them . . . and I'm going to find out what's going on!"

Jenny had for a moment said nothing, and then:

"Why? It doesn't really concern us."

Ah, but it did concern her. Anything connected with Crane concerned her; and if he had lied to her, she wanted to know why. For she had to settle with herself what she was to think of Crane. She had been drawn to him not only by his formidable physical charm, but by the combination in him of wealth, power and a kind of simplicity in his approach to Mourie; a quixotic dream, as it had seemed to her. To find it was all a mere attitude adopted for some ulterior motive, to have to think of Crane as some kind of shabby trickster, would be grievous indeed. But perhaps he had genuinely thought he would find the laird's treasure there; perhaps what he had found was as much a surprise to him as to her and Jenny . . .

She remembered Morag's voice:

"The treasure is not there."

Supposing she *had* known something? Supposing the rest of Mourie knew it? Then why had they let Crane go on looking?

She realised Jenny was looking at her expectantly, and said:

"Just let's say it's disinterested curiosity on my part . . . all right, all right, it's *not* disinterested. But I'm going to find out. And the first person I'm going to ask is Angus McKay."

Jenny pursed her lips. "You don't know what you're tackling.

125

But go ahead. In the meantime, I think we should say nothing about what we've found out. It would only complicate things."

"I agree."

There the discussion ended, and they drove back to the cottage.

In the afternoon, Elizabeth set off to find Angus McKay, leaving behind her a sardonic Jenny, openly sceptical of her being able to get any information from him, though she had volunteered the helpful information that lateish in the afternoon would be the best moment to tackle him. Officially, Angus was Mourie's joiner and, of course, undertaker. There wasn't much to be done in the way of joinery; and Angus was not good at sending bills. He lived, said Jenny cheerfully, "off death," funerals being the only occasions on which he was prompt with his accounts. Also, he had a small army pension, having lost part of his right foot at El Alamein.

Jenny had advised going straight to what Angus grandiloquently referred to as "my place of business." This was a black lean-to wooden shed at the end of Angus' house. It gave a general impression of sagging slightly. A small-paned window, somewhat askew, stretched the full length of the outside wall, and above the door were the words, in tarnished white, "Angus McKay, Joiner and Funeral Undertaker: all types of business p--m--ly at---d-d to," the paint of the last line having been peeled away by the weather. The door was on the latch. Elizabeth knocked but got no answer; she opened it, and went in. Inside there were long planks piled against one wall; a bench with a vice and plane; saws hanging on the wall; trestles ranged at the far end; sawdust and a smell of wood. The place was neat and tidy: much more so than the exterior would have led one to expect. A door with frosted glass panels gave access to the house through the gable wall. As she looked at it, a figure loomed darkly through the glass; then the door opened, and there stood Angus McKay himself.

"Good afternoon, Miss Elizabeth, and what can I be doing for you? Has Mrs. Lauder decided definitely to have the bath boxed in? For if so, I'll come up to measure it tomorrow."

"She hasn't said anything to me about it," said Elizabeth. "I haven't come on business, Mr. McKay."

"Well now, if it is about last night, I hope you will accept my apologies for any inconvenience that was caused you. It was just unfortunate that you happened to come along when you did."

"I'm not worried about last night—at least, not in that connection."

"Well now, I am very glad to know that. I would not have liked to think you were annoyed about it. It was all really a misunderstanding."

His voice was kind and gentle; and his eyes sharp and shrewd. Elizabeth, feeling his soft politeness swirling round her purpose like a blurring mist, took the plunge desperately and said, loudly:

"Mr. McKay, I wanted to ask you if you knew exactly where the laird's treasure really is."

When she asked him, he was crossing the workshop floor towards the bench and her words halted him. She thought his back stiffened as if he were suddenly on guard, but when he slowly turned to face her, she decided it was imagination on her part; he was relaxed and a little puzzled.

"But surely you know where it is? That's what Mr. Maclean's divers are after in the Sound."

"Yes, I know that. But is the laird's treasure there?"

"Well now, I do not know if anyone could say 'yes' to that. I doubt if Mr. Maclean himself could. He will not be knowing for sure till he finds it, will he? *But*"—for Elizabeth had begun to ask another question, and he raised his voice a little—"that is where it has always been said to be."

"Oh. Thank you very much, Mr. McKay."

She turned to leave, but as she reached the door, he spoke again.

"Has anything happened to make you think we might all be wrong in thinking it's there?"

"Old Morag, the day before she died, told me it was not there. In fact, she said she would show me where it really was."

"Did she now! And did you tell your aunt this?"

"Yes."

"And what did she say?"

127

"She said Morag was very old and didn't always know what she was saying."

"Now, isn't your aunt the wise woman! For that is just the way of it. Morag was very old and failing. Mind you, there was a time when she was wise herself, and had the sight. But she was growing feeble, and she felt it, and she was not pleased when there was talk of divers and things; and she would be wanting to make you think that she was knowing better than Mr. Maclean with all his clever modern ways . . . Well, good afternoon, then, Miss Elizabeth, and don't forget to tell Mrs. Lauder that I will be pleased to come and measure her bath any time." And Elizabeth was back in the village street, as wise as when she went into his workshop. It was clear that Angus, if he knew anything, was giving nothing away. Who else might know something? She walked up the street dejectedly. The little houses had a glow in the afternoon sunlight. Mourie looked beautiful, and if you disregarded the petrol pumps at the shop, much as it must have looked for years. Had it grown that way by chance, or had some laird laid out a "model village"? If so, he'd had an eye for comeliness. The little low houses were satisfyingly diversified here and there by two-storied houses.

She thought over her acquaintanceship in Mourie. There was Mrs. Macleod the Shop—Mourie born and bred—she could be expected to know something, and had indeed already expressed an opinion on the subject; but would she answer questions? Elizabeth decided she would avoid a frontal approach and introduce the topic obliquely. Was there anything she needed in the shop? Toothpaste—one always needed toothpaste.

The shop bell jangled as she opened the door. She was the only customer. Indeed, the shop was quite empty. The two neat display windows that faced the street—in one tins of every description built and balanced in structures of amazing ingenuity and no little engineering skill, and the work of Roddy; the other, Mrs. Macleod's responsibility, full of ladies' garments of impeccable modesty and relentlessly conventional taste such as solid tweed skirts, sensible jumpers, opera-topped vests, flannelette night-dresses, all surprisingly grouped round a trouser-suit in psy-

128

chedelic nylon—gave no inkling of the size of the shop inside. It was long and narrow, stretching into a gloom of ironmongery beyond the clothing counter, which was next the grocery counter, the most cheerful and profitable part of the shop. It was a model of neatness. Macleod's Select Emporium was a traditional village shop in the variety of its goods (Wellingtons and fishermen's boots hung like huge tropical fruit from the ceiling) but was as bright and spruce as any town shop, though it smelt more interesting, a subtle blend of paraffin, firelighters, onions and oranges hanging over everything.

Elizabeth waited for a minute or two but no one came; so she opened and shut the door again twice, ringing a peal on the warning bell. As the last busy clatter died away, Roddy came through from the back shop, peering at her as she stood against the light.

"Oh, it's you, Miss Elizabeth. Is there anything I can be doing for you?"

"I'd like some toothpaste, please."

"Surely. What kind."

"Oh, anything—Euthymol—Gibbs—"

Roddy wrapped the little package, handed it to her and rang up the money on the till. As he gave her the change he said:

"I hope you are none the worse for last night."

"I'm all right, thank you."

She looked at him. He was gazing at her with a rather touching expression of near adoration and she took a decision. She gave him one of her best slow smiles and said:

"Roddy, have you always lived in Mourie?"

"Yes, always. I was born here and I've never been away except when I had to go to the school hostel for the secondary school, and holidays in Glasgow at my auntie's."

"Don't you ever feel you'd like to get away?"

"Not often. I like it here."

"But do you find your job satisfactory? Wouldn't you like to be doing something more exciting?"

"You won't understand the position of course. Mrs. Macleod is my mother's cousin and she has no family and when she is gone I will be taking over the shop, and I have plans for expanding the business. You'll see."

"But don't you find it dull here—no pictures, no T.V.?"

"But we have dances, as you have seen, and we have the Dramatic Club and I am very fond of the acting; and there are the ceilidhs and the fishing, if you feel like it—no, I am not finding it dull. There is only one thing . . ."

"Yes?"

"There are not many girls to be choosing a wife from. In the summer there are the visitors and sometimes there are very nice girls among them. But, Miss Elizabeth . . ."

"Yes?"

"I have never seen anyone like you and I was wondering . . ."

The bell jangled loudly as a woman came into the shop. Roddy cast a beseeching glance at Elizabeth as he turned to greet the new customer; and Elizabeth wandered to the back of the shop and peered at the pots and pans, the buckets and bowls, the coils of rope and bailing scoops ranged on the shelves and floor. The customer—a loquacious woman of changeable mind—took a long time to give her order. Roddy sliced ham, gathered together flour and sugar, tea and cocoa, biscuits, cheese and oatmeal and a collection of tins, from time to time casting a glance in Elizabeth's direction as if to make sure she was still there. At last Mrs. McKenzie left, and Roddy joined Elizabeth at the back of the shop.

"You've a good stock here, Roddy."

"Yes, yes. But don't let us be talking about pots and pans and buckets. I was wondering if you would be caring to take a walk with me this evening. It is a fine day, and I could be showing you the heronry in the glen, if you're interested in that sort of thing."

"That would be nice, Roddy. I expect you know all there is to be known about Mourie and the country round about."

She looked at him, and then said:

"I've been wondering where I could find someone to answer a question that's been puzzling me."

"Perhaps I could."

130

"Perhaps you could. Roddy"—and she dropped her voice and moved closer to him—"Roddy, where *is* the laird's treasure, really?"

Roddy's expression registered surprise, embarrassment and sheer shiftiness. He looked earnestly at a row of aluminium teapots, setting one straight as he muttered:

"Where else but in the Sound, where they're diving for it?"

"But old Morag told me it wasn't there. She said she knew where it was."

"She was just havering . . . anyway, why do you want to know? It is not really any concern of yours, is it now?"

But Elizabeth saw her advantage. "Never mind why I want to know. Do *you* know anything about it?"

"And why should I be knowing?"

"I don't know, but I think you do."

Roddy looked at her desperately. "I . . ."

The shop bell jangled again, and in came Bella from the camp with Lizzie clutching her hand. Roddy definitely looked relieved, and Elizabeth said:

"I must be going—" And then, giving him a quick smile, added, "But I would love to see the heronry. I'll be at the road-end at eight o'clock tonight."

Before he could answer, she had left the shop, greeting Bella and Lizzie on her way out.

At half-past eight, she and Roddy were in Mourie Glen, sitting on a grassy slope above the burn, and looking across at a group of tall beeches which formed the heronry. The big untidy nests were half visible. Already the birds were ignoring their presence and were noisy and vociferous. They had seen two fly in, Elizabeth feeling a stirring at her heart as she saw them. She was no dedicated bird-watcher, but certain birds—herons, owls, kestrels, moor-hens, kingfishers—always moved her in some inexplicable way. She had borrowed Jenny's field-glasses, and had them ready in her hand, and would have been happy to spend the next hour or so simply looking. But Roddy was obviously anxious to talk and she herself had not come solely to look at herons. So after they had seen another two come in and had heard again the

131

clamour of the young in their nests, she lowered the glasses and said:

"Thank you for showing me them. They're very interesting."

"The wild life is very good round here. Sometimes I send a nature note to the *Courier* in Inverness and they print it."

Elizabeth looked at him with interest; there was more to Roddy than she had at first imagined. But she mustn't be side-tracked from her purpose. She had not breathed a word about the treasure so far, anxious to dissipate a certain wariness she had felt in Roddy when they met that evening. But it was time to raise the topic.

"Roddy, I'm sure you can tell me something about the laird's treasure. Is it, or is it not, really in the Sound?"

"Well now"—she was beginning to think that whenever a reply began with "Well now" she must expect something evasive— "that is where it has always been said to be."

"Roddy, that is no answer, as you very well know. Do you, or do you not, know if it is really there?"

Roddy shifted uneasily, and glanced at her.

"Is it very important to you? Though I cannot be seeing why it should be."

"Yes it is—it is indeed." The intensity of her reply surprised even herself, and Roddy responded to it.

"Then I'll tell you. But you must not be letting anyone know I told you. No, I do not think the laird's treasure is in the Sound."

"Ah. Then, Roddy, do you know where it is?"

"Please do not be pressing me to answer that."

"But I must have an answer. Roddy, *do* you know?"

Roddy was quite miserable.

"I do know where it is supposed to be. But it is a great secret, or so I have been led to understand."

"How do you know it then?"

"Because . . . you said Morag told you she knew where it was?"

"Yes."

"Well, you see, she would pass it on to Angus—Mr. McKay— him you saw the other night."

"Yes, yes, I know him."

". . . And he told me."

Into the silence came the squawking and screaming of the heronry. Elizabeth only half-heard it as she thought over his words. Roddy glanced at her and said hopefully:

"Would you like to go further up the glen?"

"After. Not yet. I want to know where it's hidden."

"But I am not sure I should be telling you. I do not think there is any need for it and it would not be right." He rose to his feet and held out his hand. "Come now, let us forget all this and I'll show you the best salmon pool in the peninsula."

But Elizabeth was firm.

"No, Roddy, I'm not moving from here till you've told me it all. Sit down again." And as he reluctantly did so, she said: "Why should Morag tell Angus?"

Roddy looked away into the tree tops.

"Because she was his mother."

"His *mother?*"

"Yes. It happened a long time ago, before she was married. His father was a visitor at the Big House . . . She went away to Glasgow and then Angus came to her in Mourie after, and was supposed to be a boarded-out boy from an orphanage in Glasgow, but och! everyone knew who he was. And Morag told him— about the treasure."

"But why did he tell you?"

"Because he is my uncle, and he has no family and—"

But Elizabeth interrupted him.

"Roddy, you'll have to make it clear and simple. I'm losing track."

Roddy looked at her and repeated reluctantly: "Angus was Morag's son, and lived with her as a boarded-out child till she married. Then her husband would not have him in the house, so he went to John McKay's house and learnt to be a joiner and John left him the business. And Angus' wife was my father's sister, so he is my uncle and they have no family so he looks on me as a son . . ."

"Like Mrs. Macleod the Shop."

"Yes, and I could have gone into his business if I'd wanted

133

to, but I did not like the idea of the funerals, so I'm going to take on the shop. But I'll get the joinery business some day and I'll put in a manager."

"You're a lucky man, Roddy, having two openings like that all ready and waiting for you . . ."

"Yes indeed. I will in all likelihood end up a man of some means."

He said it quite simply; but Elizabeth had a feeling that she was being given a hint that he might be a sound matrimonial prospect . . . She disregarded the remark and said:

"You still haven't told me where the hoard is hidden, or why Morag should tell Angus."

"Oh, it is an old story. When the laird was murdered, they took the things and they were going to take them away and then when they were passing the church, the minister came on them and pronounced judgment on them and said the hoard would be a curse to them for ever. But they were not heeding him, and they shut him up in his own byre and went on their way. But Morag's great-grandfather was moved by what was said and he took the stuff and gave it to his daughter, who was just a girl and not going away, and told her to hide it where it would never be found or used, there being a curse on it. And she was to tell no one. And the boat with the men went down in the Sound— and wasn't that a sore punishment on them? And Morag's grandmother hid it."

"But how did Morag know where it was if no one was to know?"

"Because her grandmother told her eldest child, who was Morag's father, and he told Morag . . ."

"And Morag told Angus."

"Yes."

"And Angus, having no son, told you."

"Yes."

A heron, with its long legs trailing, flew up the stream, but Elizabeth scarcely noticed it.

"But, Roddy, why should Morag want to tell *me?*"

134

"She was getting old and didn't always know what she was doing and she was upset by the divers coming."

"Then she may have told others. The whole of Mourie may know?"

"It is possible; but she would be readier to tell a stranger like yourself, I think . . . And now, shall we go and look at the pool? The fish will be rising."

This time Elizabeth rose and followed him up the path, still brooding over what she had heard. As he held a hazel branch aside for her to pass, she said:

"Roddy, if Angus knows all this, why did he let Crane Maclean go on with all the expense of getting divers and going on with the project?"

"Well now, I am wondering if Angus knows something more than others. Why should we have to keep a watch if there is nothing there in the water—though of course, most people might be thinking there *was* something there . . . It is not quite a straightforward situation."

And you can say that again, thought Elizabeth.

But for the moment she let the subject drop. She followed Roddy to the pool where the water, after forcing itself between high rocks, spread into a dark peat-brown pool that shelved up to a gravelly beach. They saw the salmon leaping for the flies and the rings of water spreading over the pool. Roddy discoursed about salmon with an enthusiast's affection. On the way back they saw roe deer slipping into the trees and an owl sailing through the branches; moths drifted past the black and silver birch trunks. Where the path was rocky and slippery, Roddy offered her his hand and she did not let it go when the path widened. By the time they got back to Jenny's garden gate, Roddy had told her the hiding-place of the laird's treasure.

CHAPTER 15

This was all very well. Elizabeth had felt quite a little glow of triumph at winkling the information from Roddy, a glow which had almost compensated for her disappointment at missing Crane, who, Jenny told her, had called when she was out with Roddy. But in the cold light of the following morning the glow had rather faded. What use was she to make of what she had so cunningly learnt? She had managed to avoid giving a strict promise that she would not pass on the information but had had to promise not to give away its source. When Jenny had asked her if she had found out anything, she had said, "One or two intriguing things about Mourie," and told her the story of Morag's relationship to Angus. It interested Jenny very much.

"I had no idea there was any connection between them—though of course I might have expected some link. They're all, apparently, involved in a complicated web of relationships, and one soon learns not to make remarks about people. They always turn out to be 'my mother's cousin' or 'my husband's sister's brother-in-law's nephew.' Yes"—as Elizabeth laughed—"I've encountered that one. But I never heard a whisper about Angus being Morag's son. That's because I'm an incomer. They do have a fanatic loyalty to each other, the real 'Mourians.'"

All this was no doubt true, but didn't help her with the problem of what to do with her newly acquired information. As the morning passed, the pressure grew stronger and stronger in her that she must see Crane. Too many questions and uncertainties were building up and as time dragged away, she became more

136

and more restless, and even angry, waiting in vain for the phone to ring.

And then, as she was coming back with messages from the shop, Crane's car drew up beside her, and he said:

"I'll give you a lift to the cottage."

They sat for a little while talking before she went in. Crane was solicitous, sorry he hadn't seen her the night before, hoped she was none the worse for the affair on the jetty; expressed again, warmly, his gratitude for her having come out that night to warn him; then, breaking off, he said:

"Is anything the matter, Elizabeth? You seem kind of—well, unfriendly; not pleased to see me."

It was true. She sensed herself awkward and ill-at-ease, uncertain. He laid a hand on hers and said:

"What's wrong?" gently, concernedly; and she blurted out:

"Crane, why do you carry a gun?"

"Why do I . . . ?" Surprise stopped his words. "How do you know I do?"

"I felt it—down at the jetty."

There was a tiny silence and then he said:

"Yes, I do carry a gun. Back home, you know, we carry them much more commonly than people do here . . . I guess I've got into the habit of it."

He looked at her.

"That doesn't satisfy you?" And as she shook her head, he said:

"You're worried about something. What is it?"

"Not one thing. A lot of things. I want to talk to you, Crane. About the diving, the laird's treasure . . . and other things."

"It's serious, isn't it?"

"Yes. I've found out things . . ."

But he interrupted her, gently but decisively.

"Don't tell me, Elizabeth. I've been finding out things too . . . perhaps the same things. But I don't want to talk about them yet."

He paused, frowning a little, and went on:

"Don't try to find out too much, Elizabeth. Sometimes it's

137

better to ignore things. You could be involved in more than you bargained for . . ."

"But that's not good enough, Crane. Why shouldn't I know what's going on? After all, it was me who found the murdered man . . ."

"But who said there was any connection between that and the laird's treasure? . . . Is that what you've found out?"

And suddenly he was looking at her with a piercing directness which she'd never seen in his eyes before.

"No—no. Nothing like that . . . I don't know why I said it . . . I just felt, surmised . . . you were so insistent I shouldn't admit to knowing it was Morag's grandson . . ."

"Ah." He was silent again. "Well, perhaps we should talk things over. But not here. Not with Mourie's eyes on us." (For Angus McKay had just cycled past on a wobbly bicycle and given them a wave and a very shrewd look.) "Tomorrow I'll call for you in the morning and we'll go for another picnic where we can be sure of some privacy . . ."

He laid his hand over hers. "Don't be too puzzled about things. I'll tell you all I can as soon as I can . . . and anyway I've other things to say to you that have nothing to do with the laird's treasure . . . Damn it, is that man *watching* us?"

For Angus had again wobbled past, calling a cheerful, "Fine day."

"Probably he is," said Elizabeth laughing, "and now I must go in."

Jenny greeted her with the news that Alice had invited them over for a meal that evening. The rest of the day was uneventful. Out on the Sound, the boats were visible, figures moving in them. A placid afternoon, and the evening at Alice's was pleasant. There were no other guests.

"I thought of asking Douglas and Crane Maclean," said Alice, "but I decided not. I think one concentrates more on the food if it's a monosexual party. Look how men go in for all-male dining-clubs."

The food and wine were worth concentrating on, for Alice was a splendid cook, and the time passed very pleasantly. Altogether,

138

Elizabeth thought, when she and Jenny were back in the cottage, a good day; though, on a closer analysis, she wasn't sure why. For all the questions which had perplexed her in the morning were still there; but there was the anticipation of the day to come, and the echo of Crane's words—"I've other things to say to you . . ."

So it was with utter incredulity that she listened to his words on the phone the following morning. When she had put down the receiver and returned to the breakfast table (for he had rung early) she was so white-faced that Jenny said in alarm:

"What on earth is wrong?"

"Nothing's wrong. Crane's leaving."

"Leaving?"

"Leaving. He's decided not to go on with the treasure hunt. He's handing over to Douglas. He says—he says he's finding the whole thing is becoming a bore. Aunt Jenny, I don't understand."

She looked at Jenny with woe-begone eyes, not far from tears; and Jenny, silently calling down curses on men in general and Crane in particular, said briskly:

"He'll probably be back, once Douglas finds the stuff—or doesn't, as the case may be."

"He didn't say so. It all sounded very final."

"Did he give reasons?"

"Just that he'd felt for a day or two that he was intruding on Douglas' scheme . . . that people were hostile . . . I don't understand. Why did he ever interfere at all? He didn't seem worried about local indifference when I spoke to him about it earlier . . . and yesterday there was no word of it."

Jenny took her cup and poured out fresh tea.

"Drink that and stop feeling sorry for yourself for a moment and listen to me . . . Did you say anything to Crane about Sandy's discovery in the cave?"

"I didn't get a chance."

"And he didn't mention anything about finding stuff that couldn't be the laird's treasure?"

"No."

"Well, perhaps he only found out last night, and realising

139

that what they were finding couldn't be connected with the laird, decided he didn't want to have any more to do with it . . ."

"But he didn't need to leave—he could have just handed over to Douglas . . ."

"Mphm. But . . ."

"But there was nothing to keep him here and I've been a fool." She looked at her aunt. "Thank you for not saying it, Jenny."

"I'm sorry about it, Elizabeth."

"So am I. But there it is. Now, I'll wash up."

She did the household chores with an energy and thoroughness that at another time would have amused Jenny, who was fully aware of her niece's dislike of domesticity. By ten-thirty the cottage was tidy and spruce, and Elizabeth said:

"I'm going for a walk. Perhaps I'll visit the camp and see the baby."

She put on slacks, a new Liberty silk shirt printed in shades of blue and purple and over it a thin sweater, and she took a lightweight anorak with her, for the weather was uncertain; and into the pocket of her slacks she put a small torch, in case she did decide to carry out a project half-formed at the back of her mind. Then she said good-bye to Jenny and set off up the road.

She did indeed mean to visit the camp. But before going, she had something else to do and before very long she was standing in the old graveyard, by the door of the ruined church, looking down at the carved grave-slab that had already attracted her attention by its age and beauty. For this was where the laird's treasure was hidden. She wasn't quite sure why she had come, for she certainly had no idea of trying to find the treasure. Nevertheless, she felt she must come and look at the place; and now she was examining it with more than idle curiosity, for it seemed as if the stone had been recently disturbed. She remembered that on that previous occasion, when she had knelt to look at the stone, she thought the turf round it had been tampered with. But she had had neither time nor inclination to pay much attention to it. Now she knelt again and

140

found it was easy to pull back the turf all round the slab. In fact, it rolled back like thick plush, the underside a canvas of pale roots. When she had done this all round, she saw that the slab looked almost like a great lid, and for one wild moment she was tempted to try to move it; but that was impossible without the help of other people and probably crow-bars. Could she perhaps persuade Jenny—or even Douglas?—to come and try to raise it? Probably not. She cast round for some kind of stick, and found a fallen twig, and prodded the ground; and after a few minutes had satisfied herself that the slab was resting on top of some kind of stone box—almost certainly an ancient stone coffin. Well, she had learnt something. She carefully rolled back the turf and patted it into place, and stood frowning down at it. For clearly someone else had been examining the stone closely, and probably fairly recently, though of that she couldn't be sure. Perhaps some anti-quarian visitor to Mourie had been trying to take a rubbing of the stone . . . nevertheless, she decided to mention the disturbance of the turf to Roddy.

But now it was time to go to the camp and see the baby. So she picked her way over the grass to the stile in the wall, and climbed over.

Only then did the watcher on the hill above lower the field-glasses and take his eyes from her.

They were apparently happy to see her at the encampment; Peg was cheerful, the baby seemingly flourishing. Sandy was not to be seen. But she walked a little further up the road, and then took a rough track that soon petered out in rough ground above the shore in a thicket of alders, and here, just as she was leaving the shelter of the scrub to move on to the beach, Sandy joined her, with a conspiratorial air.

"Ah didnae want tae speak tae ye at the tents. The women are ower curious."

He looked round, and then said in a husky whisper:

"Mair stuff cam intae the cave last nicht."

"Oh." She stood for a moment frowning a little, and then:

"Where exactly is the cave, Sandy?"

"There." He pointed to the rocky headland jutting out across

141

the white sand. "See thon line o' rocks? On the ither side
. . . Wis ye thinkin' o' visitin' it?"

"Yes, I'd like to see it."

"Ah'll come wi' ye."

"You don't have to." For she would rather have gone by
herself. She was in no mood for company.

"Aye, Ah'll come," and as, obviously, he would be offended if
she refused his company, she had to agree.

They went along the shingle together. To their right, a little
burn, a mere trickle of water, ran across the sand to the sea.
Small though it was, it had carved out a narrow glen. On the
further bank the ground rose sharply into a cliff that ran inland
up the stream and along the shore rising to the headland.
On the top of the cliff grew thick bushes—rhododendrons. Mourie
House must be somewhere up there. She asked Sandy.

"Oh aye. The Big Hoose is up there, but further back, ye
ken. There's a great high wall roond it—they tell me it wis
built efter the murder o' yon laird they're aye talkin' aboot.
It's no' easy tae get intae the Big Hoose grun'."

"Did you say there was a way through the cave?"

"Aye, there is that." He looked sideways at her and corrected
himself. "At least, they say there is." Another look. "Ye werena
thinkin' of tryin' tae find it?"

"Why not?"

"Ah wudna dae that. There's gey hard men amang that lot—
and if they're no wantin' fowk tae get intae the place, they'll
no' be vera pleased tae see ye."

"I'd still like to go."

For the half-formed idea had crystallised. She would explore
the cave. It would give her a definite aim for her walk, which
in her present state of mind would be all to the good, and she
might find out something which could answer some of the
questions puzzling her.

It was about a half to three quarters of a mile to the headland, she judged. They left the shingle to walk on firm sand,
and made quick and easy progress. Sandy kept up a flow of
conversation on such topics as how to get lug-worms for bait,

142

and the best way to cook trout on, or rather in, a wood fire. He avoided talking of salmon, but forgot himself so far as to mention the roasting of pheasant, then, realising he was on delicate ground, dropped the subject quickly. As they neared the cave he became uneasy again, and once more tried to dissuade Elizabeth from going into it.

"Once ye're past the sandy bit at the mooth o' it, it's no' easy going. And ye'll no' see . . ."

"I've got a torch."

"Ah weel, Ah see ye're set on it . . . Ah'm no' awfu' wantin' tae be seen in the Mourie policies masel' . . ."

"Sandy, I don't want you to come into the grounds with me. There's no need. I just want to have a look round."

"Ah weel, that's a' richt. But what fur can ye no' just walk in the gate? Or ask thon Mr. Maclean tae tak ye roon'. They say ye're freenly enough wi' him."

At this she stopped.

"What do 'they' say?"

"Nae offence, nae offence. It's juist Bella heard in the shop that ye were freenly wi' Mr. Maclean."

There was no use being angry with him. His eyes were bright and knowing as a pet robin's waiting for crumbs, and she decided to give him one.

"Mr. Maclean has left Mourie," she said, "probably for good," and noted with satisfaction that she had, at least temporarily, reduced Sandy to silence.

They went on towards the headland and soon reached the line of tumbled rocks which Sandy had earlier pointed out. They picked their way among the tidal pools to a stretch of smooth sand running into the cave. Beyond, the cliff descended in a wall of broken columns to the sea. Sandy jerked his head towards this barrier, saying:

"On the ither side o' that, there's a kind o' harbour—no' a real harbour; a big kind o' pool, wi' rocks nearly a' roon'. There's wan boat there a' the time; sometimes mair."

Now that she saw the round gaping mouth of the cave, she for the first time felt a hesitation. But she made her way in

143

firmly, Sandy following. Inside, the cave was remarkably dry. The sandy floor had the slightly untidy churned-up look of sand that has not been smoothed by the tide for a very long time. Dried sprigs of wrack lay about, and an odd shell here and there, mostly mussels blue and pearly.

"It isn't tidal then." She was really talking to herself, but Sandy answered her.

"No. The watter doesna' come up here."

"So we don't need to worry about being cut off." She looked round. "Where was it you saw them drop the box, Sandy?"

"Just here. No' that far in. Ah wis up there, stretched oot on thon ledge."

"I see. And they went on up through the cave."

"Aye."

"Well, I'll follow their steps. Thank you for showing me the cave."

"Ah tell ye whit Ah'll dae. Ah'm no' wantin' tae get richt intae Mourie estate—but Ah'll show ye the wey . . ." He looked a little sheepish. "Oh aye, Ah ken the wey. Ah've used it mair nor once."

He began to make his way into the darkness and said over his shoulder:

"Ye'll need your torch. Ah dinna."

The cave ran back for some thirty paces, widened to the size of a moderate room, the roof high, the walls glistening and smeared with green algae, and sprouting tiny ferns. The sand gave way to gravel and the floor began to slope upwards and apparently to end in a wall of rock. But a narrower opening turned off to the left. Sandy led the way into it. The air changed, could be felt flowing past her face, and the darkness became a twilight. Sandy stopped and, when she stood beside him, said:

"Pit oot the torch and ye'll see the wey better."

This was the simple truth for she could then see the daylight filtering down from an opening ahead. The cave had become a narrow cleft and the light came down through a growth of ferns and whin. It looked at first as if it must be impenetrable, but Sandy showed where it was possible to climb up, and where there were rough footholds in the rock and turf.

"And at the top," he whispered, "ye see the whins is withered. Juist push them aside and ye'll can pu' yersel' oot ontae the grass. It's a wee thing jaggey, but ye'll juist hae tae pit up wi' that."

"Right, I will. Thank you, Sandy."

She pushed the torch into the pocket of her slacks, and began to scramble up. Sandy slid back into the darkness of the cave and she gave him no further thought. So she could not know that he watched her as she climbed, and heard her muted gasps and exclamations as the dead whins pricked her hands. But she managed to shove the bushes aside and pulled herself out and fell on her face on short rough grass, the sun hot on her back.

CHAPTER 16

She lay for a moment and then turned over and looked up into the sky and the high clouds drifting over it, and the relentless misery that had been weighing on her since she'd heard Crane's oddly expressionless voice that morning began to lift. Perhaps Jenny was right. Perhaps he would come back. But to go like that, without a word of warning! Something must have happened to make him decide so suddenly to leave, for she was absolutely certain that the previous day he had had no such intention. She tried to recall their conversation: and it was true that however friendly, more than friendly, Crane had been, he had also been very adroit in parrying her questions . . . she had learnt nothing. But at least she was now in the Mourie House grounds and she meant to see as much as she could when she was there.

It was when she sat up, preparatory to rising to her feet, that she heard the burst of noise, and over to her left, from behind a line of trees and rhododendrons, saw a helicopter climb drunkenly into the air; moments after its grotesque shadow was over her, and the whining of the blades bemusing her. She instinctively shut her bewildered eyes and covered her ears, and did not look up until she felt the shadow was past. The helicopter had turned and was now climbing to the hills. She was shaken and slightly sick with apprehensions crowding on her. For she remembered the helicopter above her in the pass; and the helicopter that had climbed up before them when the body had gone for the second time and John the Ferry had been attacked —and here was a helicopter rising out from the woods of Mourie

House; and Crane lived at Mourie House—but no, no, no! she would not believe that he had anything to do with the mud-spattered corpse in the peat-trench.

To escape her too disturbing thoughts she jumped to her feet. Under the trees from which the helicopter had risen a man was standing watching her.

He moved forward into the sunlight and walked over towards her. Soon, with relief, she could see that it was Douglas. He gave her a friendly wave, and she waited for him to join her.

"Hullo," he said. "I thought I'd find you here."

"How so?"

"I saw you coming along the beach . . . Is something wrong, Elizabeth? You look as if you'd had a shock of some kind."

"The helicopter. It scared me. I told you I didn't like them . . . it seemed to come from just over there."

"It did." He sounded almost amused. "Didn't you know we had a helicopter on the job?"

She stared unbelievingly. "You mean, to help with the search? . . . Crane never said anything."

"Didn't he?" His tone was casual—too casual. Perhaps it should have warned her. "By the way, you know he's left?"

"Yes."

She had sat down again on the grass and now he joined her.

"He left quite suddenly. Said he was getting bored with the whole thing and preferred to hand it over entirely to me . . . he's given us the run of the house and says we can use it as long as we like."

"He gave no other reason?"

"None. He may have been a bit annoyed by the arrival of another dozen men—our backer in Glasgow sent them because he felt progress was too slow."

"Your backer must be a very rich man if he's financing a helicopter."

"Oh, he is." Again a note of amusement. "Very rich. Immense resources . . . Anyway, I'm not really sorry Crane Maclean has gone, for two reasons. One personal; the other is

147

that I didn't like the way he suddenly appeared and threw his weight about; patronising. I think the people hereabouts felt that."

"Won't they feel you're being patronising?"

"I don't think so. When—if—we find the laird's treasure and it's given back to them, they'll know it's not coming from some rich patron working off a guilt complex."

"But you won't find the laird's treasure—not there in the Sound."

She hadn't meant to tell him like this, but an immense irritation at his words provoked her. And certainly her statement made a remarkable impression. He was suddenly frowning, his mouth drawn into a hard line, and his voice was harsh as he said: "What do you mean?"

"What I said. I know the treasure is not there."

"Where is it?"

"I'm not prepared to say."

"How do I know you're telling the truth?"

"You don't. But you do know—or don't you—that what you have so far found, couldn't possibly be the laird's treasure?"

"How do you know what we've found? Did Crane . . . ?"

"Crane told me nothing—and I told him nothing. And I'm not telling you how I know."

He sat frowning down at her for a moment or two: his eyes were sharp and calculating. Then his face cleared, he relaxed and said:

"Well, if you say you know the laird's treasure is not there, I accept that; though it's a shock. On the other hand, it does explain something that was puzzling me. You're right, of course; we have found something, and it couldn't be the laird's stuff . . . And we'll have to decide what to do with it. But you haven't told anyone?"

"No." For a brief moment she wondered if she should tell him that Jenny also knew, but decided against it. She still felt, for all his seeming candour, that he was not being wholly frank: a kind of uneasiness in his manner—something was sending out warning signals to her. At the same time, she felt sorry for him, and she suddenly said:

"Douglas, why don't you pull out, like Crane? Leave it to the others to sort out the problems. Who knows, perhaps they've been using you, the local man, as a screen for their own activities . . . This backer, do you know him very well? Perhaps they thought you, the schoolmaster, the idealist who'd given up a lot to come to Mourie, would be excellent for a cover-up . . ."

For a moment, she thought he was angry, but he said quietly, "You really think they might use me like that? . . ." And then, as if dropping the subject. "You've never been to Mourie House, have you? Would you like to see it? It's over there beyond the trees."

He gave her his hand to pull her to her feet, she stumbled, and for a moment she rested against him, and he put an arm around her to steady her. Then he turned abruptly away, saying, "I wish you hadn't told me all this," and began to walk over the grass towards the house.

Again she felt uneasy, aware of something like danger. She remembered how he had looked standing by the gate in the dark. But she was being stupid: she knew him to be moody and touchy; but to her he had always been kind, and unresentful of her occasional outbursts of disagreement.

"You found your way through the cave, I think. By the way, what happened to your friend?" he asked.

"My friend?"

"There was someone with you as you came along the beach— I saw you."

"Oh, that was Sandy from the tinkers' camp. He had business of his own somewhere and left me at the cave."

"You knew about it before."

"Yes. Jenny told me about it and I wanted to explore it."

"They say it used to be a smugglers' cave—but they say that about most caves. Did you find anything?"

"Only shells and seaweed . . . Are those the chimneys of the house?"

"Yes. And in a minute, if we follow this path through the trees, we'll see the front of it."

The path across the turf from the cave exit was clearly

149

marked and appeared freshly trodden. Obviously the men went down to the beach regularly this way. Yet they also used the jetty regularly—so they had, in effect, two bases; and she remembered Sandy's remark that they kept boats in a "kind of harbour" near the cave. Still, supposing they had found something else than the treasure, supposing that was what they had all the time been after, what was wrong about it? Nothing really. Why then had she a not altogether unpleasant feeling of risk, even danger, as she walked up to the house?

Soon they could see it clearly. It was a long two-storeyed building with rectangular windows set one above the other and a small pillared portico before the door. It would have been quite undistinguished, had it not been for the west wing, added in the early nineteenth century, which, extending forward, ended in large beautifully curved windows which gave dignity and beauty to the facade. It was harled and whitewashed, the surrounds of windows and doors and the portico being left in the natural grey sandstone. Round the base of the wall ran a narrow flower-bed filled with rose bushes which gave colour to what might have been a rather forbiddingly austere frontage. Behind the house and to the east the ground was well wooded, with beeches, oaks, the odd conifer, rhododendrons. In the warm sunlight the effect was very charming.

Elizabeth exclaimed in admiration.

"Yes, it's pretty just now," said Douglas. "In winter it could be a bit gloomy with the rain coming in from the sea."

"The grounds are in surprisingly good order. I thought the house had been empty for some time before Crane took it over."

"I understand that there was a firm of lawyers who kept an eye on the place and got one of the locals to come in and keep the garden under control. Now, let's go in and I'll see if we can get some coffee."

And on this note of everyday cordiality, Elizabeth stepped through the unpretentious door into Mourie House—and into danger.

The entrance hall, as so often in an old house, was gloomy, lit only by light from the door and by glass panels in the door to the room on the left. It was stone-flagged and empty except for a blanket chest against the wall. A narrow stair, carpetless, ran up from beside the door on the left. Another door, covered with tattered green baize, was propped open by an old iron weight; beyond it a passage ran into gloom. Douglas opened the door on the left and said:

"Crane used this as his sitting-room. Find yourself a chair, and I'll see if someone can produce a cup of coffee."

The room was in marked contrast with the gloomy hall. It was a kind of casual sitting-room that in a previous century would have been known as "the morning-room." The ceiling was comparatively low. The walls were panelled halfway up and then washed a neutral cream colour. The carpet was laid on a polished and rather beautiful wooden floor; a slightly faded, but good, carpet in soft blues and pinks and beige and green; on either side of the empty fireplace in the wall opposite the door were chintz-covered chairs. The same chintz was on the windowseat that ran round the curve of the window. A round mahogany table and matching chairs were in the centre of the room and an old desk stood against one wall. On the walls were pleasant self-effacing pictures of idyllic landscapes—slightly faded, like the carpet—and on the table and mantelpiece were bowls of roses. The whole effect was of a gentle, timeless gentility, and as she looked round all her suspicions and tremors seemed utterly and entirely absurd. She sat down in the sun in the windowseat and was looking down the length of the room admiring it when Douglas came in.

"What a pretty room this is," she said, "and beautifully kept—surprisingly so."

"I expect Crane's man—Jimmy, wasn't he?—did it. Johnson's doing the running of the house now, with help of course. He's a very versatile person. He was almost, you might say, foreman to Crane's organisation of the search . . . He's seeing that we get some coffee. And here he is."

The dark young man with the long side-burns and pale eyes whom she'd seen talking to Crane on the bridge came in carrying a tray. He put it down on the large table and moved a smaller

151

one over beside the window-seat. As he went to pour the coffee, Elizabeth turned and looked idly out into the sunlit garden.

Against the trunk of the big pine tree on the far side of the lawn, a man, wearing a leather jacket and jeans, was leaning looking straight across at the window, and at her. Casually cradled in his arms was a rifle.

Chilly with alarm, she turned to look back into the room. Johnson was placing a cup on the table beside her. She saw and instantly recognised his hand. Tattooed on the back, the grotesque scar of a blue and red anchor: the hand that she had seen clutching the air as she thrust it from her car, on that first day, up in the pass.

Her throat dry, she stared, transfixed. The hand, having released the cup, was laid flat on the table, and as Johnson leaned forward his pale eyes looked into hers and his voice, harsh and grating, said:

"She knows my hand. She can't deny it. Look at her." Without turning his head he spoke to Douglas. "Show her what you've got, boss. Show her it!"

She was aware of movement at the edge of her vision, and another hand, Douglas' hand, laid something on the table in front of her. She dragged her eyes from Johnson to look.

It was the photograph of Morag's grandson.

She almost heard the click of the trap closing on her.

CHAPTER 17

It was Douglas' voice that jerked her out of her frozen stillness.

"I guess you know whose picture that is, Elizabeth, and where it came from. Don't bother denying it. I know you were at Morag's house the day before she—died, and I'm sure you saw it there. And of course you recognised—didn't you?—that face when you saw it again up in the peat-trench."

"Just like you knew my hand just now." Johnson made the statement in a flat unemphatic voice; it made her shudder.

"In fact, Elizabeth," went on Douglas, "you know too much. I wish you hadn't told me all you know. But you have, and we can't ignore it. It's essential for us that people should think we're looking for the laird's treasure, not anything else. We can't afford yet to drop the pretence."

"That's why we got rid of him." Johnson put a long finger on the photograph. "He knew. So did the old woman."

Still the safe flat unemotional voice. She daren't look at him, but kept her eyes on Douglas.

"In your case, I don't think we need go so far." He half-raised his hand at Johnson's grunt of protest. "If we can keep you out of the way for the next couple of days, we shouldn't need to worry about what you know or don't know. Let's say it depends on you. Keep quiet, give no trouble and you'll be all right."

"It'd be simpler," said Johnson, "just to get rid of her."

He might have been pointing out that her coffee was cold, so casual was his tone, and she hated him for it.

"But I don't think it's necessary," said Douglas, "not if all goes as we hope. We'll keep her here. There must be a room upstairs that would do."

"Sure there's a room. I still say it'd be simpler the other way."

"No." Douglas' voice was decisive. "She'll stay here."

"And do you really think," said Elizabeth, her voice sharp with anger, "that you'll be able to keep me shut up here, and no one wonder what's happened? The police will be notified in a matter of hours."

The two men looked at each other and smiled: a quiet, confident, knowing smile that made her skin creep with apprehension.

"I think not," said Douglas. "Someone is going to have seen you walking along the cliff by yourself; and there are dangerous spots along there. They'll all be pretty sad to think you fell over; but if you ever do get back, they'll be all the more glad to see you. Well, I'm going to be busy today. For one thing, since you've shown us where the treasure is . . ."

"How did I do that?"

"You were seen visiting the graveyard this morning, and being very interested in that old stone, and prodding round it. So I'm guessing it's there; and we're going to look at it a bit more thoroughly than you did. First, we'll see you settled. You go ahead, Johnson."

Her feet sounded dull on the stone floor of the hall, hollow on the uncarpeted stair. Johnson led the way along a corridor, stopped at a door, opened it and switched on a light; a dim, naked bulb hanging from the rather low ceiling. It was a fairly large square room with striped wall-paper, showing lighter patches where furniture had been moved. An old four-poster bed dominated it; on it was a mattress. There were two high-backed chairs, and a carpet on the floor. An old-fashioned tiled fireplace was set into a carved natural oak mantelpiece. Heavy shutters were closed against the window, and padlocked. The room smelt dusty and airless.

"This is the best bedroom, I reckon," said Johnson. "I guess it'll do."

Douglas looked round.

"I guess so. We'll get you some bed-clothes. And a small table for meals. Get a better light fixed, Johnson. Our guest will no doubt be glad of some books to read." He hesitated fractionally and added: "Believe me, I'm truly sorry things have turned out like this. I hope you'll only need to be here for a day or two—what happens to you depends on yourself. And Johnson, just remember Miss Elizabeth is to be treated with courtesy, and if you or anyone else so much as touches her, it'll be the worse for you. Understand?"

"Sure." The flat, laconic reply was also a sneer, and again she felt her spine crawl with fear, sensing into what an alien world she had fallen, where killing and threats of killing were commonplace.

Douglas seemed to be expecting her to speak, but she said nothing. Johnson stood aside to let him out, followed him, shut the door, and she heard the key turn.

Then she sat down on one of the chairs and let her body slump, aware of the physical exhaustion that went with nervous strain. Oddly enough, for the moment her fear had gone, partly because of the relief of Johnson's being no longer there; his presence had an almost paralysing effect on her; partly because Douglas' words did, she believed, give her a certain amount of protection. No; what she felt was indignation and incredulous astonishment. It was just not possible that she should be sitting a prisoner in Mourie House. Such things didn't happen —well, not to people like her. Abductions, murders, they happened to other people, names in newspapers, stories that you followed, God forgive you, with detached interest . . . but they didn't happen to you.

Only now they had.

She realised she was gnawing at the forefinger of her left hand, and before panic could take over from anger, she jumped from the chair and began to examine the room.

Not that there was much to examine; it could all be seen at a glance—bed, chairs, fireplace, shutters, and, in a corner, along from the fireplace, a cupboard door. No doubt it was locked; but she would turn the handle to make sure. The door opened; it was not a cupboard, but a room of some kind. She could dimly see the end of a long, low piece of furniture. She felt for a switch, found it, but when she flicked it down, nothing happened. How maddening! She remembered her torch, took it from her pocket and switched on. The beam caught a startling spatter of green-leafed water-flags and yellow water-lilies embossed on white tiles. She swung the light round; the oddly shaped piece of furniture was an old-fashioned bath. She was, in fact, in a rather splendid if highly idiosyncratic bathroom.

In other circumstances, she would have rejoiced in it. Even as it was, she could appreciate its happy absurdity. It was the size of a small bedroom. The walls were tiled to the ceiling; and embossed with an improbable watery landscape—flags, water-lilies, moorhens' nests and moorhens among bulrushes, rising in perspective halfway up the wall to blend with a blue sky overlaid with curly and slightly bulbous clouds. The enormous coffin-shaped bath was boxed in with the same tiles. The oval hand-basin was perched on a sheaf of ceramic reeds and bulrushes; the water was to spout from an open-mouthed brass fish, sadly in need of polishing. The pedestal of the seat, approached in a truly thronelike manner up three shallow tiled steps, was also embossed with bulrushes. The mirror of the massive marble-topped dressing table beside the bath was so painted with watery vegetation as to be almost useless. On the wall dividing the bathroom from the bedroom was a little wrought-iron fireplace, set into a wooden mantelpiece pullulating with large-mouthed, curly-tailed, scaly fish.

The unabashed flamboyance of it all cheered her up; and when she turned a tap, and the brass fish, miraculously, eventually ran hot, she felt momentarily quite lighthearted.

"If I had soap, I could have a bath. But I haven't. And I think I hear footsteps, so I'll get back to the room."

When the door opened, she was sitting on a chair with folded hands. She had expected, and dreaded, that it would be Johnson. But it was a small thick-set man who carried a bundle of sheets and blankets and pillows. A scar pulled together one side of his face, and he had a cauliflower ear. As he kicked the door shut behind him, he said in a richly Cockney accent, "Don't try no funny stuff, miss."

"I won't," said Elizabeth. She watched him dump the things on the bed and as he made to go, she said:

"Mr. McBain said I was to have a stronger light here, and something to read. And I want a towel and soap."

He looked at her with a kind of admiration.

"You're a cool one. All right, I'll get them."

He leered at her and went off grinning. "Gor blimey! A towel and soap!"

She busied herself folding the blankets and sheets into neat piles till he came back with two towels, a cake of soap, a small table and an electric bulb. Then she watched in silence while he stood on a chair, took out the old bulb and replaced it with the new one. When he had finished, he grinned again and said facetiously:

"Will that be all, miss?"

"As a matter of fact, no. I'd like that bulb you've just taken down put into the bathroom there."

"Bathroom? D'you mean to say . . . ?" He opened the bathroom door and said: "I can't see where the light is."

"Haven't you a lighter or matches?"

There was no answer, but she heard a click and saw the wavering light of the flame, and heard a gasp at what it revealed. He came back, took a chair, and in a moment the bulb was in.

"All ship-shape, and your lunch will be along soon." And he left, to her relief, for his clumsy parody of the attentive servant was sub-insolent and faintly nauseating.

The new light was quite bright enough for reading by, and she decided to ask again for books when her lunch was brought. It was now about twelve-thirty and she thought it wouldn't be long in coming. She was tired of sitting on a chair, so she propped two pillows behind her back, and sat cross-legged on the bed, leaning against the head, and settled down to try and think the whole thing out.

She decided that for the moment she was in no personal

157

danger. What story had been passed along to Aunt Jenny she could not tell. It was probably something along the lines Douglas had indicated; it was upsetting to think of Jenny's distress but it was true that when—if—she returned, the greater would be her relief and happiness.

The very fact that she felt she could rely on Douglas' influence to protect her, at least temporarily, was, she had to admit, a revelation. Her thinking about Douglas had been thrown into total confusion by the events of the last hour or so. The rather stodgy, prosy schoolmaster, earnestly dedicating himself to the enriching of the cultural life of a remote village, was a sham, a pretence to cover up his position of authority. That he was in command was evident from his over-ruling of Johnson's suggestion that she be quietly eliminated; he must be supremely sure of the outcome of what they were doing, absolutely certain that he and the rest were going to get away—get away completely and successfully—if he could afford to overlook, as it were, what she knew and could tell, if she got the chance.

And what exactly were they up to? They had obviously used the legend of the laird's treasure as a blind: to keep Mourie on their side, with its mouth shut. In her earlier remarks to him, she had been not far from the truth. Clearly, they had found some other wreck, had known of it beforehand, were dredging up a great deal of loot. As to the legality of such an enterprise, she knew nothing. In this case, legality would be a very minor consideration, since whatever they were after was so important to them that they murdered people simply to maintain secrecy . . .

And Crane? Where did he fit in? He had said he had found things out . . . but he could not have known that Douglas and Johnson were responsible for the killing of Morag and her grandson; otherwise he would not have simply gone away without doing anything at all about it. But why, then, had he been so perturbed by her recognition of the body, why so insistent she remain silent? Was he too not what he seemed?

Perhaps he did know about the murder of the old woman and had decided it was simply not his concern. Was he also using

158

Mourie and its people and its legends merely as a means to an end?

Her head was beginning to ache, and she slipped from the bed and began walking up and down. The padlocked shutters, the sense of confinement, threatened to become unbearable. Perhaps the bathroom window was not padlocked . . . but it was, and though she shook and pulled at the bar, it was no use.

Back in the bedroom she began to feel hungry and was quite pleased to hear footsteps coming along the corridor. It was the ugly little Cockney again, carrying a tray on which was an omelette, roll and butter, a little bowl of fruit, cheese and a pot of coffee. Under his arm he had three books. He put down the tray with a mock bow, and offered the books.

"Brought you some books, miss. I took the first three from the shelf, and hope you like them."

He gave her a grin and went out, leaving her holding *The Rosary* by Florence Barclay, *Bulldog Drummond,* and *My Tiger-Hunting Days* by Lt. Col. Murdo H. Rintoul, D.S.O.

Her hands were hot and grubby and she took the towels and soap and went to wash. As she dried her hands, she looked idly round—and up.

In the bathroom ceiling was a small trap-door.

She stood staring at it with the towel dangling from her hand. For here was a way of escape.

To counteract the beating excitement within her, she made herself fold the towel very precisely and hang it and the unused one neatly on the towel-rail. Then she went back to the bedroom, sat down at her tray and ate her lunch mechanically, not tasting a thing. When she'd finished, she pushed back the table and sat sideways on the chair, thinking.

The trap-door would lead into the attics and doubtless had been put there to give access to a cistern. This was certainly not the only bathroom in the house, and there was in all probability another trap-door somewhere—so that it might be possible to pick one's way along the attic, down through the other trap-door and ultimately to freedom.

If one didn't meet anyone, if one could cross the open ground to the trees, if one were willing to run the risk of being shot in the back . . .

After all, why? Douglas had more or less promised her she would be unharmed and let go free if she did nothing for the next day or two. Then he and the rest would be gone; she needn't ever tell anyone she knew he and his associates had caused two murders . . .

And she would live for the rest of her days knowing she had acquiesced in evil. She suddenly had a vision of Morag lying alone and lifeless; she must at all costs get away and tell what she knew.

But telling wasn't enough. It would be pointless and galling to run the risk she would be running, if Douglas and the rest got away after all. If only she had an idea of what their plans were; then perhaps some way of preventing a getaway could be found . . . She began to toy with wild ideas of finding herself in a position where she could overhear plans—like Jim Hawkins in the apple barrel—all nonsense, of course, as she fully realised.

Wide Boy, as she had christened the Cockney, came and removed the tray, made some facetious remark, and left her, still brooding over her problem.

A few minutes after, Douglas came to the room, and before he'd gone, with careless arrogance had told her what she wanted to know.

She was roused from her thoughts by the sound of the key turning in the lock, and looking up, she saw Douglas standing in the doorway. Her first thought was: He's different. For, seeing him framed against the dim light of the passage, she noticed the cruel downward slant of his mouth and a hard calculating gleam in his eyes as he looked at her. When he spoke, she sensed a sharp anger beneath the level voice.

"Who else did you speak to about the laird's treasure, Elizabeth?"

She had risen to her feet and spoke back firmly.

"No one."

"She's lying." Johnson's laconic voice. He had appeared in

the doorway behind Douglas, his pale eyes bleakly watching her, and now she was afraid.

"I'm not." She addressed herself to Douglas, refusing to look at Johnson. "Why do you ask?"

"Because we've just looked in the place in the churchyard, and there's nothing there." It was Johnson again who spoke, and by the little movement of Douglas' shoulders she sensed his irritation.

"I know nothing about it. Perhaps it never was there. Perhaps I was told wrong."

"Someone had taken up the stone, and filled up the cavity with fresh earth and leaves." It was Douglas this time who spoke. "Are you sure you didn't drop a hint to anyone?"

"No, I did not."

"Maybe the person who told you went and took the stuff." Johnson again. How she hated him! "Who was it told you?"

She said nothing, and after a moment's pause, he went on:

"Perhaps you told Maclean where it was." He turned to Douglas. "Mebbe that's why he went off so suddenly. With the stuff."

"I did not tell him anything." She heard herself shouting the words, and added quietly, "Crane Maclean doesn't need to run off with any—stuff."

Before Johnson could speak again, Douglas forestalled him. He was still watching her, but less furiously, frowning and nibbling at a finger, and he said:

"She's right and besides, we can't go chasing round after the treasure at this stage. Someone knows we won't find it: but that doesn't mean he has any idea about what we *are* after."

He turned to Johnson. "We'll carry on as if this hadn't happened. Tell the men so, and get on with it."

When Johnson had gone, he closed the door and said: I'm sorry all this had to happen. It won't be for long, I promise you. By tomorrow—that's Saturday—or Sunday at the latest, we'll be gone and it'll all be over."

It was his placid dismissal of the whole affair, as if it were

161

the merest holiday enterprise, that sparked off her indignant exclamation:

"Do you really think you're going to get away with everything just like that? I don't know what you've found, but it must be something pretty big. Do you honestly believe you can just take it all and go?"

"Yes I do. Who else but you knows we're not looking for the laird's treasure? Yes, I know. Someone knows we're not going to *find* it—that's a different thing. Besides, our plans are well laid. But you don't know what these are, do you, Elizabeth? Nor what exactly we are taking away."

"I don't want to know. What difference can it make?"

And she waited, hoping he would tell her.

"It makes no difference to your present situation. That's why I can tell you—because you can't do anything about it. What we came to find, and have found, is gold coin and bullion from a ship in the Sound, worth—well, a lot. I'm not going to say how it got there, but nothing, *nothing,* is going to stop us getting that away. And it isn't, you know, just a question of private individuals. Oh no. This is far beyond that." He pulled forward a chair and sat astride it as he spoke. "It used to amuse me to realise that you all thought I was nothing but the village schoolmaster—oh yes, I've got my degree all right; and my Harvard doctorate; and everyone swallowed the story that I'd come to Mourie out of sheer idealism, to waste myself there . . . You rather looked down on me, didn't you? A dull, prosy fellow you thought me, especially after Crane Maclean with his money, and his oh-so-noble idea of restoring the laird's treasure to the poor and deprived of Mourie, appeared on the scene."

She was astonished by the hatred that suddenly distorted the mocking tone of his voice; not only hatred—jealousy too. Douglas McBain was jealous of Crane Maclean—and on her account. It added a further wearisome complication to the situation and she remained silent though aware he was waiting for her to speak. As she said nothing, he went on:

"His interference complicated things for a little. It wouldn't have stopped us. It was fortunate for him he got bored and went

162

off . . . just as it's unfortunate for you that you had to go blundering along finding out what was in no way your business. Our plan is very simple. The helicopters come down, we load the stuff on, they go, we go, Mourie left behind, none the wiser. Except for you, Elizabeth." He looked at her meditatively. "And maybe Johnson is right. Maybe I'm being a fool . . . Would you be prepared to promise, if you're let go as soon as we've gone, not to say a word for twenty-four hours?"

She pretended to consider.

"I might. But apart from me, I still think you're taking risks, if so much is at stake."

"We've kept the plan simple. That's what technology can do . . . smooth difficulties. Besides, if we think there's any risk of interference from outside, we have other plans. Did you ever think how vulnerable Mourie is, as a place?"

To this she made no answer. He stepped towards her, looked keenly at her, and then drew back.

"I'm sorry," he said again. "It would have been good if things had been different . . . But if you don't do anything stupid, you'll be all right. I promise."

When she heard the grating of the lock, she sat down again, weak after the suspense, almost dizzy at the thought that now she did know the plan and its object. She must try her hardest to get away—it was an inescapable responsibility laid on her. As soon as it was dark enough—and that would be round about eleven or twelve—she would try to get into the attics, and find a way out. Then it would be simply—simply!—a case of making her way back to the village, reaching a telephone, contacting all the resources that could be called on to deal with the situation.

Meanwhile—she looked at her watch—meanwhile about eight hours must pass. She settled herself again on the bed and began to read *My Tiger-Hunting Days*.

163

CHAPTER 18

It wasn't Wide Boy who brought her evening meal, but a thin, tall, fair man with cadaverous cheeks and a missing tooth whom she had noticed once or twice in Mourie. He put down the tray without saying a word and only looked at her, sideways. She thought she heard voices raised in discussion during the brief moments while the door was open. Once it was closed, the heavy silence returned. For that had been one of the most trying things about the long afternoon hours: the total absence of sound from outside the room. The heavy shutters closed off any noise from the open air, and in the house there was nothing. *My Tiger-Hunting Days* had been soporific and at one time she dozed off, waking with the feeling that there had been some kind of sound in the room; and aware of a quiet footfall outside. Afterwards there had been nothing till the arrival of her meal; and this time she had been able to appreciate the cold chicken and fresh fruit salad. When it had been removed, she got down seriously to planning what she must do.

The trap-door, looked at from below, didn't seem likely to give trouble. She remembered the trap in the bathroom at her home; it had been quite a thrill when she was a small girl to haul herself up through it and into the mysterious realm of the attic to see if the cistern was frozen. She was tempted now to bring a chair, climb up and try to open this trap-door. But the risk of being caught doing so was too great.

The hours crept past. Abandoning Colonel Rintoul's unfortunate tigers, she tried to lose herself in the solemn nonsense of *The Rosary*. At nine o'clock Wide Boy brought her a cup of

164

coffee, said, "Good night," cheerfully, and then, leaning close, too close, to her, said, "If I was you, miss, I'd jam a chair under your door handle tonight," and went off whistling.

This alarmed her a little. She had hoped she could count on the night being without interruption. But she decided to follow his advice and did jam a chair against the door. Then she made up the bed with the bed-clothes—if anyone did come in to check on her, it would give the impression she was reconciled to spending the night there. She ran a bath, hoping that anyone passing and hearing it would decide she was settling down for the night. At ten, thinking of escape stories she had read, she put a pillow in the bed and heaped clothes round it, so that at a cursory glance the bed would look occupied. Then she put out the light and waited in darkness.

This was horrible. Like the silence, the darkness was total and absolute. After about ten minutes she moved into the bathroom, closed the door, switched on the dim light and sat there. She tried to keep the minutes from dragging by counting the number of lilies, bulrushes, fishes, etc., in the decor. By a quarter to eleven she could stand the waiting no longer.

She went back to the bedroom and listened. Absolute quiet. She removed the chair from the door (if they had to batter it down to look in, her ruse of the pillow in the bed would be no use). She returned to the bathroom, placed the chair under the trap-door, took off her shoes, stood on it, and stretched up her arms.

Thank God! She could reach it, for she had dreaded having to move the heavy dressing table and standing on it. She pushed up, and felt the trap yield. Gently she tried to shift it sideways to the left. It wouldn't budge. But it moved easily to the right, and from the black rectangular hole came a little gust of dusty, stale air.

She stepped softly down from the chair, switched off the light, bolted the door, pulled out her torch and lit it. Up on the chair again, she gently placed the torch on the edge of the gap, pushed her shoes in, and pulling on her hands and levering her feet against the wall, she pulled herself up and in.

165

She swung her torch round. It was much as she had expected —old roof beams, faded and worm-eaten here and there; between them, equally old planks, warping in places, and with the nails from the slates sticking through. At one end, beyond the ceiling of the bedroom, rose a stone wall, the original wall of the house before the wing had been added. In the other direction, the attic stretched for what seemed a long way. The beam didn't reach to the end.

All this she saw in a mere moment. Then she carefully replaced the trap-door, managing to jam the free end with two old slates lying near it.

Now to go down the length of the attic and hope she would find another trap-door. She stuffed her shoes into her pockets and began to pick her way over the rough joists in her bare feet.

Ahead of her, she saw a short length of rope dangling from a joist. But it wasn't rope. It moved and curved as the rat turned from the light and disappeared into the shadows ahead; and at that her courage did fail her, and she almost turned back.

But she went on, treading quietly, treading cautiously, once almost falling on to the plaster between the joists when she stepped on a sharp splinter in the wood. She kept the beam pointing straight ahead, preferring not to see rats, if there were any lurking in the shadows on either hand. Twice she heard the scrabble of claws and surely that shadow at the foot of the support beam there was moving? But she simply refused to look and concentrated on picking her way noiselessly over the beams.

But there was no other trap-door, and the light was playing over a solid wall at the far end. Her heart sank.

But it rose again when she saw that it was a wooden partition and that there was a narrow door in it. If only the door was not locked . . .

It wasn't. As she cautiously lifted the old latch and pushed, the door swung outwards but with a startlingly loud creaking. She switched off the torch and stood in the darkness.

No sound but the thumping of her heart.

She stepped through the door and into a smallish room, with

166

a plank floor, a big cistern in one corner, some old chairs, an iron bed-stead, a big trunk—a typical attic dumping ground.

It also had a small attic window. She saw this when the torch-light passed over it. She could only hope no one outside had noticed the momentary beam. She looked out of the window, down into a shadowy kind of courtyard formed by the two wings of the house. In the twilight she could see some kind of structure almost in the centre. It puzzled her at first, and then she recognised it as a well. She could just distinguish a shadowy figure coiling up a rope, as if he'd just been hauling up a bucket. How odd to take water from an old well when there was an adequate system in the house . . . Could there be animals to water?

Anyway, she had no time to waste on such questions. Carefully shading her torch with her hand, she picked her way among the junk to the other end of the room, and another door. It too was unlocked and opened directly on to a narrow wooden stair which led straight down to a wooden landing from which a grey light filtered up. No sound came from below.

But there *was* a sound: not from below; from behind; someone was hammering on a door and shouting.

They must have come back to check on her, and found her gone, and that would be the bathroom door they were battering. She heard the crash of its bursting open.

As quickly and quietly as possible she began to go down the stair. The landing was a half-landing, and the stair continued down and came out on a stone-flagged passage, apparently little used and feeling damp to her feet. It ran at right angles to another, along which a light was shining. She must be in a wing of domestic offices built out at the back of the house and not now used. Surely there would be a door. Where? At the end of the passage?

But it wasn't at the end. It was on the side of the passage, and bolted with two great rusty bolts. They rasped and screeched as she pulled them and she had to take two hands to the big iron key, and it might have defeated her if she hadn't heard the house begin to buzz with angry noise as the alarm was given, and the stair thumping with predatory footsteps. Almost crying from the pain as the iron bruised her hands, she wrenched the key round, pulled open the door, and was out in the dark twilight of the clear midsummer. A belt of woodland loomed up ahead, and she sprang into the shadow of the trees and leant against a tree trunk for a moment to draw breath and think what to do.

She had intended, if she got away unseen, simply to make for the road and get back to the village as quickly as she could. But certainly the road would be watched—everywhere would be . . . If she could hide for a space till the immediate pursuit had spread out . . . She must stay in the trees. Why not up in a tree? Out of her unconscious mind floated a sentence—was it from *The Jungle Book?*—"Men seldom look up when they're hunting." She looked into the branches above her. She was standing beneath a magnificent oak.

She began to climb. Some fourteen feet up she found a broad bough on which she could stand, with her back against the trunk, and she tried to force herself into complete stillness.

For through the leaves she could see lights here and there —the windows of the house blazing up one after the other. Then she heard a shout, "The old back door is open!" and a muffled thudding of feet on cobbles and grass. More shouts; steps; and voices beneath her. Douglas—"We've got to get her. She'll make for the village. By the road or the shore."

"I said you should have got rid of her." Johnson's flat voice.

"This time we will." A cold fury in the words.

Steps moving away. Voices dying away. The sound of cars starting up. Silence, and the wind stirring in the leaves. She felt weak with momentary relief and with dread for what might come. There must be some way out of Mourie grounds that would avoid road and shore. Up towards Mourie Beg perhaps. Up on the moor. Then perhaps she could come down on the village from the hill direction. She had got her bearings now: the shore was there, the drive there; Mourie Beg lay up there.

She came down from the tree as silently and almost as quickly as a squirrel, blessing the passion she'd had for climbing as a child. Keeping well in among the trees, she began to make her way inland in the direction of the moor. She found a little path and followed it, having put on her shoes in case she tramped on thistles and thorns. Every few yards she stopped, and twice thought she heard voices, but distant. Then she heard another sound; water trickling over stones. The path skirted a huge tree trunk and in the less-dark where the trees parted she could just see a narrow plank bridge with a single hand-rail. While she stood hestitating whether to cross it or not, dreading leaving the friendly darkness, she heard a fairly large animal stirring in the overgrown rhododendron bushes which bordered the burn on her left. At the same time, two figures loomed up on the path beyond the bridge. This was no time to wonder about animals. She slid into the rhododendrons and found they opened into a tiny clearing beside the water.

From the burn rose a dark figure that pulled her to the ground and laid a hard and leathery hand over her mouth.

Above the hand, she could see the face.

It was Sandy.

His head was cocked as if he was listening. Then he relaxed and took his hand from her mouth and said in a small whisper:

"Ye're in trouble." A statement, not a question.

"Ah thocht ye were. The wood is fu' o' folk trampin' aboot. Are they efter ye?"

Elizabeth nodded.

"Aye. Weel, we'll juist try tae jouk them. Bide a wee till Ah get the fish."

He disappeared down the bank and came up with four trout. "It's a fine wee burn fur the trout. Aye. Ye'll be wantin' tae get back tae the hooses."

"Yes. But they're watching the road and the shore."

"Aye. Ah'm no much wantin' tae ken whit it's a' aboot, but Ah dinna like thon man. It wud please me fine tae slip ye through his fingers. Weel, the first thing is tae get oot o' this place. An' that's easy done if we tak tae the watter an' follow the burn. Sae, tak aff yer shoes and juist follow me."

169

The water was icy. Sandy went ahead and she followed as closely as she could; some stones were very slippery, the smaller pebbles hurt her feet. But the burn ran through thick shrubs, like a tunnel, and when the pools were deep, Sandy showed her where to find a foothold on the bank. It was a fairly noisy burn, and the extra splashing they made was scarcely noticeable. But as they neared the road, things became less easy.

The protection of the shrubs and rhododendrons ended abruptly and the burn ran through a stretch of rough grass and disappeared into a narrow arch in the boundary wall of the grounds, the arch, in fact, of the bridge that carried the road to Mourie Beg. There was no cover at all between the ending of the shrubs and the archway. Down on the right was the house, almost every room lit up, and with figures every now and then going in and coming out. Worst of all, as they peered from the bushes, they could see the dark shapes of two men crossing the grass towards the burn, and one of them at least carried a gun of some kind in the crook of his arm.

"Ye'll no can get ower the wa'," whispered Sandy. "Ye'll need tae get under the bridge. Noo listen. The burn changes course half way through the bridge, and turns tae the richt. Sae keep yer haun' on the wa' as ye gang through. An' anither thing—there's a kin' o' hole in the bed of the burn juist whaur it changes course. It's no' deep enough tae droon ye but it'd reach amaist tae yer airmpits. But if ye keep tae the richt ye'll be on the edge of it."

"Do you mean I've to make a dash for it?"

"Naw." Sandy peered out again. "Ye'd be seen. Ah'll try and get them oot the wey. Then ye can get under the bridge. But wait fur me at the ither end." He looked out again. "Ah'll let them see me noo."

He slipped out from the shadow of the bushes, crouching.

There was a shout, quite close at hand, and Elizabeth shrank back into the shadows.

"Stop!"

A pause, and then she heard Sandy's voice.

170

"It's me, Sandy frae the camp. Ye ken me, mister."

"So I do. You been poaching? What's that you've got there?"

"Ach weel, it's juist a wheen troot Ah got in the burn up there . . . ye can hae them, though it'll mean the wife and bairns gaun hungry . . ." His voice had become an insinuating pathetic whine.

"Oh, keep your fish. We're after bigger stuff tonight. You haven't seen a girl sneaking about in the grounds, have you?"

"A girl? Wearing troosers? Aye. She went by up there. She near tramped on me."

"That's her! Which way did she go?"

"Ye ken the plank bridge up there? She went up the burn above it . . . she'll no find it easy going."

"Why, thanks! Come on, Jake, we'll get after her."

"Wull Ah come wi' ye?"

"No, we know the place."

She heard the muffled sound of feet running on grass, and then Sandy was back beside her.

"Awa' wi' ye. Ah'll wait here a bit, and if Ah see ony mair comin', Ah'll heid them aff."

She ran over the grass by the water's edge like a hunted hare, and into the safety of the arch. It was pitch dark there and the wall was slimy to touch. She kept her hand on it and felt the wall curve to follow the changing course of the burn. At the same time her left foot, feeling forward, lost touch with the bottom; she lurched, lost contact with the wall and splashed wildly as she almost fell forward into the water. But she found her footing when the water reached halfway up her thighs, though the current, surprisingly strong, pulled hard on her legs. She hoped the burn would become no deeper. Nor did it. Another yard or so and she was in shallower water and could see the faint curve of the other side of the bridge. When she reached it she waited and soon there was a stirring behind her, and added splashing in the water, and Sandy was there.

He spoke in her ear.

"They're on the road. Ah had a bit look. Ah dinna ken whit's

171

gaun on, but it's something big. Yon fellies wis cairryin' machine guns. We'll hae tae be gey carefu' no tae be seen. Ah think the best thing is tae get back tae the camp. Ah ken the way, and Ah'm thinkin' they'll no be likely tae bother us yins there. Juist you follow me as close as ye can an' we'll jouk them . . . Wheesht!"

He caught her arm in warning as footsteps and the sound of voices passed overhead. Then with a whispered "Come on" he went ahead down the burn, now shaded by low-growing alders and hazels. After about two hundred yards he climbed on to the left-hand bank, and stretched out a hand to help her after him.

"Pit on yer shoes noo, fur we're in amang the whins an' it's jaggy."

It was horrible pushing her wet feet into her shoes but she managed and soon they were picking their way among clumps of whin that grew at random. To Elizabeth each looked like the next, but Sandy picked his way quite confidently through them. After about ten minutes he stopped, sniffed and said: "That's the fire at the camp," and indeed she could recognise a faint tang of woodsmoke.

"Juist you wait here and Ah'll go on an' see if a's weel there. They're no likely tae come in here amang the whins an' Ah'll no' be long."

He disappeared between two clumps and she was left alone. The sound of the sea came faintly to her—they must be quite close to the shore. Otherwise there was no sound to be heard. It was a perfectly calm and tranquil summer night. The peacefulness of it all after what she had just come through was almost like a blow. A total weariness suddenly overwhelmed her and she slumped to the ground in the shadow of the whin and waited for Sandy's return in a numb unawareness of anything except of the cold of her soaked slacks clinging to her legs. But her ears registered the wary approach of his steps and she dragged herself to her feet. Sandy peered at her with concern.

"Eh! Ye're far through. But juist a wee bit further an' we'll be at the tents. There's naebody aboot but oorsels."

He took his arm to guide her. And then it happened.

A gigantic thud up in the hills, a split second of silence and a huge rumble of sound vibrating over Mourie and the sea and into the hills of Skye.

She felt Sandy's hand begin to shake and tremble and when he spoke his voice changed to a hoarse unsteady whisper.

"Let's get back, let's get back quick."

They crossed rough grass and reedy patches of squelchy bog and came to the trees, through which the light of the fire flickered. Soon they were standing beside it and Nancy had taken control of things.

"Sit doon, Sandy, by the fire. It's a' richt!" She put her hands on his shoulders and shook him. "It's a' richt, Sandy!"

Sandy looked at her blankly, but he stopped shaking and crouched by the fire. Nancy turned to Elizabeth.

"Ye'd best get into the tent. Sandy says there's fowk efter ye."

But Elizabeth hesitated. "Is he all right?"

"Aye. He'll be fine. He was once buried efter a quarry-blasting and since then anything like that sets him aff . . . Ye heard . . . ?"

"An explosion? Yes."

"Some o' thae navy things up the coast, nae doot. But come intae the tent . . . Ye never ken wha micht be aboot."

She took Elizabeth over to the tent where the baby had been born. Inside a hurricane lamp had been lit. The baby was asleep in a basket and Peg was sitting on the mattress wrapped in an old tartan shawl, and looking worried. Nancy explained:

"She's feart they're efter Sandy fur the poachin'."

"They're not. It's me they're after. I . . . it's too tangled a story to tell you, but they're wicked men. They've killed one, or more likely two, people."

She was surprised at her own coolness as she spoke. Her feeling for Douglas was dead. She didn't feel anger or fear; just total detachment.

"I've got to get back to the village. But they're watching the road and all the approaches."

173

"We'll get ye back—some way. We'll keep ye as lang as we can, but come daylicht they'll maybe come tae search the camp, and they micht be gey naisty if they thocht we'd helped ye."

"I've thought of that," said Elizabeth. "I'll stay no longer than I can help."

Nancy looked at her.

"Sit doon. Ah'll bring ye some tea; and we'll get ye hame, dinna worry."

Peg moved over and Elizabeth sank down beside her. She was cold and shivering, and Peg said, "Hey, tak it," and took off the shawl and flung it over Elizabeth's shoulders. It reeked of woodsmoke and sweat but it was gratefully warm. Peg ran a hand over her soaking trousers.

"Ye'd better get tae the fire and dry yersel," she said.

It seemed a sound idea, and Elizabeth went to the tent opening and then remembered it might be better to keep out of sight. Nancy was busy by the fire with kettle and mugs, making tea. Sandy was already holding a mug and drinking. She wondered if she dared join them and was on the point of leaving the tent when Bella appeared running through the trees. At the fire, she said breathlessly:

"There's men there"—she pointed behind her—"wi' guns. Ah think they're coming here."

Nancy put down the tea-pot.

"Into the tent beside the weans. Pit yer heid beneath the blanket, let on ye're asleep, an' dinna speak a word. You, Sandy"—for he had risen to his feet in alarm—"sit doon again. An' juist tell them ye've been at the fishin'—an' ye've seen naethin'—except whit ye telt thae men at the Big Hoose."

She came over to the tent and found Elizabeth inside the entrance.

"I'll go," said Elizabeth. "I'm not going to get you into trouble."

"Na, na. We'll manage. See—get ye on the mattress there. Turn yer back tae the licht—pu' the shawl ower yer heid— here . . ." She flung a patchwork cover over Elizabeth's knees. "Hide thae breeks ye're wearing an' tak the wean . . ."

174

She lifted the sleeping baby from the basket and pushed him into Elizabeth's arms, hissing to Peg:

"Dinna say a word. Get on there an' lie doon an Ah'll dae the speakin'."

She turned the lamp low and the three of them waited. Soon there was a sound of twigs cracking under heavy steps and loud voices.

"Still awake, mister?"

And Sandy's voice: "Ah wis at the fishin'."

"Uh-huh. We're looking for someone. We're looking hard and we're going to look in your tents."

"Ye've nae richt . . ." A pause. "Ah weel—dae as ye please."

"We will. You look, Joe. I'll stay out here in case anyone tries to leave."

Nancy was peering out from the tent.

"He's in Bella's tent . . . but the weans'll stay quiet, Ah'm shair o' that . . . he's oot noo."

"Well?" The same arrogant voice.

"Just a couple of kids and a woman asleep."

"Try the next one."

"That's Mysie's," whispered Nancy.

There was an outraged squawk, followed by shrill cries and a screeching of eloquent abuse. Also the sound of metal clattering and a yelp of pain. Then Joe's voice protesting.

"All right, all right. I'm getting out . . . No girl there; only an old witch of a woman."

"Witch is it! Ah'll witch ye!" Another metallic clatter. "Get oot o' here afore Ah curse ye into Kingdom Come!"

"Just look in there, Joe, and we'll go."

Nancy made a swift movement over to Elizabeth and tickled the baby's chin. He woke and began to wail. Nancy stood between Elizabeth and the light from the lamp, and didn't turn as a short thick-set man carrying a gun came into the tent.

"Well?" She shot the word at him like a bullet.

"I'm looking for a young woman . . ."

"Ye'll no be meaning my dochters by that? Her there on the bed is tryin' tae sleep after a day on the road. An' her here is

175

tryin' tae hush a wean that's ill. An' Ah'll thenk ye"—she swung round in a magnificent gesture of indignation—"tae leave honest folk tae theirsels, and gang seekin' yer kind o' young wumman somewhere else."

The baby's whimper became a loud cry of hunger. Elizabeth crouched over it, crooning. Joe gave a helpless glance round, and retreated.

"There's a sick baby in here . . . no sign of the girl."

"O.K. Let's go."

The sound of their going died away. Peg sat up and put the baby to her breast. Silence and relief flooded the camp, broken only by complaining murmurs from Mysie's tent.

Nancy waited for a moment or two and then peered out.

"They're awa'! An' Ah think Ah know hoo we'll get ye back tae yer auntie's . . ." She put her head out of the tent and called softly: "Sandy."

Sandy came over and into the tent.

"Thon's a bad lot," he said. "They pointed a gun at me . . ."

"Aye. Bad as they come," said Nancy, "but listen noo. This is hoo we'll get the lassie back tae her auntie. Awa' you, and harness up the powny tae the cart. Peg here'll drive the lass *and* the baby tae Mistress Lauder's—if they're stopped, Peg'll say she's taking her sister and her sister's sick baby tae the nurse. Gin ye keep the shawl ower yer face—and tak aff yer breeks and pit on a skirt, naebody's likely tae look ower close at ye."

But Peg was unenthusiastic.

"Ah'm no wantin' tae gang—or tak the baby—mebby they'll shoot us."

"Ye'll have tae gang—tae feed the baby. Ah dinna think there's ony danger o' shootin'. Ye'll drive and dae the speakin'. An' Miss Elizabeth here'll hae the baby and mak oot she's ower worried tae sae a word . . ."

It seemed as good a plan as any. The rough brown pony was found and harnessed to the little flat cart. Elizabeth was given a skirt; her slacks, rolled in a bundle, were shoved under the two folded sacks on which she was to sit. The baby was wrapped up and she was shown how to hold it in a fold of her tartan shawl.

176

The little thing had fallen asleep again, full and content. A still unwilling Peg climbed on to the cart, took the reins, and they moved off up the track in the grey dawn light, to join the road into Mourie.

The little cart bumped and rocked. It was very uncomfortable and the shawl kept slipping from Elizabeth's head. But at last she managed to pull it well over her face, and anchored it in position by wrapping it tightly round her arms. Then she was worried in case the baby, lost in the depths of the shawl, would smother; by the time she had arranged it so that air in what she thought would be sufficient quantity could reach him, they were approaching the bridge. Two men, armed, were lounging against the parapet. Peg whispered sideways to her:

"Ah'll dae the speakin'."

Peg was evidently prepared to play her part confidently, and when the men moved forward to bar their way, looked at them without any cringing. Peering out from the shadow of the shawl, Elizabeth saw that one was Joe, the other a lean man who squinted and had a pinched cruel mouth. He spoke.

"You from the camp? Where do you think you're going?"

"Tae the nurse's. Ma sister's wean's awfu' sick—near chokin'. Let's get on, mister, and dinna hinder us."

"Let me see the baby."

He stepped forward with outstretched hand. Elizabeth shrank back, a purely instinctive movement, but it made him hesitate for a split second, and Peg raised her voice.

"Ah'm tellin' ye, the baby's near chokin'. Dinna keep us back. Ma sister'll go mad if onything happens tae him . . ."

Her voice rose to a shrill shriek that split the quiet morning air and Joe intervened.

"I told you about it. It's a sick baby all right. Let them past."

"Ye'd better," said Peg, flapping the reins on the pony's back, and they jogged over the bridge.

Once round a bend in the road, she persuaded the reluctant pony into a moderately swift trot, and in an unexpectedly short time they were at Rose Cottage, and Elizabeth was ringing the front door-bell.

177

Jenny opened it, gaped in blank astonishment, pulled her inside, and went out to help Peg lead the pony round the end of the house and tether it to the fence.

When Peg and she went into the sitting-room, Elizabeth was sitting in a chair, still holding the baby wrapped in the shawl, and with tears of exhaustion and relief trickling down her cheeks.

CHAPTER 19

Peg took the baby gently from Elizabeth, and crooned to it. Jenny unwrapped her from the shawl and said:

"It's all right. You're back home. There's nothing to be upset about."

Elizabeth looked at her in numb amazement. How could she possibly say there was nothing to be upset about? But then of course Jenny knew nothing about Douglas and the murder of Morag, and gold to be taken away secretly—only she knew it, and so she couldn't, yet, let it all slip and forget it and sleep . . . which was all she wanted to do.

Instead, she sat up and said harshly:

"But there is everything to be upset about." She looked up. "First, switch off the light, Aunt Jenny. Anyone passing could see everything in here . . . and they mustn't. They mustn't know I'm here."

Without a word, Jenny switched off the light. The early daylight was kinder to Elizabeth's eyes, and she said more calmly:

"Aunt Jenny, everything is wrong. I—they had me shut up in Mourie House, and I got away, and they would have killed me if they'd got me, and Sandy saved me and took me to the camp— and then Peg brought me here . . ."

"But you're safe here."

"No I'm not." She clutched Jenny's hands. "Listen. Douglas and the rest aren't looking for the laird's treasure. They never were. It's something else. Thousands and thousands of pounds. And nothing, nothing is going to stop them getting away with it.

179

So he said. I don't care about that. But he—they—killed Morag and Morag's grandson . . . Aunt Jenny, Douglas is a murderer."

She stopped, clutching Jenny's hands, her eyes bright with tears, her face white and pinched. Jenny was silent for a moment and then said:

"Are you sure you know what you're saying? . . . All right"—as Elizabeth dropped her hands and opened her mouth to protest—"then we must phone the police station."

"Aunt Jenny, you haven't understood! Hamish McIntosh can't do anything about it—they've got guns—they've—they don't care *what* they do!"

"That's as may be," said the ex-matron of Scotland's most famous teaching hospital, "but he is the law, and he can get help. I'm going to phone him now."

Elizabeth watched her helplessly. Supposing she couldn't make anyone understand what was going on? Jenny was holding the phone with obvious and increasing irritation. "Really, this exchange is ridiculous . . ."

Into the silence came Peg's voice from where she sat by the window.

"There's twa men coming tae the door."

The speed with which Jenny dropped the phone showed that she had been more affected by Elizabeth's story than she had admitted. Elizabeth herself sat paralysed, gripped by an overwhelming clutching terror. Steps approached the front door. The bell rang gently.

"Get down the passage to the kitchen."

Jenny's voice was a mere whisper. Elizabeth didn't move.

"It's no use. They'll get me whatever—I can't—I can't move."

Jenny shook her by the shoulders.

"Don't be a fool . . ."

The bell rang again. Then they heard the door being opened. Two or three steps in the hall; the sitting-room door swung back. Two men framed in it.

Elizabeth, crouching back in the chair, gave a sob. Jenny, standing like a menacing sentry, relaxed, and Peg sat down again.

For it was Angus and Roddy who came in.

180

"What is going on here? Why did you not open the door?" Angus was gruff. Then he saw Elizabeth. "Well, if it isn't Miss Elizabeth, back home safe and sound. Where have you been all this while?" Then as she turned her woe-begone face towards him, "What is wrong?"

"Plenty," said Jenny, "if what Elizabeth said is true. Can you tell them, or shall I?"

Elizabeth told them, wearily and bleakly; and the two men took her very seriously.

"You say McBain said Mourie was vulnerable?" asked Roddy thoughtfully.

"Yes. He said, did I realise how vulnerable it was? I don't know what he meant."

"I still think we should ring Hamish McIntosh," said Jenny. "I was trying to do that when you arrived."

"No harm in that, I suppose," said Angus, "but perhaps not much use either. I'll try to get through, if you like."

He lifted the phone, listened for a moment and said: "It's dead."

"Nonsense," said Jenny. "It's just the exchange. I've had trouble before, trying to make a call at night."

"No, it is quite dead. I wonder now . . . Roddy, as Miss Elizabeth has been found, I think we'd better get back home and try to have some sleep."

"But will Miss Elizabeth be quite safe here?" said Roddy. "I would be happy to stay . . ."

"I do not think McBain will be harming her now. He must know that once she got back to Mourie she would be telling all she knew." Angus turned to Elizabeth. "So there is no point in getting rid of you now. He would have to do away with an awful lot of people. And he is not likely to do that—at least I do not think so. But then, we do not really know him at all, do we? Though I always thought he was not quite what he seemed; he was not just like any of the schoolmasters I have known—but I understand they are different nowadays, and the children liked him . . . but he will have to keep any news from getting out of Mourie until they are safely away, and that is why I am wondering about the phone . . . You see, if they put the exchange out of action . . . the steamer doesn't call for three days . . . they could soon make the ferry-boat useless . . ."

"And that only leaves the road," said Roddy, "and if they set up a road-block . . ."

They all looked at each other.

"You heard it too—the explosion?" asked Angus.

Jenny nodded.

"Then, if they've blocked the road as well as taking all those other steps, Mourie is in a state of siege."

As the word, with age-old connotations of war and violence, starvation and death, hung in the air, a puzzled, anxious voice said:

"Ah'd like tae get back to the camp." And Peg stood up and gathered her shawl round her. Elizabeth felt guilty, for she had momentarily forgotten Peg and she thought Jenny had too. But it was Jenny who spoke reassuringly.

"I don't think you should go back just yet, Peg. I'll get a bed ready for you and you'll stay here for a little. You wouldn't want the baby to get hurt, if you met any of the men from Mourie House. They'll know at the camp that you'll be quite safe with me."

"Aye. But they'll no be daein' onything bad tae the fowk at the tents?"

"I'm sure they won't. There's no reason for them to harm anyone—as long as they're left alone to get away with their stuff."

Out of her weariness, Elizabeth heard herself say:

"But they must not get away. They've killed two people. You see that, don't you? Roddy? Mr. McKay?"

"Yes, I see it." Roddy spoke soothingly. "But I think it must wait till morning. We are all needing sleep. In the morning we will get hold of the others and see what is to be done."

After Jenny had seen them out and locked the door, she said to Elizabeth firmly:

"Upstairs and to bed. You're worn out."

Elizabeth rose obediently. As she had a foot on the stair she said:

"How did Roddy and Angus McKay come to be up at this hour?"

"They'd been looking for you. When I became anxious about you, I rang various places and eventually called Mourie House, and was told you'd last been seen going down to the cliffs, and they'd send someone to look for you. When Roddy heard about it, he went for Angus and they went to search up and down the shore." She kissed her niece lightly on the cheek. "A lot of people were concerned about you."

Elizabeth woke from a deep sleep with a tremendous start. The shadowless light of a cloudy day filled her room, and so did the sound of a loud booming voice.

It came from the road outside. She went to the window, and standing well back, peered out. A Land-Rover was being driven down the road by Joe while Squint-eyes, standing in the back was speaking through a loud-hailer.

"Mr. McBain is holding a meeting at the top of the quay. You are all asked to attend. Mr. McBain is holding a meeting at the top of the quay . . . You are all asked to attend. Mr. McBain . . ."

Downstairs Jenny greeted her gloomily.

"I thought that row would waken you. You should have had a much longer sleep. How do you feel?"

"A lot better, though still a bit tired. Will you go to the quay?"

"I don't want to, but perhaps one should know what's going on. Peg's still asleep. If I'm away when she gets up, make her some breakfast."

Jenny was gone only half an hour, and when she returned, Joe was with her—a slightly shame-faced Joe, but a Joe with the authority of a gun cradled in one arm. Jenny marched indignantly up the path before him, and into the kitchen, and in answer to Elizabeth's look of panic, said:

"Don't worry, Elizabeth. You're to be a hostage; along with most of the men of Mourie. This man is to take you. Douglas spoke straight to the point. You might say, in fact, that he took us all into his confidence. He laid all the facts before us. They'll have completed hauling up their gold from whatever wreck they've

183

found by tonight, and will then leave; by helicopter, in relays. They've cut the telephone, sunk the ferry-boat, blasted rock on to the road. Oh yes, and locked Hamish McIntosh up in his own cell . . . We are cut off, and just to make sure there's no 'funny stuff,' as he called it, they've rounded up most of the men and put them in the school—as 'hostages.' "

There was a concentrated fury in Jenny's voice which Elizabeth had never heard before. Meanwhile, Joe was showing some impatience mingled with embarrassment. She guessed Jenny had been eloquent on the way to Rose Cottage.

"You best come right away," he said. "The Boss is in a mighty bad temper and mostly because of you."

"All right, I'm coming."

The Land-Rover was outside, Squint-eyes now in the driving seat. Joe got in beside her, and in minutes they were at the school.

Mourie School, an old building, had been brought up to date by the installation of electricity, storage heaters and indoor lavatories. An asphalt playground surrounded it on three sides. The back of the school and the high back wall of the playground formed one long line of masonry on the hillward side, the playground sloping down to the road. As they stopped at the playground gate Elizabeth could see Roddy and one or two others being escorted through the school door. Inside the building were two classrooms, with windows placed high in the walls, so that childish eyes might not be tempted to look outside and be diverted from the stern world of learning within. In the larger of the two rooms, gloomily seated at desks too small for them, were most of the men of Mourie. Elizabeth knew most of them, having seen them coming and going in the village. Angus McKay was there and, to her surprise, beside him at the desk was Alice. Everyone looked grim and gloomy, and scarcely anyone so much as glanced at her as she was pushed into the room. But Alice got up and said in her clear English voice:

"I *am* glad to see you—well, not glad you're here, but glad of your company. I can't think why they brought me here, except

184

that I just happened to be standing outside the shop talking to Mr. McKay when they came along. Come and sit beside me."

She sounded quite cheerful; in fact, as Elizabeth looked at her, her chestnut curls rampant, her slim little figure in a royal-blue sweater and ski-pants, her eyes bright, she got the impression that Alice was positively enjoying the situation. But as Alice stopped talking and she took her place beside her, she realised how very quiet the room was. Occasionally someone cleared his throat, but mostly they sat looking down at their hands clenched between their knees. No one looked at her, and hostility filled the room like a mist.

Roddy was behind her, and she turned and said to him in a low voice:

"What's wrong? Are they blaming me?"

Angus overheard her.

"I don't, my lass. But some here will be thinking that if you hadn't let yourself be caught by McBain—or if you hadn't gone interfering into things—we might not all be sitting here rounded up like sheep in a dipping-pen. But I'm not blaming you. It might have happened this way anyway. We should maybe have let it be known sooner that we knew what was going on."

"Let it be known sooner? What do you mean?" Surprise made her voice sharp and several heads were raised. Angus moved a deprecatory hand and said:

"Hush now. We don't know who might be listening."

"Well, what do you mean?" Her low harsh whisper carried across the room. Everyone was listening now. But before Angus could answer, the door opened, and Douglas stood there, Joe and another man armed behind him. Again she was struck by the change in him. The schoolmaster, part of the community, passing the time of day with acquaintances in the street, and yet a little apart too, was quite gone. Instead, arrogant and sneering, he was someone from an alien world. She noticed that after a quick glance from under lowered brows, no one looked at him. For a moment his eyes, full of cold hostility, met Elizabeth's, but she turned her head and didn't look at him again.

185

His words were precise and scornful.

"No one's going to get hurt if you just stay quiet till we've gone. Some of the women will bring you food. But don't try to get out till we let you." A pause. "Or you'll be shot—dead."

The door slammed and left a deep silence, broken by Angus' whisper:

"It's a bastard he is and no mistake."

"But what are you going to *do?*" said Elizabeth.

"What can we do?"

"We can't just let them get away with it."

"Well, we had been hoping that indeed we would not be letting them get away with it *all*. But now I'm not so sure . . ."

"Mr. McKay, I don't understand. I'm not talking about the money or the gold—I'm talking about what they've done."

She whirled round and looked at Roddy.

"Or haven't you told them?"

"We haven't had time," said Roddy. "We've just been brought here and they got us out of bed."

She turned back to Angus and raised her voice:

"It's not the money that matters. They're killers. *They* killed the man I found up in the hills: he was old Morag's grandson— and they killed her too. Now do you see why we must do something?"

Now the silence was different; shocked and angry. A voice said: "John the Ferry?"

"I'm sure they did that too."

There was a murmuring and now they were all sitting upright and someone said:

"It would be a good thing if we could hand them over to the law . . ."

"If you're meaning Hamish, I don't think that would be much use," said a voice, "and anyway, I understand he's locked up in his own cell."

There were one or two appreciative grins and the tension relaxed a little.

"But I don't see how we can do anything," said a voice from the back of the room. "We cannot very well be stopping the

186

helicopters and we do not even know where they keep them—and the simple truth is that they have guns and we have not."

They murmured agreement, almost, Elizabeth felt, with relief at the thought that, having satisfied themselves that any effort was impossible, they might do nothing with a clear conscience. But before she could raise her voice to refute this, there was a sound of footsteps from outside and a voice raised in protestation. The door opened, and a figure stumbled in and almost fell. Roddy caught him by the arm and he stood there awkwardly, twisting in his hands a grubby cap which had fallen as he stumbled. He wore thick-soled shepherd's boots, shapeless trousers, a tweed jacket dark with dirt, and an open-necked shirt. His hair was shaggy and fair and he needed a shave, and was looking round uncertainly, almost desperately, his light eyes sliding from one to another. Elizabeth could not remember ever having seen him before, but he seemed to be known to the company.

"Man, how did you come to be here?" asked Angus.

"I was walking down the street, and two men with guns jumped on me and brought me here. And I have done nothing, nothing at all."

"Don't worry, Towny. You'll be in good company. They're keeping us all here till they can get themselves away. They're bad men, Towny, but you're safe here."

"Are you sure I am? I haven't done anything . . ."

His voice rose to a wail.

"It's all right. Come and sit down and be quiet."

"Who is he?" whispered Elizabeth to Roddy.

"Towny came here as a boarded-out child from Glasgow years ago—that's why he's called Towny. He's not quite right in the head; and he lives alone in a little cottage away up a glen between here and Ruaidh. He helps with the sheep at lambing time, or he'll help unload cattle from the boat—and he roams the hills and does a bit of poaching. Sometimes he'll not be seen for weeks, and then he appears down at the shop . . . He's quite harmless and it's ridiculous to bring him in here."

Someone who had climbed up on a desk to look out of the window said:

"Here's Mairi Macleod coming with two big baskets. Will it be food?"

It was. Joe and another man escorted her into the room and she put down the two baskets and said:

"I've tried to think of everything. You can make tea in the school kitchen here, and there are mugs that the children use. Be careful, Roddy, when you unpack the smaller basket." She looked round the room. "Are you all right here?"

"Sure they're all right," said Joe, "and you can get back to the shop now. The Boss is quite happy for you to bring in food, but he doesn't mean that you stay here talking."

In the larger basket were bread, butter, cheese; slabs of chocolate; a bag of apples; sugar, tea. In the other were bottles of milk and, wrapped in a convincing camouflage of old newspapers, two bottles of Glenlivet single malt whisky.

"And isn't she the sensible woman!" said a voice. "She knew we would be needing something to keep our courage up!"

"Just that," agreed Angus. "But we'll not be using it just yet. And I'll just be putting it in this desk, here, for it would be a pity if any of our gaolers were to see it and be tempted."

Alice and Elizabeth went to the little pantry-kitchen and brewed up tea. When everyone had a mug in his hand, Alice said:

"Before Towny arrived, Mr. McKay, we were talking about what we could do . . ."

"So we were," said Angus, who seemed to have assumed the rôle of leader, or elder statesman. "Someone was saying that there wasn't much we could do, since we don't know where the helicopters are, let alone trying to destroy them . . . Towny, what is the matter with you?"

For Towny had spilt the tea out of his mug and was now gaping at Angus and saying:

"You must not do anything to the helicopters, Mr. McKay, you must not."

He laid his hand on Angus' arm, drew himself close to him and whispered in his ear.

Angus' expression as he listened changed from exasperated

188

kindliness to sharp-eyed interest. When the hissing agitation of Towny's voice ceased, Angus patted him on the shoulder and said:

"It's all *right*, Towny. There's nothing to worry about." And then to the room at large, "Towny knows where they keep the helicopters."

"Where? How? Is it far?"—they remembered to keep their voices low, but only just, and Angus gestured them into silence.

"Quiet! He found the place when he was out on the hills one night . . . It's the Old Man's Kiln . . . He says there's more than one: he's seen them."

There was a stunned silence; a voice said softly:

"Aye, it would be a good place."

"Where is this?" Elizabeth whispered to Roddy.

"It is up in the hills—I'll explain in a minute." He raised his voice. "Why didn't Towny tell us about this before?"

"He was terrified into saying nothing. One of McBain's men caught him coming away from the Kiln and told him if he ever went there again, or if he told anyone what he'd seen, they'd burn down his cottage and then shoot him. He's always been a scary creature so he said nothing and hasn't even been down to the village since . . ."

"So now we know where they are," said Alice.

"What difference does that make?" said Willie McAlister. "We're cooped up here, and no way of getting out. They've men watching the school, and I'm not feeling like being a hero and making a dash for it . . ."

Through the mutter of agreement rippling round the room, Elizabeth whispered to Roddy:

"You said you'd explain . . ."

"You know the hill that rises up from the moor behind the school? The one that rises to a kind of huge wall of rock?"

"Yes."

"Well, it really is a huge wall. It surrounds a hollow—a crater, I suppose it is. Inside there's a roughly oval grass-floored space. There's a break in the wall of rock—an old water-course, I think, by which it is possible to get inside. Otherwise

189

it would be extremely arduous to climb up and down the other side. I must say it was very bright to think of putting the helicopters there. Even if we weren't shut up here it would be almost impossible to get at them."

Angus was speaking to the room in general.

"Well, we now know where the helicopters are. Now you can just set yourselves the task of trying to think how we could get at them—it'll while away the time, though I doubt if it'll be much other use . . . the machines might as well be in the next world as in the Old Man's Kiln and us here. And I'm thinking we could do with something to eat—if Miss Elizabeth and Miss Merriweather would be so kind . . ."

"Of course." Elizabeth jumped up. "We'll make toasted cheese for everyone. Coming, Alice?"

Roddy carried through the basket, and they began to make toast on the electric cooker. Alice said:

"I'm quite attached to this little kitchen. You know I did a spell as teacher here, and I used to nip in here and brew up a cup when things were quiet enough in the classroom—I decided that as I was helping them out by doing the job, I needn't be too orthodox about how I did it . . ."

Roddy, taking down mugs from the shelves, said:

"The school's very different from when I was here. It was a dark kind of place and could be very cold in winter."

"How was it heated?" asked Elizabeth idly.

"There was a boiler that heated hot water pipes in the classrooms, and we used to hang our wet coats on them and the place would be full of the smell of wet wool, like a sheep-fank on a rainy day."

"The cloakrooms are heated now," said Alice. "Electricity must have made a big difference. But the old boiler-house is still here. I was shown the door when I came to teach. It's kept padlocked."

"The old boiler used to break down," said Roddy, "and sometimes the coal wouldn't come and if it got too cold, we would be sent home, so we didn't mind. Once the Inspector arrived, and found the school empty and he was going to put in a bad report, but Mr. McNab, the headmaster, said if he would wait in a classroom, he would collect the children back. And by the time he had got them gathered, and I'm not saying he hurried himself, the Inspector, poor man, was blue with cold. So we were all sent home again and there was no report."

"Getting coal here must be quite a problem," said Elizabeth. (For the idle conversation was soothing and relaxing; the pretence of normality, therapeutic.)

"It was an occasion, when the coal came," said Roddy. "We used to be allowed into the playground to see it arriving, for Mr. McNab liked to superintend the operation. It came in a big green lorry, and it had to be backed up the track behind the school wall there and tipped up just at the chute into the boiler-house and we sat on the wall and gave the driver cheek . . ."

But Elizabeth interrupted him.

"Did you say there was a chute into the boiler-house?"

"Yes. A little square door at ground level in the back wall. The coal was tipped there and then Murdo Mcphee shovelled it in and sometimes we helped. A grand dirty ploy."

"But Roddy—if the boiler-house is still there, the chute will be there." She almost choked on the words. "Where coal came in, people could get out! We could escape!"

"We could! Why not?" Alice was enthusiastic.

So was Roddy. "If the chute is still there, if we can open it." His voice dropped. "But it's padlocked. And they would be sure to take all the keys away when they brought us here."

"Padlocks can be broken," said Alice.

"With what?"

"Perhaps," said Elizabeth quietly, "we could go and look at the boiler-house door."

It was at the end of the short corridor which ran from the entrance past the two classrooms. An ordinary door with a bolt and a padlock through the ring of the bolt. It wasn't a particularly big padlock. Roddy ran a hand round it.

"It is not very strong—if we had an iron bar of some kind, it could be broken."

"'An iron bar!" Elizabeth echoed the words ironically, and

191

they stood looking at each other helplessly. Then Alice brightened.

"Come here, Roddy." And she turned and went back down the passage, and opened a door into a large cupboard, really a store-room. On shelves down one side were books and stationery. Against the other wall was propped discarded equipment—old scratched grey blackboards, ancient maps, waxed and yellow, two high chairs—and in the dimness at the far end, two enormous coal buckets, and in them long-handled shovels, tongs and pokers.

"Relics of the days of the open fires," said Alice, seizing a poker. "See if this will do, Roddy."

It did. Roddy thrust the point through the loop of the padlock, gave a quick wrench, and it burst open.

They looked at each other triumphantly, and Roddy laid his hand on the padlock to lift it from the bolt, but Alice said:

"Wait a minute. We can't all go in. Suppose any of Douglas' lot came in to the school, and noticed we weren't in the room or saw this door open . . . We must keep some kind of a watch."

"Right you are," said Roddy. "I will keep watch at the entrance here, in the shadow of that door. You stay here, Miss Alice, and if anyone is coming, I'll signal, and you can tap on the door, and Elizabeth here will just stay in the boiler-house, and if they ask where she is, we'll say she's in the ladies'. All right?"

"Right."

He went down the passage and stationed himself where he could look into the playground, but was himself not easily seen. Alice and Elizabeth took off the padlock, slid back the bolt and opened the door. It creaked alarmingly and swung outwards above a flight of worn and gritty stone steps. Elizabeth felt for a light switch and found it just inside the door. The light was as feeble as could be, but it showed her the steps, and the outline of the old boiler, squatting in the middle of the cellar. Alice closed the door behind her and she picked her way down the steps. The air smelt fusty, earthy and sooty.

She stood by the boiler and looked round. That must be the back wall ahead of her. And there was the chute! Up near the roof, a solid little square wooden door with a rusty bolt and hinges and the wood beginning to rot round the edges. Under it were some lumps of coal and a layer of dross trodden solid. If they could reach it, if it opened, then here was a way of escape.

Back in the corridor beside Alice, she helped her to replace the padlock so that it looked untouched. Then they all three went back to the kitchen, excited and jubilant.

"We can all get out," said Elizabeth, "if we can open it." But Alice was cautious.

"What would be the point? They'd find we'd all gone—turn nasty, start shooting. No, we've got to be more subtle. Now we know it's there, let's get back to the others, and plan a campaign."

"Just that," said Roddy. "Is the food ready? Then let's go in with it."

Taking up the trays, they formed a triumphant little procession and went into the classroom.

CHAPTER 20

But the jubilation was short-lived, for just as they put down the trays on the front desks in the classroom and before they could say a word to anyone, they heard the entrance door being opened with a crash, and a moment after, Joe and Squint-eyes were standing in the classroom door. Joe looked a trifle mutinous. Elizabeth was beginning to feel a kind of ridiculous affection for him, if only because familiarity was blunting his original fearsomeness, although she knew he was as nasty as the rest. None of the others could produce in her the cold terror that Johnson roused and she was thankful that he had not appeared among their guards. Squint-eyes was being bullying and loud-mouthed.

"I've some good news for you, folks. My friend Joe is going to stay right here with you; just to see that you all stay good little boys, and good little girls"—with a leer at Elizabeth and Alice—"and if you try any fancy tricks on him, he's going to shoot without giving any second chances. Mr. McBain figures it'd be better to have someone keeping an eye on you, seeing you're so many and might get to thinking up something among yourselves. So be nice to Joe and he'll be nice to you."

And with a sardonic smile all round, Squint-eyes left. They heard the bang and clang of the school door as he closed and locked it.

Joe swung himself on to the teacher's desk that stood on a little dais, cocked the gun in a meaningful way, and looked at them with mingled bravado and sheepishness. No one spoke or even looked at him; they collected tea and food in silence

194

and sat eating as if he weren't there. It was a splendid display of imperturbability, but Roddy, Alice and Elizabeth were in turmoil of frustration.

That's torn it," said Elizabeth out of the side of her mouth. "How on earth can we tell them with that in beside us?"

"If we could rush him," whispered Roddy, "knock him out . . . ?"

"Too risky. At first sound of a shot, the others would be in on top of us."

They ate in moody silence. No one in the room was speaking. The only sound was Joe's soft whistling—a maddening sound. Roddy took up a plate and offered it to Angus. Angus took a slice and munched it solemnly. Presently he took the tray and began to collect empty mugs. When he came to the girls he said very softly: "Come and wash up—now."

But as they left the schoolroom Joe called after them: "Say, where do you think you're going?"

Angus answered him courteously. "I am taking the mugs to the kitchen for the girls to wash up and I am hoping you will not object."

"O.K. But make it quick."

In the kitchen, as they clattered the crockery in the sink, Angus said, "What is it? Roddy says you've found something."

They told, swiftly and briefly. He stood tapping a knife on the draining board, frowning.

"We must try to get at the helicopters," said Alice. "If they're put out of action, we've at least delayed their getaway—they'll be cut off . . ."

"Except for their boats," said Elizabeth.

"Except for their boats. But the helicopters are the main thing."

"You're right," said Angus decisively, "they're the most important things."

"But we can't plan anything with that man there," said Elizabeth.

Angus gave her a meditative look.

"I am thinking we can manage . . . I'll get back now, for I

195

would not like him to be imagining we were plotting anything . . . Just give me a few of these mugs."

When they followed him into the schoolroom a few minutes later, the atmosphere had totally changed. Instead of cold silence there was a gentle buzz of conversation.

Angus was talking to Joe and they heard him say:

"You would have no objection to us having a game of cards, would you?"

"No; if you can find the cards."

"Well now, I think Mr. McBain has a pack in his desk here that he took off a wee boy who was playing with them instead of doing his sums . . . so if we could get at the drawer . . ."

Under Joe's very watchful eye Angus fished out from the desk a grubby pack of cards and he and three others, including Willie McAlister and Kenneth the Post, pushing two desks together, settled down to play. Roddy and the others gathered round to watch. Before he dealt, Angus produced the bottle of Glenlivet, and poured a small drink for each player and then, as if on an impulse, he offered a generous tot to Joe.

"Well now, will you join us in a drink? It is an unfortunate situation we are in, but you are only doing as you have been ordered, and there is no need for ill-feeling . . ."

"That is a very sensible attitude to adopt, Mister . . ."

"McKay."

". . . Mr. McKay. I don't want to see any trouble, and I'm sure you don't, so we'll drink to that."

He downed the drink in two swift gulps and handed back the mug with the remark:

"And that's not a bad liquor either, Mr. McKay."

Elizabeth, seeing the expressionless stare of the eyes that watched him drink, felt a chill run through her, and Alice beside her whispered:

"The poor fool!"

The game began. It was whist—played with a ferocious intensity that produced a sudden sharp exchange in Gaelic, bringing Joe to his feet.

196

"None of that. There's to be no talking in your heathenish local lingo. Speak English—or keep your mouths shut."

"Of course." Angus' voice was silkt. "We are forgetting ourselves in the excitement of the game—you know how it is. But it is bad manners to speak Gaelic when there are those present who do not have it . . . Another drink, to show it's understood?"

Joe did make a gesture of refusal but the mug was in his hand before he could say anything. He went back to his perch on the big desk and the game went on.

So did the Gaelic. In a low whisper between the loud exclamations in English. Alice and Elizabeth joined the group round the players, and to Elizabeth—no card player—the game seemed crudely played. At the end there was an argument; voices were raised; more Gaelic spoken. This time Joe did no more than wave an admonitory finger, which Angus took as a request for another drink, and politely pouring it into the mug, returned it to Joe with a friendly "Slainte—that is our word for good health," and when Joe looked at it bemusedly he said reassuringly, "Drink it down. Good single malt never did anyone harm." And Joe drank.

The game went on; they were less careful about the Gaelic. Roddy leaned over Angus' shoulder, pointed to a card in his hand and said something. Someone opposite spread open a newly gathered trick and replied. Towny was pulled forward to look on and he too commented on the play. Joe did once or twice sketch a gesture of protest, then he gave up, finished off his drink and appeared to be studying with interest the stuffed wild-cat in the glass case on the far windowsill.

Presently Roddy came to stand behind the two girls. They could just hear his whisper above the chatter of the card table.

"It's all fixed. Towny and I will go—Towny knows the hills better than anyone and he trusts me. He wanted Angus to go with him, but Angus is too old; we will need to be as quick-footed as possible. Once we've got to the Old Man's Kiln we'll do what we can to put the helicopters out of action—if we can get near them: Towny says there's what he calls 'tins of oil'—

197

aviation spirit I guess—mebbe we can set it off . . . And then we'll try to make our way beyond the road-block and get help. Anyway, this is the idea: in a minute or two, the game will stop, there'll be an argument, and in the confusion Towny and I will slip out. A second or two after, you will go out. Then the four of us will go to the boiler-house and you'll help us to get out—right?"

"Right."

Suddenly Angus threw down the cards and rose, the Gaelic spluttering from him. Voices were raised and a subdued tumult rose. Roddy and Towny disappeared, Elizabeth and Alice followed. Roddy and Towny were standing by the cellar door. Without a word the bolt was released and the door swung open. Soon all four were standing in the dim light looking up at the chute.

"I'll have to climb on Towny's shoulders to reach it," said Roddy. "I think I could jam myself on the ledge while I work at the bolt"—for the little door was heavily recessed into the wall.

Towny had understood. He braced himself against the wall, Roddy climbed on his shoulders, and up on to the ledge. The bolt was stiff and rusty, and his fingers fumbled helplessly at it. Then Towny produced from his pocket a huge pocket knife fitted with an absurd tool for taking stones from horses' hooves— with this very blade Roddy opened the bolt.

"I'll have to stand on your shoulders to open the door, Towny."

He took off his shoes, flung them down, and lowered himself on to Towny's shoulders to open the door. It swung inwards groaning, and behind it came a trickle of earth and pebbles. On the outside was a tangle of grass and weeds and brambles.

"This is good cover," said Roddy. "Steady, Towny, I'm going up."

He knelt on the ledge, pushed aside the undergrowth, and peered out.

"Not a soul in sight, and the hillside bare. If we can get to the bed of the burn, the cover is good. I'll lie up in the heather just across the track. Do you understand, Towny?"

"Yes, but . . ."

"I'm going; bring my shoes."

He wriggled out of sight, and Towny straightened himself and said:

"How am I to get up?"

"You'll have to stand on my back and pull yourself up," said Elizabeth, and she and Alice between them got him up, and watched him vanish through the opening, leaning back to pull the door to behind him before he disappeared. In three minutes they were back in the big schoolroom. Across the confusion, Angus looked at them and they nodded. He raised his voice, the hubbub died down and he turned to speak to Joe, standing clutching his gun at the edge of the dais.

"It is a true saying that cards are the devil's own snare! Look at the disturbance we have been having and all because of them! But it won't happen again. Let's have a drink to show there's no ill-feeling." He poured a drink into each of the mugs on the card table and then filled Joe's, raised his drink and said "Slainte" and watched appreciatively as Joe raised his mug with a slow sweep of the arm and drank.

Angus came over to the girls.

"They're away," said Elizabeth.

"Ah. Then there's nothing to do but wait," said Angus.

"But the boats," said Elizabeth. "Shouldn't we be doing something about the boats?"

"I'm not sure what we should be doing about that. We don't want to be chancing it too much . . . Joe here might suddenly take notice of what was happening . . ."

"I shouldn't think," said Alice drily, "that he'll take notice of anything for some time."

"I am not sure." Angus looked at Joe with the calculating eye of the expert. "If we give him more he might come to a fighting state . . . I am hoping he will just be feeling very happy and peaceful and not bothering . . . But for the boats. If we wait till we see what happens at the Old Man's Kiln?"

There was a noise from the dais. Joe was no longer perched on the desk. He was sitting on the edge of the dais, slumped

199

against the desk, his gun held very loosely, his eyes closed; and a silence fell on the room.

"We could get his gun and tie him up," someone whispered.

"Aye, we could. What about it, Angus?"

But Angus shook his head. "Roddy and Towny are away to the Old Man's Kiln. And we don't want to upset McBain's men, because we're thinking it might be a good idea to get at their boats too."

"Are any of you good at the chess?"

It was Murdo MacSween, an older man who had the first croft out of the village, a small boat and a capacity for seemingly spending all his time propped up on the jetty smoking, and at the same time earning an apparently adequate living. His jerseys had no darns in them, his boots no patches; his house was always neatly whitewashed; and his wife, a timid little grey woman who scampered out of sight round the end of the house whenever she saw anyone on the road, had as nice clothes as anyone in Mourie.

He repeated his question to the astonished faces turned to him.

"Are any of you good at the chess? . . . My brother in Edinburgh taught me the game, and a very good game it is and grand for passing the time and many's the game Cathie and me play when it's too rough for going out in the boat . . . Well, taking into consideration what Willie here said about the guns, and the fact that we're hoping Roddy and Towny will be finishing off the machines up there—I am thinking we have pretty well reached checkmate with these men outside."

"How might that be?" asked Angus in a gentle voice, looking at him under his brows.

"If the machines are destroyed, if the boats are put out of action, they will not be able to get away from Mourie."

"No. That's the idea."

"But we will none of *us* be able to get away either."

As always, the bold statement of the unremarked obvious produced a silence.

A voice whispered:

"And they have the guns . . ."

200

"Just so."

"You're forgetting one thing," said Alice impatiently. "Roddy and Towny are going to try to get through the hills and bring help. So we're not really checkmated—there can be another move. What we have to do is to make sure that if and when help comes, that lot are still here. So I say we must do something to the boats."

"Just so." Angus lapsed into a brief silence and then said: "I think we'll wait till Mairi Macleod brings in another basket of food. It won't be long now, and I am hoping and thinking they will let her come in alone—otherwise it will be awkward with Joe in that state. I was telling her to take a look round and see what was what. She will be able to tell us if they have a guard on the boats at the jetty . . . and then we'll set about dealing with them." He smiled a little. "Nothing violent. We learnt a long while ago here to fight without violence."

It seemed a sensible enough plan. They settled down to wait, and in a surprisingly short space of time, Mairi Macleod appeared with another basket of supplies. This time to their relief she came into the room alone, and was greeted by Angus with a flood of Gaelic. Others joined in with comments and interjections. Then she turned to Elizabeth and Alice and said:

"Mrs. Lauder said I was to ask how you were doing."

"Not too badly," said Elizabeth. "What about Peg and the baby?"

"They're back in the camp, none the worse. Now I must be going, for there's things to be done. Angus will explain . . ."

Which he did, as soon as she had gone, gathering them at the end of the room, away from Joe, who lay gently snorting as he slept.

"There is one man, armed, watching the boats at the quay. There's three motor-boats—and Murdo's boat. The wee rowing boats don't matter. Mairi thinks she'll manage fine to get him away from the boats for a little . . . maybe a little of the strategy we used on Joe. Man, is not whisky the wonderful thing? But like fire, like fire—a good servant but a bad master." And he absent-mindedly emptied the bottle into a mug and drank.

201

"So—where was I? Oh yes, once he's out of the way, she'll be hanging out a white dish-towel with a red stripe on her washing line that you can just see out of the window over there; isn't that so, James?" He repeated the question in Gaelic to a bored young man perched on a windowsill and got a nod of agreement. "And when we see it, someone will slip out by our escape hatch and go to the jetty and put them out of the way of sailing . . ."

"Who would go?" said Willie McAlister.

Elizabeth and Alice looked at each other.

"We'll go," said Elizabeth. "We've been in and out of here so often Joe wouldn't notice, if he did surface."

"That is so," said Angus, slowly. "And they will not be watching the road now, and if you are careful . . ."

There was an uneasy murmur in the room and a voice said:

"It is not right to let women go."

Alice spoke in its direction.

"I think it must be us. They're bound to send someone to relieve Joe, and they might not miss Towny and Roddy, but four men being gone they very well might notice. Besides, they wouldn't be so likely to think we had gone."

"I think you're right," said Angus, "but I am just wondering . . ."

"If we'd know how to put the boats out of action?"

"Just that."

"Sea-water in the fuel tanks," said Alice promptly.

"It's no problem."

Angus nodded.

"Just so. I had forgotten you were a bit of an expert."

Alice looked a little self-conscious but said coolly:

"It's not all that risky. There's good cover, one way and another, all down the jetty."

"The men watching the school might see you," said the same voice.

"We'll be causing a diversion here," said Angus. "I would not be letting them go if I thought it was too dangerous."

Time passed. Silence fell, tension built up. Then James on the window ledge said:

"She's hanging it up. A dish-towel with a red stripe."

Two minutes afterwards, Elizabeth, Alice and Angus were in the boiler-house. Alice was hoisted first on to the ledge, opened the little door and looked out into a green tangle of grass and bramble, through which filtered the glow of the late afternoon light. Parting the tangle, and drawing a sharp breath as the prickles scratched blood, she poked out a cautious head, and then whispered down:

"All clear. I'll do as Roddy did and wait for you in the long heather across the track." Then she pulled herself out of sight.

"My turn now," said Elizabeth, and waited for Angus to brace himself against the wall so that she could clamber up on to his back and shoulders, but he made no move, saying:

"You will be careful, I hope. These are very bad men."

"Oh yes, I'll be careful."

Looking at him, she thought: He *knows* something. So she said:

"What did you mean by saying Alice was 'a bit of an expert' when she talked of putting the boats out of action?"

"Did you not know? During the war she was with the Resistance in France." And in reply to her astonishment he added: "One can never know what unlikely things people may have done—and that applies to more than one in Mourie. Take Mr. Maclean, for example—I think there was more to him than appeared—and I would not be surprised, not surprised at all, if you were to see him again much sooner than you're thinking just now . . . But you are keeping Miss Alice waiting, and I don't think, in the circumstances, that that is a good thing."

This was true. So with questions and surmises buzzing through her head, she clambered up with his assistance and through the little door. As she turned to close it, she saw him looking up with bright calculating eyes. Then she slipped over the road, swift as a weasel, to join Alice.

203

CHAPTER 21

"I thought you were never coming," said Alice. "Let's go."

They raised cautious heads from the heather and looked. All clear, and they were over the track and in the shelter of the school wall. It gave them cover from those watching the school, but they could be seen from the back doors and windows of houses stretching towards the shop. Alice whispered:

"We're very visible from that direction."

"As long as none of *them* see us, it's all right," said Elizabeth.

And so it was. They came to the end of the wall where it finished at the road. Alice peeped round. A little to the left, the jetty ran down to the water. To reach it, and the shelter of the sheds, they must cross the road diagonally. This was the moment of greatest risk; and it was at this point that a row started up in the school behind them. There was a smashing of glass, and shouting, and heavy feet thudded over the asphalt of the playground.

They didn't need to say a word to each other. In seconds they were over the road and in the security of the gap between the old warehouse and the sea-wall. They edged their way down the length of the wall and peered round the gable of the old shed, at the three motor-launches. There was not a soul to be seen near them. A quick glance up to the school showed an empty playground.

"Now!"

And the two of them were in the nearest boat, steadying themselves against its swing as they jumped down. They set to work quickly and silently. In a matter of minutes they had topped up the fuel tanks of all three of Douglas' boats, and Murdo's, with sea-water, and were back across the jetty and squeezed between shed and wall again, panting, flushed with the excitement of danger surmounted and mission accomplished.

"We've done it!" whispered Elizabeth.

"Good for us," said Alice. Then suddenly she was serious, and said: "But it was too easy."

"Meaning . . . ?"

"Just that. It's all going too smoothly. If you think what's at stake . . ."

"You mean the money?"

"Of course. The amount alone is enough to mean it won't all end tamely like this." She paused. "It's been too—too good-humoured so far. They're not a bunch of amateurs. They're dangerous, ruthless men . . . What should we do now?" She stood thinking, pulling at her lower lip with the thumb and finger of her left hand.

"We've got to get away from here," said Elizabeth. "The guard may be back any minute."

"Of course," said Alice. "Could we reach Jenny's house?"

"I think so. Back up the side of the school and along behind."

As they crept up the line of the school wall, they could hear a confused rumble of angry voices inside. They followed the wall round, past the chute and then crept under the shade of a thick fuchsia hedge and a stone dyke and so reached Jenny's back wall and the little wooden gate into the back garden.

Jenny, finding them in the kitchen, said:

"Get out of sight of the window. Upstairs, I think, would be best."

She took them into her room, where a tiny window in the gable gave them a view of the school and the hills beyond, and there they told her what was going on.

"So there's a good chance that they'll be trapped here and not able to get away?"

"If all goes according to plan," said Elizabeth. "If they put the helicopters out of action. And if the boat, or boats, in the anchorage beneath Mourie House are made useless."

Jenny looked at her.

"And who's going to do that?"

"I am."

"You can't." But her words lacked conviction.

"I must. I know where they are. There's no one else."

Alice had been listening. "I'll come too."

"No. There's no need. I think I know how to get there without being seen. There's no need for two . . ." She turned back to Jenny. "It's not even all that dangerous. With this rumpus at the school here, I don't think there'll be anyone back at the Big House. Anyway, I must."

"Here's the Land-Rover from the Big House coming now," said Alice, who was looking out of the small window. "It's going to the school."

Douglas and two others got out of the Land-Rover when it stopped in the school playground. In his stride, the stiff turning of his head, Douglas' anger was manifest. The three went into the school, and for a brief space of time the playground was empty. Then the school door swung open and out came Douglas and the two men, dragging between them a bewildered and shambling figure. It was Joe. Even across the distance they could see the attempts at protest and the terror that pulled his head from one side to another as he pleaded.

"No, oh no!" said Elizabeth, "they're not going to . . ."

But they were. They propped him against the wall under the high school window and held him against it; and Douglas drew out a gun and shot him. As Joe's body slid down the masonry and slumped on the asphalt, the echo ran round the playground and died into a deep silence.

At the same moment, from high on the hills above the school, where a wall of black rock rose up to crown the height, a column of dark smoke climbed into the air and hung like a gibbet in the sky.

Elizabeth saw it.

"That smoke . . ."

"It could be a heather-fire," said Alice.

206

"Heather smoke is white or blue," said Jenny. "That's a chemical smoke—from the Old Man's Kiln."

"The helicopters . . ."

"Yes."

"Then, if I'm going to Mourie House, I must go at once—before *they* see it and realise . . . I wish there was some way we could hinder the return of the Land-Rover."

"You mean, block the road?" said Alice.

"Well, yes, but it's obviously not possible."

"But it is. With a bicycle." She turned to Jenny. "In the cattle grid. Remember?"

"Of course." Jenny explained to a bewildered Elizabeth. "Alice managed to get her bicycle jammed in the slats of the cattle grid one day, and held up two cars, the Mourie Transport Co, the main van, and the coal lorry—it's a perfectly feasible idea."

"I can't go and get my bike, but you can, Jenny. If any of them try to stop you, you can say your car has broken down and you're going to a baby or something . . . then you can give a wobble on the grid and stick."

"All right," said Jenny, "I'll do it."

As soon as she had gone, Elizabeth crept out again by the back gate. The low dyke kept her from being seen from the road. Then she took to the thickets of low birch and alder; with luck she would gain the bridge and so reach the grounds of Mourie House.

She dare not look back along the road, but when she reached the thickets, she heard the noise of a car being driven at speed down the road, and she crouched and waited. There was a screeching of brakes, and silence. Aunt Jenny must have managed it all right, and a furious and frustrated Douglas was presumably now struggling with the jammed bicycle.

She reached the edge of the burn just below the bridge and took to the water. The grounds seemed deserted as she looked out from the shadow of the arch. She would trace back the way she had come with Sandy—up the bed of the burn under the bushes and then along the path to the back of the house.

She made her way upstream. There was a hum of insects, the

207

cool sound of water—and all round violence, evil, death. She shivered uncontrollably, aware suddenly how tired she was, mentally and emotionally battered. She stumbled, almost falling headlong into the brown peaty water, and decided she must sit down for a little on the bank. Now, for a moment, she could think of Angus' words—that she might see Crane again sooner than she thought. What did Angus know? Clearly much more than she had thought. All along she had been aware of the people of Mourie, the "real" Mourians, playing some kind of part in what was going on, apparently passive—and yet, and yet . . . But Crane—what could Angus mean?

She had found a crumpled tube of fruit gums in her pocket, and popped two in her mouth, and chewing on the sticky sweetness made her feel better. She rose to her feet again, and stopped puzzling over Angus' remark. What she was doing needed all her concentration. The path couldn't be far away.

It wasn't. Ahead of her she saw the plank bridge and soon she was sitting on it putting on her shoes. Under the trees there was a great stillness and no sunlight, but away to her left, it was bright beyond the tree trunks. The silence, the path twisting through the dark green rhododendrons and laurels made her feel uneasy and very much alone, but she went on, the soft surface of the path deadening her steps. Soon she was standing beneath the tree in which she had hidden, looking across the stretch of grass to the house. The well she had seen from the attic was clearly visible, almost central in the area defined by the main block and wings of the house. The grey stone wall of the shaft was about three feet high.

She stood looking at it, uneasy, prickly. The house was apparently deserted. There wasn't a sound . . . or could she hear a car in the distance coming along the road? If so, she must get down to the beach and the boats as quickly as possible. But she didn't move, some kind of sixth sense, some irrational reluctance keeping her still in the shadow of the trees.

As she stood there, she was suddenly rigid with terror. Over the edge of the well, something was slowly rising; something round, dark, hairy . . . the head and shoulders of a man. His hand appeared and grasped the parapet and he hauled himself up and over.

For a moment she saw him straight on. It was Johnson; Johnson, assured, calm, cruel. His actions were swift, secretive and very purposeful. He had a rucksack on his back and now he slipped it from his shoulders, fumbled in it and pulled out two smallish oblong parcels; he put one in each pocket of his jacket, and dropped the haversack down the well; a small soft sound echoed up from it. Then he reached into the well and drew up a narrow rope-ladder. Only then did she see where it had been hooked into stanchions in the stonework. He coiled it up, and dropped it in, and the same quiet thud resounded from it. He picked up two other packages from the base of the well-head, crossed to the right and disappeared round the end of the house, the crunch of his feet on stone suddenly deadened as he reached the turf.

There was silence. The sound of the car had died away. Elizabeth came out of the shadow of the trees and walked softly over to the well. It would only take seconds to look down and see what was there. It was clearly being used as some kind of hiding-place; and surely it could only be for the stuff from the wreck. When she was halfway to it, she heard the noise of a car again. She must hurry. One glance would be enough . . .

But as she reached the well-head there was another sound: feet on gravel. She swung round, but Johnson's hands were already at her throat, his cold grey eyes glinting down at her.

He was immensely strong. Instinctively and ineffectively, her hands pulled at the iron fingers. Through the buzzing in her ears she heard his words:

"This time I'll kill you. You should have kept out of this. It went wrong as soon as you came blundering in . . ."

The hands tightened and tightened and the humming in her ears grew to a roar and in her eyes was darkness lit by bright flashes. She fought, hopelessly, feebly; felt the pressure on her back as he forced her across the parapet of the well; felt her strength ebbing, and then there was a thudding throb in the darkness; the cruel pressure was gone; the roaring died away, light returned. She slid to the ground by the shaft, and was aware of struggling bodies close to her. She could see feet twisting and turning. Then a scream, a heavy thud, and a long groan. Silence; and when she looked up, Crane was leaning on the parapet looking down in the maw of the well, panting hoarsely.

She could not believe it, but stayed huddled on the ground, gaping at him; but he turned to her, and lifted her up, and held her close, murmuring as he ran his hand over her hair:

"I shouldn't have gone away . . . it seemed a good idea, but . . . you might have been killed."

"But I'm not." Her voice was hoarse. She wanted to forget everything, just to be there with him; but she could hear the car again, closer. So could he.

"What now, Crane?"

"I don't know what's been happening along there at the school . . ."

"The helicopters are out of action; and the boats. There's just the boat moored off the beach here . . ."

He held her at arm's length and looked at her searchingly.

"I must stay here, in case Douglas comes here—as I'm sure he will. But the boat . . ."

"I'll go. I know where to go. There won't be anyone about, not now." She gave a little shuddering glance at the old well, now full of a dreadful silence.

"All right. But be watchful and wary."

Without another word, she slipped away through the trees, which soon thinned out beyond the wing of the house. Soon she was on the grassy paddock dotted with alders, that stretched to the cliffs. She found a little path and followed it, running lightly. It joined the broader path she had followed from the cliffs with Douglas the day before—only the day before? Through the low trees she could see the hollow where the cleft ran down to the caves; and for one brief moment she thought she saw through the bushes something moving ahead of her—a man? Or a cow? Or a sheep? Impossible to tell. But Crane's words rang in her ears: be watchful and wary.

So she paused, panting, at the top of the cleft, and looked

back. No one was in sight, but she could hear the noise of the car quite clearly. It must be quite close to the house. From the cave there was no sound at all.

She began to clamber down into the darkness silently, and stood at the foot of the cleft, listening. Was there an echo of steps dying into silence? Soon she was in the cave, listening again. Not a sound. With the help of her torch she stole as quietly and quickly as possible to the entrance and stepped into the mellow light of early evening.

The shore was deserted and silent. Not even the sea, very calm, and breaking in tiny ripples, made any noise. Not a soul in sight. She leaned into the silence, looking and listening.

Over to her right was the ridge of rocks beyond which, according to Sandy, the boat would be waiting. She began to run towards it and saw in the firm sand a man's footprints; how freshly made, it was impossible to say.

She was at the rocks, began climbing, reached the top of the ridge, and peeped over. On the other side, the rocks went almost sheer into the sea, with just a narrow ledge to give a footing. Across the deep dark water was another precipitous ridge. It was like a miniature fjord, and at the landward end was closed by the cliff beetling above a tiny strand. The exit to the Sound was through a narrow channel between the ridge opposite and a reef of ugly rocks that curved round from the side where she stood. At some time one or two iron rings had been battered into the rocky ledge, and to one a motor-boat was tied. It lay there on the smooth dark water. What was she to do?

She could untie it and cast it adrift; better would be to do as they had done to the others at the jetty. She looked round again from the top of the ridge. Nothing stirred in the landscape except the sea-birds. She climbed down to the ledge and began pulling on the rope to draw the boat towards the landing. The rope looped into the water. To get a better grip, she knelt down and reached down to grasp it and pull. It was quite heavy and difficult to handle and she began to pant a little with the effort.

A hand came over her shoulder, laid itself over hers to help;

211

a man's hand; Douglas' hand, for when she turned her head, there he was looking at her with calculating and unloving eyes.

"We'll soon pull her over," he said, "and then we can set off. I could kill you now, and drop you into this nice deep water. But I won't. Not even although you and your prying and your worrying over the death of a worn-out old woman—oh yes, I guessed—have spoilt everything we've worked for—and more than you'll ever know. But at present you could, possibly, be useful—perhaps as a bargaining point—perhaps other ways. And at any rate I'm not leaving you for our noble selfless American to enjoy."

All the time he was hauling on the line, holding her hands fast against the rope. Now the boat was tapping on the rocks, and he swung her up in his arms and into it.

"And don't try anything silly."

She sat without moving, for it was clear that he would kill her without any qualm at all if he felt like it. Now he was busy untying the rope. The sinister little fjord was quite silent again.

Then she heard it. A man's voice shouting:

"Elizabeth!"

And before Douglas could reach her, she screamed—a cracked, mindless, hoarse scream cut short by a blow across the mouth that sent her whimpering against the side of the boat. But her scream had worked. Feet rasped on the rocks and a man's head and shoulders appeared against the sky. Crane.

When he saw her, he hurtled over the tumble of stones, and flung himself on Douglas, just as he finally untied the mooring rope. There was a flailing of arms and a sickening sound of blows; then a grunt of pain, and Crane lay sprawling on the ledge while Douglas sprang into the boat and pushed off. He went to the controls, and in a moment the engine putt-putted into life. Elizabeth, despairingly watching Crane lying limp on the rock, saw him stir, stagger to his feet, and swing his head from side to side, searching. She saw him stoop, lift a huge stone in both hands and catapult it after the boat. It smashed heavily

212

against the rudder just at the water-line. The boat rocked momentarily violently. Douglas didn't even look round.

Crane stared after them. She saw his expression of fury change to fierce anxiety. He cupped his hands to his mouth, stood at the edge of the ledge and shouted:

"McBain! You fool! Watch the current to seaward. Between the rocks! Watch it!"

But it was no use. She could feel the water grabbing the boat and she could see that here it was not smooth and still; the water was dimpled and turning on itself. She saw Douglas pull at the wheel and say: "She doesn't respond . . . the rudder's damaged." He turned it desperately to one side and another. The boat had swung round; it was being carried sidelong on a racing tongue of water. She heard Crane shout again. Douglas left the cockpit and was looking over the side when they smashed against the wicked outcrop of rock that barely broke the surface where the sea curdled through to the Sound. The boat tilted, jarred again, and Douglas fell with a shout into the eager water. The current carried him past the bow. She heard him shouting: "I can't swim. Help me! Help me!" and she leaned over and held out her hand. But it was no use. His cold fingers brushed hers, but the water carried him past, and where the surface gently lifted and boiled as the currents met, his white face disappeared beneath a crest of creamy foam.

She shrank back against the edge of the boat that was tilted up on the rock clear of the water. The other edge was beneath the surface; water moved and slapped against her feet, but the boat, jammed on the rock, was, for the time at least, steady. She heard Crane's voice again, faint but clear: "Don't move. Stay quite still. I'm coming."

She was frozen with cold and fear and couldn't move, not even to turn her head. She was aware of nothing but the dark sea, the water, gentle and sinister, slapping at her feet, the echo of Douglas' cry. Then a voice again: "It's all right, I'm here," and Crane clambered off the half-submerged ridge beside her. He took her in his arms and murmured reassurances. Speechlessly she turned and hid her face in his wet, cold shoulder.

Above the small sound of the water she heard another noise—a droning, familiar, to-be-dreaded noise. Over the cliff-edge came a helicopter, low, hovering, seeking. She looked up, shuddered, and her hands clawed at the edge of the boat as she moaned with the realisation of defencelessness and failure.

Crane understood. "It's all *right*, Elizabeth. It's one of ours. It's the police helicopter."

CHAPTER 22

The party had grown in an unforeseen and amiable way, as parties tended to in Mourie. Mrs. Macleod the Shop had asked Jenny, Elizabeth and Alice to come in for a "wee drink" after business hours. Roddy, of course, was there, and Angus and Kenneth the Post and various others. Towny was there, a transformed man, neatly dressed and looking round contentedly, for he was something of a hero since he and Roddy had outwitted the guards at the Old Man's Kiln, destroyed the helicopters and contacted the authorities after a difficult climb down the other side to a shepherd's cottage and telephone. Now Mrs. Macleod's sitting-room, a pleasant room above the shop, with windows looking over the Sound to Skye, was full of voices and a thin tobacco smoke that drifted out of the open windows into the warm damp air; for a fine rain was falling. After three days of excitement and comings and goings, Mourie was back to normal —well, almost back to normal. The telephone was restored to working order; a replacement for the ferry-boat was operating; work had begun on opening the road, the policemen and CID men who had been asking questions, and poking about, and taking statements had gone. So had the band of divers and the rest of Douglas McBain's crew; they had gone off under police escort, pending further enquiries; and Joe's body, and Johnson's, had gone too. Mourie, relieved that all this was past before the influx of summer visitors, and not a little cheered by the news that John the Ferry was "going to be all right," was relaxing. The fishery cruiser that Elizabeth could see now from Mrs. Macleod's window riding at anchor where the diving boats had

215

been stationed, and the presence in Mourie of two or three quiet men in naval uniform and two or three in discreet plain clothes, were evidence enough that normality was not totally restored; but evidence also that the wreck and all to do with it were very firmly no longer to be any business of Mourie's.

The room hummed with conversation, relaxed and easy, with an added zest to it because of danger past.

Elizabeth sat on a stool by the open window looking out on the Sound, calm and pearly under the soft rain. She still felt tired, but now it was a pleasant lassitude, not the fatigue, and distress that had gripped her for two days after Douglas' death. Then she had not been able to banish the vision of his white face and beseeching hand as the water had gathered him into itself. Aunt Jenny too had been shocked by the recent events, for she had liked him, found him congenial; and took hard the realisation of how totally she had mis-read him. She admitted to Elizabeth that his death had been in a sense a relief, for the cold-blooded shooting of Joe haunted her.

The rest of Mourie took his drowning pretty well in their stride. Angus, coming over to Elizabeth now, offering a glass of whisky, typified the general attitude. "Here is a good drink," he said, "and you look as if you could do with it." He raised his own glass—"Slainte"—and waited till she had drunk in reply. Then he began to talk of the past few days.

"It is a terrible time we have had, and yourself not least. But it was a fearful ending that man had, to be swallowed up like that by the sea." He took a meditative mouthful of his drink. "It was a judgment."

The old-fashioned phrase, which she'd used often enough facetiously, took on a new aura of truth. For Douglas had been wicked and cruel and ruthless; had caused the death, among others, of a young man, a harmless old woman, could easily have killed her . . . and yet she felt his death as a waste—he had been highly intelligent, his passion against the injustice of Clearances surely not all fake? The children had genuinely liked him . . .

Angus answered her thought.

216

"Not but what there was something in him . . . but we will never be knowing what set him off on the wrong way. Did you hear what they did to that silly man they sent to watch us? What was his name now—Joe?"

"We saw what they did—from a window in my aunt's house."

"Yes, yes, a terrible thing."

"But it was you made Joe drunk," said Elizabeth. "You're as responsible for his death as they were."

"Not quite, though we might be said to have contributed to it in a small way. But what else could we have been doing?"

Elizabeth had no answer. For of course once the violence and death had begun, there was no end to it.

She realised Roddy had joined them, and was speaking.

"How are you feeling now?"

"Tired a bit."

"Has Angus been telling you how they got out of the school with no bother at all at the end?"

"I haven't had time," said Angus. "We were talking about Joe."

"A pity about him," said Roddy, "but tell her what happened."

"After they had shot Joe," said Angus, "McBain called us all out to the playground, and drew up his men, and told us if anyone was to try to get away, he would be shot at once. And it was a queer thing, but up until then I was thinking of him as really someone we should be afraid of; but when he was going on like this, I thought: He is playing at being a great and powerful man, and he is not. And I was suddenly very fed-up and angry, and I shouted: 'You are talking nonsense, Douglas McBain. If you look over there you will see the smoke rising from the Old Man's Kiln, and that is your helicopters that is on fire, and you are as much in a trap as we are.'"

Everyone in the room was listening now, their faces turned towards Angus. He raised his voice.

"And at that, there was a kind of roar from them all, and they looked at each other and you could see they were very perturbed, and they were turning round to McBain with a nasty look in their eyes. I will say this for the man, he was not at a loss, for he said, quite cool and collected: "There is no need to panic. We did not have just one means of getting away. There are the boats. You will take them to the beach below the house and we'll put the stuff on them there, and a rendezvous for an emergency like this has been arranged. So get down to the boats and I will go in the car and we'll meet at the house. And there is plenty of time, so don't panic.'"

Angus paused and took a mouthful of his drink.

"So they went down to the jetty and he jumped into his car and went off down the road . . ."

"And found himself blocked at the cattle grid." Alice was quietly triumphant. "That was my idea, though I must say Mrs. Lauder here carried it out splendidly."

"I managed to jam the bike in pretty deep," said Jenny. "It took some time to get it out."

Angus took the interruption tolerantly.

"That is so; and it was a very ingenious idea . . . It was really very interesting to watch what happened at the boats. They just could not believe they would not start. They were taking off their jackets and turning handles and banging switches: and two of them even got into the water and were diving underneath . . . Oh yes, it was a very interesting sight. But when they saw it was no use they were very angry, very angry indeed. And they came storming back up to the school and things looked ugly; they looked very ugly. Some of them went down the road after McBain, but he drove off before they caught up with him. The rest of them made for us, and they were very angry, and I did not like it at all . . ."

Angus paused dramatically, savouring the moment of suspense.

"And then?" said Roddy.

"It was Willie here who had a very bright idea. He said: 'If you want to get away, you could go as far as Lustaig by car, and then there is a track over the shoulder of the hill to a road with buses.' It was a stroke of genius, for he guessed once there they would not return but would spend their time looking for the track, which does not exist. Some of us said they could use our cars, and they went away and we walked back to our homes. And all in all I think we handled the situation very well."

He drank to the resourcefulness of Mourie, and so did they all, with a murmur of approval.

Well, that's how some of it happened, thought Elizabeth. But it doesn't explain at all how Crane came to be at Mourie House. And none of it says a thing about *why* all this happened. Shall we ever know? She looked at the company. Perhaps Angus could explain some of it; probably Crane could. But Crane wasn't there. She had seen very little of Crane since that time on the rocks when she had turned and clung to him as the helicopter passed overhead. He had caressed and soothed her back into a semblance of calm, for she had suddenly been shaken by wild sobs that threatened to become uncontrollable. Then he had helped her back to the security of the beach and up to Mourie House and the car that took her to Jenny's. Since then he had been much involved with those who had suddenly found Mourie so interesting—the polite strangers in civvies, the naval men. She had seen him once or twice, but always when someone was about. Once or twice she had thought he was almost trying to avoid talking with her. Oddly enough, this didn't worry her. She knew that sooner or later he and she would meet and decide—decide whether what was between them was real and true, or merely the play of circumstances.

She had been gazing out of the window, lost in her thoughts, but now a change in the quality of the sound of the voices in the room, an exclamation, "There you are! How are you?" made her look round. Crane was standing in the doorway.

He raised a hand in greeting to them all and said to Mairi:

"I'm sorry I'm late. I've been on the phone to Jimmy. He went to London to report to the embassy on what's been going on. I said it wasn't possible for me to go myself as I still had things to do here."

Elizabeth could feel the eyes swivelling as he made his way over to her. Mourie was taking a great interest in her and Crane at the moment.

"I have just been telling Elizabeth here," said Angus, "how

219

we got out of the school, and she agrees with us we were very smart fellows, don't you, Elizabeth?"

"Yes indeed," said Elizabeth. "But what I really want to know now is, how did Crane here happen to be in Mourie House just at the right time for me?"

The buzz of voices died down, and someone—Willie McAlister?—said: "Indeed, and that's something we'd all like to know."

"It's rather a long story—"

"If you give us time to fill our glasses, we will not be minding that." There was some laughter, a clinking of glass, a general air of settling down. Crane sat on the floor by Elizabeth, gave her a private, conspiratorial glance, and began.

"One—or was it two?—days after we went fishing at night, and I met you all on the quay when we returned"—there was an exchange of sheepish glances at his words—"I had a conversation with Elizabeth here, in which we agreed that we should meet the following day, so that she could tell me one or two things she'd found out—and, by the way, I don't know yet what they were." He looked at Elizabeth enquiringly, but she shook her head and said:

"Later."

"All right. At that point of time, I still wasn't sure whether what they'd brought ashore on our fishing expedition—oh yes, you were all absolutely right, it wasn't just a fishing expedition. You all kept such a vigilant watch on what was going on that it wasn't possible to bring anything ashore without being noticed: and Johnson and the rest were very insistent it should be brought unnoticed—I still wasn't sure whether what they brought was the genuine laird's treasure or something else. All kinds of excuses had been made by Johnson to hinder my seeing it— 'Mr. McBain would have to be there too: he'd put it away at once in a safe place because he didn't altogether trust the boys,' and so on. I hadn't heard any hint of any plans for moving the stuff out of Mourie, and that seemed to indicate it was the legendary treasure they'd got hold of, and it was simply to be handed over to you people here . . . Then two things happened,

220

after I'd left Elizabeth that afternoon and gone back to the house. A number of men arrived in a mini-bus—about eight of them, saying they'd been recruited for McBain by his sponsor, the mysterious magnate in Glasgow. To me they seemed totally unnecessary, and I wondered if they were some kind of security forces—and then one of them, not knowing the set-up, told my man Jimmy that 'the stuff' was to be moved out over the weekend, and they were there to make sure nobody interfered. So that cleared one problem and created another."

"Meaning you now knew it *was* something other than the laird's treasure they'd found?" said Jenny.

"Yes. That was now clear. But obviously Jimmy and I were now a problem to them—they couldn't start sending the stuff out if we were around. So . . ."

"So they'd have to get rid of you?"

"Exactly. So I decided we'd go of our own accord, when they still didn't know we were aware of anything else going on but the hunt for the laird's treasure. I announced I was bored and was washing my hands of the whole affair and going away with Jimmy. Actually, we meant to go only as far as Melldaig down the coast, Jimmy was to stay there near a phone, and I was going to hire another car, come back under cover of darkness and stay here over the weekend keeping an eye on things, but, I hoped, unseen."

"And where did you think of staying?" said Roddy.

"With Angus here." He raised his voice as a little ripple of surprise ran round the room. "I told Angus I thought something underhand was going on and he agreed to keep me at his place, and say nothing. He too was anxious to have things cleared up."

"But Angus . . ." said Elizabeth, and before she could go on, Roddy said swiftly: "Your glass is empty," and as he took it from her to replenish it, he gave her a warning glance. For of course, she must not let it be known that it was he who had told her that Angus knew where the laird's treasure was. Angus was looking consciously virtuous and Elizabeth was aware of a gentle bemusement stealing over her—partly due to the whisky no doubt, but partly also to a sense of being lost in a tangle

221

of knowing and not knowing, of motive and counter-motive; an intensification of what she had felt at her interview with Angus in his workshop.

"Well, I see all this," said Jenny to Crane, "but why weren't you taken into the school with the rest?"

"Because the road had been blocked before I got over it in the car. So I had to make my way down on foot—I figured something was going on, and took to the moor when I was nearing the village. So I came very cautiously to Angus' place, just before they came to pick him up. I hid in a coffin."

"A *coffin?*" Alice was really horrified.

"I have one or two always in stock," said Angus placidly. "Just in case."

"You must remember I knew nothing about helicopters and so on—Angus hadn't time to tell me. But I decided I'd try and get into Mourie House to see if I could find whatever they'd got from the wreck—but I didn't manage till fairly late on in the day—I got there not long before Elizabeth—and you know the rest. Thank goodness I was there."

He laid a hand on Elizabeth's, and she said:

"Thank goodness indeed. I understand now how you were there when Johnson . . . But how did you come to the boat in time?"

"You remember we heard a car. I thought it was McBain coming. It was actually two cars we heard. It was Roddy and Willie here who came to Mourie House. They told me Douglas McBain had gone off ahead in the Land-Rover—they'd found it just inside the gate—and it seemed clear he'd made straight for the boat—so I made for it too—just in time."

There was a moment's hush in the room, and then conversation broke out again; people moved about; groups broke up and reformed; as if at the end of some kind of performance, as if an episode had been completed. Only Angus remained, leaning against the window, silent and thoughtful, looking into his glass. Nor did Crane move from beside Elizabeth.

Finally Angus spoke:

"You have no information about McBain himself, have you?

He was a strange man—not altogether bad, as I was saying here to Elizabeth—but I would be interested in knowing something about him."

"Well, I do know a little. The authorities on both sides have been making enquiries. He really was a graduate of Edinburgh and Harvard. He came from a grim background in Central Scotland—his father chronically disabled in an industrial accident—and made his way by brains and work. But he seemed to have some kind of a grudge against life and the powers-that-be—and with him it seems to have taken the form, not of "working for the revolution," but of wanting to dominate society—by acquiring power—and he seems to have thought that was most easily done by grabbing riches."

"That's true," said Elizabeth. "He once said as much."

"They think now that he was involved in one or two shady financial episodes in the States—but he had a splendid cover in being the dedicated academic type. There's even hints of the Mafia . . . Anyway, when the brains behind the attempt to get the stuff from the wreck were looking for a team, he was an obvious choice—local background, etc. And it was easy for him to play the part, because a lot of it was genuine. His passion over the Clearances I'm sure was genuine. But he clearly was no amateur at the business—and ruthless as they come."

But that isn't all the story, thought Elizabeth. We've a right to know "why" as well as "how." So she said clearly, but not loudly:

"But that's not all. The really big questions haven't been answered—or even asked. What were they looking for in the Sound? And why?" Everyone was looking at her as she went on. "And you could tell us, Crane, couldn't you?"

He straightened his shoulders, looked up and round as if making a decision, and said:

"Well, I guess you ought to know, seeing you were all involved in the affair. To begin with, I want to make it clear that I originally came over here with no other purpose but to find the laird's treasure and hand it back to you folk. And in fact if I find it, that's just what I will do. But Douglas McBain was

223

using the story as a cover for something quite different. And I must warn you that I can't tell you all I know, nor how I got to know it—you'll understand why later. Maybe it's possible that some of you know something of what I'm going to tell you already. But Douglas McBain wasn't interested in the laird's treasure, except as a cover."

"What was he after, then?" Mairi Macleod asked gently.

"Ah, that's a long story. Some of you may remember an episode in the First World War, when it was rumoured a ship had gone down in the Sound and two or three bodies were washed ashore. Since coming here, I've heard talk of gold coins, sovereigns, being picked up . . . though I've never been able actually to find anyone who admits to having such a thing . . ."

"Mysie's charm!" It was Jenny's turn to draw attention, but when Crane looked a question at her, she shook her head.

"The local legend was that these came from the laird's treasure. But—and this is where it's difficult to go on, because there's so much that can't be said—the ship that foundered—or was torpedoed—was carrying currency and bullion to—well, to a country which, though a very poor country, occupied a geographical position of supreme importance to the Allied side—the United States by this time was in the war, and in fact supplied some of the bullion. And this country—oh, let's give it a name; say, 'Anonia'—while not on our side, had indicated a willingness to transfer its support if . . ."

"You mean, we were buying them over?" Roddy's tone was scornful.

"Yes. You can see that this was a transaction of 'supreme delicacy,' as the diplomatic professionals say. In other words, the whole affair was so dicey that fantastic security was observed, 'usual channels' short-circuited, paperwork reduced to a minimum. And when the ship went down—and no one knew how it did—the records were destroyed. It had never happened."

He broke off. Angus refilled his glass, and Crane went on:

"The whole affair was non-existent—until a few months ago. Then Anonia sent a nasty little note to your Foreign Office saying they'd heard from an impeccable source that you were

224

going to salvage the coin and bullion; and they took a dim view of this, because it was really theirs, morally if not legally. Colossal cheek, really, but all very awkward because (a) no one really knew anything about it at this end, and (b) Anonia was still at its old game and though usefully supporting Britain and her friends in current world problems, was quite capable of switching its support to others . . . So your Foreign Office quietly contacted our State Department, because, of course, we were involved as partners in the original deal, and exchanged lengthy and non-meaningful notes with Anonia, and feverishly tried to find out all it could about the original arrangement and the loss of the ship; and finally narrowed it down to being one of several lost off the West Coast in the latter part of 1917. And that was as far as they got . . ."

"But how do you know all this?" said Roddy, wary and suspiciously.

"Ah." Crane uncurled his long legs and stood up. He looked out of the window and then swung round to face them. "Some of you know that my family business is in electronics, and I travel a lot for the firm; and sometimes, I've done work for the State Department in the course of my travels. Don't ask me for details. Anyway, I'm known in various U.S. embassies, and have friends in them. Well, on my way here, I spent a few days in London, and one of my friends from the embassy came to see me. Of course I told him I was coming here—and why—and, to cut a long story short, I was asked, when I was in the West here, to keep my eyes and ears open—no more. For by this time they'd managed to establish that the Anonians were quite definite that an attempt was to be made to get the stuff up, and as neither our government nor yours was involved, it could only be an illegal operation. So I said I would do what I could, but it wasn't to involve anything particularly active . . .

"Then two or three days before I left London, I was at a party, and my hostess, a kind woman, when she heard I was coming to Mourie said, 'But how extraordinary, there's someone else here who's going there,' and she promptly took me away

225

from a charming girl I was talking to and introduced me to Peter Macdonald—you know him?"

For a smothered exclamation had come from Angus.

"I don't know. It's possible."

"He told me he'd a connection with Mourie—his grandmother lived there. And he was feeling rather ashamed that he hadn't gone to see her more often, for he thought she must be going a bit senile, since he'd had a very odd letter from her, asking him to come, because some man had come to Mourie and was going to salvage the laird's treasure from the sea, and it wasn't there, and he must come and be told the truth about it. So he was going off to Mourie to see her. Well, I wondered if this might possibly have anything to do with the Anonian business, mentioned it to the embassy, and came on here.

"When I got here, and found everyone believing in the story of the laird's treasure in the Sound, and Douglas full of his indignation at the Clearances—and I do believe he was genuine in that—and everyone saying poor Old Morag was a bit deranged, I decided it was all straight and above board. Except for the body on the pass. Peter Macdonald was red-headed, like myself. So it could have been him. But no one had seen or mentioned any red-headed person having been in Mourie, and after I'd been here a couple of days I couldn't believe anyone could come here and not be noticed, so I just concluded he'd not yet come—he hadn't been specific about time. And then— and then Elizabeth recognised the body in the peat as Morag's grandson. So I *knew* that Peter Macdonald must have stumbled on something pretty big. And the way Douglas dropped out of it all, though he kept close contact with Johnson in secret— Alice told me—it all added up."

"But, Crane"—Elizabeth could keep silent no longer—"if only I'd told you—Aunt Jenny and I knew it wasn't the laird's treasure in the Sound. We saw one of the coins that was found— an Edward VII sovereign—and anyway, the laird's treasure never was there. It—"

But Angus interrupted her.

"So Elizabeth here had been finding out all you wanted to

226

know. What a pity you couldn't have co-operated sooner. It would have spared us a lot of bother. And what will be happening now to all this gold and stuff?"

"I don't know," said Crane. "It's in the hands of the professionals now. My guess is that someone in Anonia found out about the original agreement and the amount involved and organised a private attempt to get his hands on it—and found in the legend of the laird's treasure a wonderful cover story. Probably learnt of it from Douglas—and once Douglas had got himself appointed here, it was quite easy. But someone, I think, must have sold information to the Anonian government and they seized the chance to put pressure on our government to get the stuff . . ."

"And because of all this shabby—no, slimy—diplomatic nastiness, Morag had to be killed. It's wicked, wicked," said Elizabeth. "I don't care about their gold—as far as I'm concerned they could have had it and all power to them. But to kill Morag—and her grandson—and poor silly Joe . . ."

"Why were they needing to kill Morag?" asked Mairi Macleod.

"They were afraid," said Crane, "that she did know where the laird's treasure really was, and could, at a word, blow apart their cover story, and force them to give up the diving. I'm sure that's what happened with Peter—she must have told him the truth and he let Douglas and the rest know he knew it."

"But why up the pass? Why put his body in the roller?"

"I guess they arranged a rendezvous up there," said Crane. "He kept himself very secret here. Maybe Morag made him do it. I guess he didn't want to be seen and the top of the pass would be a good place."

"And the road-roller," said Roddy, "would be a landmark. For the helicopter Elizabeth saw as she came up the pass. It was to have picked up the body. But the mist foxed the whole thing, and they dragged it off and buried it in the peat."

"And when it was found again," said Angus, "someone, Douglas perhaps, must have told the helicopter to pick it up. He must have telephoned Mourie House, and they radioed . . . But why did they leave John the Ferry?"

"I think they thought he was dead," said Crane. "But Peter

227

Macdonald had to be removed in case someone linked him with Morag and so roused suspicion about her death . . . They had so much at stake that nothing could be allowed to stand in their way . . . You were lucky, Elizabeth."

"Was I?" said Elizabeth. "Oh yes, they didn't kill me. But I think I caused Morag's death . . . Wait—I told Douglas—on the night of the dance—that she was going to show me where the treasure was—and that night she died; and they killed her."

She looked round in misery and saw their eyes trying to reassure her—kindly, but admitting the truth.

Crane laid a hand on her shoulder.

"You can't take the responsibility for another person's evil," he said.

"If you are thinking along these lines," said Angus heavily, "then I am just as responsible as you are. For if I had told her I had taken away the treasure from its place, she would not have been bothering you about it."

There was a stunned silence.

"I think I should be telling you," he went on, "those of you who don't know, that we were never very sure that Douglas McBain was really after the laird's treasure. Some of us were never very sure about him at all—his fine story about coming here with his grand university degrees to help the deprived natives—no, it had not the ring of truth. And when he was bringing all these strangers to help find the laird's treasure, we wondered some more. We were remembering the old story about the ship in the First War, and Mysie is not the only one to have a sovereign from it. I've got a handful of them myself in the house, picked up long ago. But we thought we would just let them get on with the business of looking for the stuff and when they found it we would let them know we were aware of what they were up to and perhaps some arrangement could be come to. But it would not have done at all if they had found the laird's treasure—and sometimes secrets can be told"—his eyes flickered over Roddy's face—"and fobbed us off with that while they took the wealth from the sea. So as a precautionary measure I removed the laird's stuff."

Elizabeth looked at them. They sat there nodding agreement. All the time they'd known what was really going on . . . She spoke to Roddy:

"And when you told me about the hiding-place of the treasure, you knew it was empty."

"Yes. Angus told me. He thought I ought to know."

"Then why . . . ?"

"I thought you wanted very much to know where it had been hidden. So I told you. And I knew it didn't matter very much, though I was breaking a promise, because it wasn't there any more."

She gave up, caught Jenny's eye and thought: Did I ever say life here was simple and straightforward?

But Mairi Macleod was speaking.

"It sounds to me, Angus McKay, as if you were planning blackmail?"

"Well now, I wouldn't put it like that. But seeing the kind of men they turned out to be, maybe it's a good thing I didn't try any negotiations with them."

"And what about the treasure?" she went on. "Mr. Maclean?"

"I guess it's mine," said Crane, "by the terms of the purchase. And I'm going to do just as I said—give it back to the descendants of the evicted crofters, as some recompense."

There was a small appreciative murmur, broken into by Roddy's voice, loud and emphatic.

"I'm tired of always hearing about the bad lairds in the past," said Roddy. "I'm tired of hearing about the past at all. We are living here not too badly, and we beat that McBain and his lot into the dust, and we did it with our own things—our language and our drink and our brains. And we can manage fine by ourselves and are not needing charity from outside."

"Bravo, Roddy, it is in Parliament you will be before long," said Willie McAlister. "But I agree. We are not enjoying ourselves with this talk. Let us forget it all."

Which they proceeded to do very successfully.

CHAPTER 23

"Stop here," said Elizabeth, and Crane drew the car into the little lay-by. The red road-roller was gone; it had suddenly been moved, in accordance with one of the unpredictable whims to which county road departments seem prone. "I'll say good-bye here," she went on. "This is where it all began and this is a good place to round it off."

"Isn't it a very gloomy place?" said Crane, looking unenthusiastically over the great slabs of rock, the peat-bog, the scree, the savage hills.

"It can be and it was. Not today." For the sun was shining from a cloudless sky and the wet rocks reflected a steely blue light, the tiny trickle of the burn sparkled and the sphagnum moss was brilliant. "If I leave you here and walk back, I'll be able to enjoy the wonderful moment when this is behind and the islands and sea and Mourie below—Aunt Jenny's Shangri-la."

"I like Aunt Jenny," said Crane. "I hope she likes me."

"She's beginning to. I think she's very angry with herself for having been so wrong about Douglas—she always rather prided herself on being able to read character."

"I was taken in myself to begin with," said Crane, "and I think it was understandable. He wasn't just a bad man—he genuinely had this almost fanatical feeling about the Highlands. I thought he was falling for you and was afraid you might . . ."

"Fall for him? Never!" She spoke vehemently and then laughed. "I thought of him, not as bad, but as boring—which from the point of view of falling in love is much worse."

"And what about Roddy?"

"Oh, poor Roddy! I feel a little guilty about Roddy."

For Roddy, meeting her by the shore one day, had tentatively and rather touchingly, proposed.

"I don't suppose you could be finding it in you to settle down in Mourie?" he had said. "I will be having a good business, in time; if you could see your way to marrying me?"

He took her refusal philosophically.

"I was thinking it was too much to hope for, but there was no harm in asking."

It was clear that the rest of Mourie had decided she was to marry Crane. There were meaningful glances, arch smiles. Even the tinkers were interested, uttering sly and sidelong wishes for "guid health and a kind man" when she went to thank them for their help. Aunt Jenny had come to approve the idea. But Crane himself had never once mentioned the word "marry."

Now he was saying:

"Do I bore you?"

"You know quite well you don't."

"Well, then—"

"You know that too, Crane."

For after the days they'd spent together in Mourie, walking and picnicking, bathing and lying talking in the dunes, if he didn't know by now that she was deep in love, he'd never know.

"I guess I do," he said, and kissed her.

When he released her he said:

"When I get back from the States—that'll be in about three weeks—we'll be married."

She began to laugh.

"You haven't asked me yet!"

"Did I forget to? I'll ask you then. And that'll please Mairi Macleod, who hasn't missed a chance for the past two weeks telling me that Mourie House needs a mistress." He was suddenly serious. "You'll like living in Mourie, won't you? Not all the time of course."

"I'll love it," said Elizabeth, "especially in the Big House. I've grown very fond of it."

For she and Crane had been into every nook and corner of it.

231

And whatever dark and tragic doings had happened there in the past had left no trace of gloom—it was essentially a house for happiness.

"That's settled then," said Crane, briskly. "Now I must go."

She got out of the car and as she leant in to kiss him good-bye, her eye caught the wooden box laid on the back seat.

"The treasure! D'you know, I'd forgotten about it. What did you finally decide to do with it?"

"I'm taking the things to Edinburgh to be valued, and then they'll be sold. Not for very much, I'm afraid."

"I suppose not."

A pair of silver candlesticks, a silver salver, a little bag of sovereigns, a gold watch, a signet-ring—and that was the laird's treasure. When the bundle, wrapped in a stained plaid, had been untied in Angus' house, there had been a silence, not of disappointment, but of awe. Mairi Macleod had spoken for them all when she said:

"And those men did murder and were drowned for that!"

"I'm thinking," Angus had said, as he lifted a tarnished candlestick, "that it is better to believe an old story than find the truth of it."

If anyone was deeply disappointed, it was Crane; but it had been decided to sell the things and use the money for something for Mourie.

"Have they decided what to spend the money on?" said Elizabeth, as she looked at the box.

"It depends on how much the things make. One suggestion is a clock above the window of the shop—'for it is a great want not to be knowing just what the time is,' as Willie McAlister said, and I believe he really thought he meant it . . . And now good-bye, my love—for three weeks. And let's be married in Mourie, and everyone can come."

"Sandy and the rest too?"

"They'd be welcome!"

She watched the car out of sight and then turned to begin the walk down to Mourie, her step light and her heart dancing.

232